Tingles raced up Cassandra's arm. The odor of the cleaning oil, leather and something completely male filled her senses.

She tried to concentrate on Wolf's instructions, tried to follow them. Had he felt anything? He continued teaching her how to load the pistol's two-barrel chambers, apparently unaffected.

She could feel his warmth radiating off him in the quiet interior of the stable. He reached around her from her back and his hands closed over hers to adjust her hold on the weapon. The gun was cold against her skin, but his hands were warm—the skin of his palms calloused from hard work. His breath on her neck did crazy things to her senses. Everywhere they touched—hands, arms, shoulders—was on fire. Her heart raced in her chest.

She looked up at his familiar face, so close to hers. He stopped talking. He might have stopped breathing.

Author Note

Lauri Robinson and I have loved writing this series set in Oak Grove, Kansas. The town and its inhabitants have become so real to me that I wish I could go there and visit them in real life! I am confident that all of them will find their happy-ever-after.

The heroine in this story, Cassandra, is a woman whose joy of life has been snuffed out by circumstances beyond her control. This is her journey back to herself and finding her inner strength again.

The hero in *Wedding at Rocking S Ranch* is my type of hero. A strong, independent yet caring man. Raymond Wolf was inspired by a strong, tough and yet gentle hero in my own life—my father.

I hope you enjoy their story.

Happy reading!

KATHRYN ALBRIGHT

Wedding at Rocking S Ranch

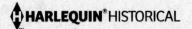

Recycling programs
for this product may
not exist in your area.

ISBN-13: 978-1-335-05176-9

Wedding at Rocking S Ranch

www.Harlequin.com

Printed in U.S.A.

Kathryn Albright writes American-set historical romance for Harlequin. From her first breath, she has had a passion for stories that celebrate the goodness in people. She combines her love of history and her love of story to write novels of inspiration, endurance and hope. Visit her at kathrynalbright.com and on Facebook.

Books by Kathryn Albright

Harlequin Historical

The Rebel and the Lady
Texas Wedding for Their Baby's Sake
Wild West Christmas
"Dance with a Cowboy"
Western Spring Weddings
"His Springtime Bride"

Oak Grove

Mail-Order Brides of Oak Grove
"Taming the Runaway Bride"
The Prairie Doctor's Bride
Wedding at Rocking S Ranch

Heroes of San Diego

The Angel and the Outlaw
The Gunslinger and the Heiress
Familiar Stranger in Clear Springs
Christmas Kiss from the Sheriff

Visit the Author Profile page at Harlequin.com.

Dedicated to my father,
who has championed my writing career from the beginning and who, when I was barely up to his knee, introduced me to a love of stories with his amazing tales of a young girl and her flying horse.

Prologue

Oak Grove, Kansas, 1878

Raymond Wolf rammed the oil-soaked cloth down the rifle's barrel for one last coating, making sure the path was smooth and slippery without any catches. It had to be perfect if it was to be his best friend's wedding present.

The long swab pressed against the farthest end of the shaft, and at the same moment, something squeezed in Wolf's chest. An invisible weight descended, as if the very air pressed down on him. Maybe he had been working too hard. He'd had that large order to finish for Dodge City last week, which demanded all of his time. This was the first chance he'd had to work on Doug's rifle.

The sensation grew stronger. Doug's face filled his mind. He set the rifle barrel on his workbench and clutched the turquoise stone at his neck. The small workshop, the snow falling outside the front window, all faded away into a gray mist. Then his friend's face faded too. Something had happened.

"Wolf?" Jackson Miller spoke from the doorway, breaking into the strange fog. Miller stepped inside quickly, followed by another man—a stranger—and shut the door. "Got a man here looking for you."

Wolf released his grip on the stone and struggled to shake off the premonition. He stood and backed away from his work area, staring at the hammer, trigger guard and bow drill that lay on the table. Absent only a moment ago, now the strong scent of oil and varnish filled the air once more.

Miller stepped farther into the room and removed his flat cap. "Are you all right?"

Wolf looked up, still slightly dazed. "Miller," he said, acknowledging his neighbor.

Then his thoughts cleared, and he noticed the short, pudgy man in a gray suit peering around Miller's shoulder. Wolf wiped the oil from his hands on an old rag and slowly removed his shop apron, hanging it from its neck loop on the peg beside the window. He turned back to the two men. "What can I do for you?"

"Raymond Wolf?" the stranger asked, his gaze dubious.

Outsiders always took a moment to adjust to his looks. Confusion happened first, quickly followed by suspicion, and then the lingering unspoken question: Why wasn't he on a reservation with the rest of his tribe? And more than that—was he dangerous? Wolf counted it ironic that along with his appearance, the profession he had fallen into—gunsmithing—also made them nervous. It was ironic and, if he was truthful, satisfying.

"Excuse me. My name is Franklin Masters. I...uh...

have some unfortunate news regarding an acquaintance of yours. A Mr. Douglas Stewart."

Wolf blew out his breath and braced himself. He knew what would be said before the man continued. His friend—his blood brother—wouldn't be coming home.

Chapter One

Alexandria, Virginia

Cassandra Stewart slipped her hand through the crook in her father's arm and leaned on him for support as she descended the grand staircase of her parents' estate.

At the bottom of the stairs, her mother stood beside their housemaid. "I don't like this, Cassandra. Not one bit. Are you sure that you want to do this today?"

"No. I'm not sure, but I've put it off for far too long. It's been ten months since Douglas has been gone."

"You are still weak. Just the work of dressing has taxed your strength."

She smoothed the wide silk belt at her waist. It matched the dress she had donned. How she hated the color black. "The attorney said it was necessary as soon as I was feeling well enough. Today is a good day. I feel stronger. Besides, Mr. Edelman went out of his way to travel all the way from the city to take care of things. It is time."

Father patted her forearm—his way of showing support, both physically and emotionally. He was ready for, as he stated, "the entire disaster of her marriage" to be over and done with. He wanted his little girl back and for life to return to the way it once had been before she ever met Douglas Stewart Jr. Father simply wanted to protect her—his only child—and this was his way to do it. He had no idea that she could never go back to life as it once was. Not after all that had transpired. Douglas had changed everything in her life. So had the loss of their baby.

The house echoed with the whispers of her two great-aunts. While she'd been confined to her bed, they'd discussed her in the hallway just beyond her bedroom door. A wayward woman—tainted—they'd called her, speculating whether the death of her husband was a punishment from above because she'd blatantly gone against her parents' wishes and the mores of decent society to marry so quickly. Most couples were engaged a year before the wedding ceremony.

Cassandra consoled herself with the knowledge that their own marriages had been long and lonely, as their husbands both sought to escape their daily harping and criticism. Her own marriage, although only a few short months, had been a wonder, and she would be forever grateful to have had that time with Douglas. Yet her great-aunts' harsh judgment stung her conscience. She had never been good enough to suit them. A disappointment—that's what she was.

As she walked slowly down the hallway, a chill coursed through her. She pulled her tatted shawl tighter around her shoulders with her free hand. Despite the heavy heat of the midsummer afternoon, she was still cold. The meeting shouldn't take long. All she had to do was sign the official papers, and her late husband's land would then be ready to sell. She might have sold it long before this, releasing the burden of a property she'd never seen, if not for Mr. Edelman's insistence that he make sure that no will existed.

And then there had been her daughter. Cassandra had held out hope that the property would be a legacy to pass on, but her daughter had come early—much too early. Her chest tightened at the memory. She didn't want to dwell on it, yet couldn't help herself. Hope had become despair. And a mad fury had overtaken her. Douglas had been reckless to participate in that boat race. He'd thought himself invincible in all things. The very quality that had drawn her to him had also been the death of him.

Well, today would be one more snip in the rope that tethered him to her. A rope that she both loved and hated at the same time. Her heart had ached for so very long—nearly a year now. Her hopes and dreams had all been dashed the moment the boat he'd crewed with his friends had collided with another.

As she entered the library, Mr. Edelman turned from the floor-to-ceiling window that overlooked the lawn and the Potomac River. He was a short round man, with light gray hair and eyes to match. "Good afternoon, Mrs. Stewart."

At the sound of her married name, her father's grip tightened on her hand. After all this time, it still bothered him.

"Thank you, Father." She released his arm and sat down in the chair he held out for her on one side of the massive oak table. "Mr. Edelman. Thank you for making the journey today. Please take a seat."

Her mother and father took seats on each side of

her at the long table as if to bolster her for what might be coming.

"Indeed, it is no imposition. It is always a treat to get away from the city for a short break in routine, especially in the oppressive heat of summer." He cleared his throat and took a seat across from her. "I prepared the paperwork several months ago and simply set it aside, awaiting this moment when you would be ready. All that is needed is your signature in several places."

He set his leather satchel on the table and withdrew a stack of papers. "Most of your late husband's finances are tied up in the property. Since he left no will, as his wife, you inherit everything. Once the ranch sells, you should have enough money to choose where you want to live and live there quite comfortably."

Mother gave her a quick side hug. "You will stay here. As you have since the…incident."

It wasn't an incident… It was a marriage. But the courtship and wedding had happened so fast, and then the marriage had been over just as fast. *No one's fault*, the captain had written in his report of the boating accident. If not for the months of morning sickness that followed and the lingering ache in her belly, Cassandra might have wondered if the marriage had happened at all.

Mr. Edelman placed the first paper in front of her, along with a pen.

Something he'd said gave her pause. "You must be exaggerating the extent of his holdings. Douglas said it was a very small farm. He only had a few cows. Certainly not sufficient enough to keep me for more than a year."

She picked both papers up and started to read. Halfway down the page she realized she hadn't understood anything and started over. The inked letters swam before her, the words meaningless.

Mother leaned toward her. "I'm sure Mr. Edelman has everything in order, dear. He's very reputable, and your father has already looked over everything."

Cassandra stared at the line where she was to put her signature. It was all so very final—putting her mark there. She should simply sign it and let it go. There was already a potential buyer in Denver waiting for word from her. But all that she could think of was the last time she'd seen Douglas. He'd been in so much pain toward the end, but he'd asked her to do one last thing for him.

Mother leaned toward her. "Sign the paper, dear. Mr. Edelman is waiting."

Cassandra looked up and caught the worried glance her mother sent her father. Another chill slithered through her. Why did she feel so torn about this? Had she procrastinated, not because of her health, but because of the promise she had made to Doug? Was that the real reason she had put off this moment?

"Before I sign this, I have one question."

"Yes?" Mr. Edelman said.

"Will I be able to stay on the property after these papers are signed?"

He looked momentarily surprised. "Well…no. Any further contact with the property would be handled by Mayor Melbourne in Oak Grove. He is the attorney there. He has agreed to handle the sale upon receipt of these papers. There would be no need for you to travel there yourself."

"But…what if I choose to?"

Father shook his head. "We've been through all this. You are not strong enough to go."

"But I will be. Not tomorrow, or even next week. But someday."

Mr. Edelman leaned back in his chair and laced his fingers together over his girth. "I didn't realize that you had reservations about selling your land. Perhaps you should explain."

Your land. How could it be hers if she'd never seen it? Never walked upon it? "You see…after his accident and just before he…he passed, my husband asked me to go to the farm. He wanted me to live there—to stay for an entire month. I'm sure he hoped I would come to love it and stay, but, of course, that is not possible. I would not want to be there without him."

"Your parents didn't mention any of this when they retained my services."

Of course they hadn't. Discussing it in front of Mr. Edelman was their ploy to make sure she felt even more pressure to bend to their wishes.

"It would be sensible if the property were nearby, but to travel all the way to Kansas…" her father interjected.

"Yes, yes," Mr. Edelman said. "Highly irregular for a young woman of means. Not a good idea to travel on your own. There are ruffians and scallywags out West."

Cassandra nearly smiled at the exact same words her parents had used when trying to stop her from marrying Douglas. Surely the great Wild West held all sorts of people, not just the social miscreants mentioned time and again by her family and close friends.

"Douglas spoke of the place only a few times," she

said. "He looked forward to showing it to me, but then the boating accident happened."

"It really is for the best, Cassie," Mother said. "You belong here. Not halfway across the country stuck on a cow farm with a bunch of rough men."

Her mother's words left little uncertainty as to her true feelings. Cassandra glanced up at Mr. Edelman. No doubt he'd heard of her situation, bantered up and down the seaboard by gossipy society matrons. Mother's inference did not help the slightly tarnished, although completely undeserved, reputation that she'd acquired by marrying Douglas so rapidly.

She suddenly realized that her fingers were clenched around the pen and her teeth were clamped together. Even her chest was tight. She had loved Douglas honorably. It wasn't fair for others to judge her otherwise.

With that thought, something in the cold ashes of her core sparked. A wisp of the determination she'd once possessed began to glow inside her. Douglas's memory didn't deserve to be brushed aside and forgotten as if he'd never existed, as if he were an "unfortunate incident." Their marriage had happened no matter how hard Mother and Father tried to sweep it under the rug…and push her to forget it.

She was angry that he'd left her alone and reeling from the consequences of his careless behavior, but she still loved him. Their short marriage had been wonderful. Maybe she should do as he asked. A promise, after all, was still a promise, even after death.

She set the pen down, her movement slow and deliberate. "I want to see the grave and make sure that my husband's interment—" how she hated that word

"—was handled appropriately. I believe I will make the journey after all."

The silence that followed her announcement reverberated like the last gong of a bell.

"Well then," Mr. Edelman said after a moment, glancing from her to her parents. He gathered the papers together in front of him. "If you are sure that is what you want, I'll get these in the post to the attorney in Oak Grove. They'll be waiting there for your signature after you have fulfilled your promise to your late husband."

"Why can't I carry them with me?"

He looked unsure. "It's irregular."

"It seems sensible to me. They are, after all, *my* papers."

"Very well. When you arrive in town, simply leave them with Josiah Melbourne." He started to close his satchel when he stopped. "Oh, yes. Here's one more item." He withdrew a small box and handed it to her.

The crude wooden box was the size of a small rectangle jewelry case and without any decoration. She turned it over. Her husband's initials—DLS—were burned into the bottom. "Where did this come from?"

"Mayor Melbourne said it was found among your late husband's papers."

She frowned. "Why am I only seeing it now?"

"We thought it an oddity," Mother said quickly. "It's just an ugly box. Nothing of consequence."

"But it was important enough to Douglas that he kept it with his legal papers." Cassandra smoothed her fingertips over the letters. The box was an amateur attempt at woodworking. Was it Douglas's first attempt? She knew so little of that part of his life. Now she guessed it made scant difference.

"I took the liberty of opening it, thinking it might hold something of import regarding your late husband's estate," the attorney said, indicating she should go ahead and open the box. "As you will see that was not the case."

She opened the lid.

A folded piece of paper lay on top of a few small assorted items—a lock of auburn hair tied with a bow, a bullet and a leather thong with a small turquoise stone. On the very bottom was a feather. Mementos, she supposed. She wished Doug were here to explain their meaning.

She opened the paper and found a note in her husband's script, written with a steady, strong hand.

Wáse'ekhaar'a—
You will know what to do.
Wira'a

"This isn't for me," she murmured, confused. They certainly were strange names.

"We could put it in the post," Mother suggested. "There is no reason for you to hand carry it all the way to Kansas. You belong here."

Cassandra closed her eyes. "Mother. Please. I will simply take it with me. Someone there will surely know what it is all about." She turned to the attorney. "I'm sorry to have brought you all this way only to stop short at the last moment."

"Quite all right." He leaned toward her, his gray eyes kind. "Your mother and father do have your best interests at heart. You are obviously still recovering from your illness, and it is an arduous journey to travel so far." He stuffed the papers and the box carefully back in the satchel. "If you change your mind and end up staying here, then send me word and we will talk again."

"Thank you, Mr. Edelman."

He stood, as did her parents. At the library door, he stopped. "Please consider, Mrs. Stewart. A promise made to a man on his deathbed isn't legally binding. God would not hold you accountable for trying to ease the last few hours of your husband's life. Good day." He turned and headed down the hall, followed by her mother and father.

They would, as a matter of course, hold a whispered conversation out of her hearing, trying desperately to figure out a way to keep her here. Whatever plan they hatched would come to naught. She was getting stronger. She had to do what *she* thought was best.

"God might not hold me accountable," she whispered into the empty room. "But I do."

Chapter Two

Autumn, 1879

The Kansas Pacific train blew its whistle, announcing its arrival into Oak Grove. Cassandra Stewart gripped her reticule tightly against her chest, her nerves on edge. The squeal of brakes and the sudden hiss of steam as the engine slowed did not help to ease her anxiety.

It had taken all her courage to remain on the train at the last station in Salina. All she'd wanted to do was disembark and wait for the next train back to Alexandria. Nothing here was as she imagined. There were no trees, no beautiful parks or lovely brick buildings, no rolling hills or quiet waters. Only prairie on one side of the train and stockyards—empty at the moment—on the other side.

What have you brought me to? she asked silently, thinking of her late husband. She didn't expect him to answer her from across the chasm; it was just that she felt so very alone now. If he had accompanied her as they'd first planned, this journey would have been a great adventure. Without him, she could no longer view it as such. It was only a duty.

Thus far, regard for his memory had kept her on the train and steady to her course. It hadn't been so long ago that she was the bold one in her family and among her friends. What other woman at twenty-one years of age did she know who skipped the traditional year of waiting and married a man after only five weeks? Tongues had wagged. The gossips in town had had their day, and she hadn't cared. In her mind, love had its own calendar and could not be denied.

Her father viewed her penchant for adventure differently. To him, she was simply impulsive and willful. Or—as her dearest friend, Chloe, had been quick to point out—foolish. Cassandra had scoffed at her words then, but after all that had happened, maybe her friend was right and her great-aunts too. Maybe, as Aunt Tilly had said when she was little, she was being punished.

She remembered the day. She had scrambled through the fence after a cat, tearing her dress on a nail and muddying her stockings and shoes. She had crossed two streets and become lost by the time she finally caught the frightened animal. The cat had clawed her neck and tore her pinafore in an effort to get away from her. After wandering the streets for what seemed like hours, the grocer's wife had helped her find her way back to the house.

A hellion—that's what you have on your hands, Aunt Tilly had told her mother. *You must curb her penchant for constant adventure and excitement. It is unbecoming in a woman.*

If her great-aunts were right, and it was her willful choices that had brought on all her heartache, then maybe doing this would fix it in some small way. The loss of Douglas and their baby had been retribution almost more than she could bear. When her month was completed, she would return home and bow to the wishes of her family. Perhaps then life would go on.

Doug's death had tamed her right down. Now all that remained was to keep the promise she'd made to him. There were so many other things in their short life together that she had been unable to control. This, his last request, was something she could do. She would keep her promise, and then perhaps once it was accomplished and she was released from it, she would be able to move on with her life.

"Ma'am?" The conductor walked down the aisle toward her. "This is your stop. It's as far as your ticket takes you."

She glanced out the window once more at the rustic wooden buildings and the dirt street. "It may as well be the ends of the earth."

He gave his short beard a thoughtful stroke. "Now, Oak Grove ain't all that. It must have a few good points or people wouldn't stay." He brought her hatbox and parasol down from the overhead compartment, and handed them to her and then headed back to the door.

She squared her shoulders. She could do this. Moving to the doorway, she let the conductor help her down to a box he'd placed for the purpose of disembarking, and then down again to the wide planks of the platform. The harsh wind whipped the black ribbons of her bonnet and blew a small tumbleweed across her path. No one else on the train got off. Her trunk and carpetbag were the only luggage sitting there—a forlorn statement in her mind.

The conductor released her arm and tipped the brim of his cap. "Good day, ma'am." He swung a leather satchel over his shoulder that contained mail for Oak Grove residents and strode toward the station office, disappearing through the doorway.

Cassandra took a deep breath and turned to survey the small town. From her vantage point on the platform, she could look straight down the main street. To her left stood a large livery stable. To her right stood a two-story building with a sign—Wet Your Whistle Saloon—above the batwing doors. Tinny piano music filtered out from somewhere inside. Farther down the street, past the laundry and bathhouse, there appeared to be a hotel and restaurant.

Fourteen days ago, she'd written two letters. One to Mr. Barker, the foreman in charge of the Stewart property, and the other to a Mr. Wolf, a friend her late husband had mentioned a time or two. Mr. Wolf's address had been in town. Between the two men, she thought that at least one would have been here to meet the train…and her.

She sighed. All right then. She would figure this out. It wasn't as if the entire process was an insurmountable obstacle. She would get there on her own. Traveling to the property shouldn't be all that difficult. All it required was to hire a wagon from the livery and a guide.

Wolf stood unmoving on the shaded boardwalk in front of his parents' dry goods shop and watched the woman on the platform. The sun slanted just above the horizon, casting her in silhouette and stretching her shadow like a sharp-angled ghost down Main Street. The black netting on her expensive-looking hat covered her face. The black feathers on top were arranged artfully and yet tall enough to brush the underside of her opened parasol—a parasol fancied up with black lace and satin trim. Quite the sight for a simple town like Oak Grove.

He had a good idea who she was. Cassandra Stewart—the woman Doug had fallen so hard for. She was the reason Doug had dug his heels in about returning to the ranch. The way Wolf saw it, because of that she was also the woman who had had a hand in his death.

What was she really doing here? Her short note had only mentioned seeing the ranch and checking on Douglas's grave site. There had to be more to it. Nobody traveled halfway across the continent just to see a piece of land. Especially some rich woman who looked to be more used to Sunday socials and carriage rides in a manicured park than a wild prairie.

"All aboard!" the conductor called out from the train steps. The engine rumbled and the wheels creaked as they forced the massive metal beast to move. A whistle blew—a loud, sharp sound—startling the woman and making her grasp her parasol tighter.

Sanders, standing at the doors to the saloon, noticed her too. He started toward her, doffing his hat as he approached. "Daniel Sanders, ma'am. Help you with your bags?"

"I thought there would be someone here," she said, her voice wavering with uncertainty. She glanced once more down the main street. The action gave away her apprehension.

Did she expect to be taken care of? Was she a hothouse flower whose only purpose was to look pretty? He couldn't see Doug marrying someone like that, but it had been several minutes and she hadn't moved from the platform.

Torn between giving in to the urge to assist her and his feelings of distrust, Wolf hesitated. He didn't want Sanders bothering her, particularly if she was Doug's widow. Even though he had reservations about her, it remained that she was Doug's choice. That meant, in Doug's stead, he owed her assistance. Besides, it wasn't like him to deny any woman simple courtesy. Reluctantly, he stepped off the boardwalk, drawing her gaze.

"You need a place to stay?" Sanders inquired. "You are welcome at the saloon. Got a couple of vacated rooms upstairs right now."

She flashed a startled look at him. "Thank you, but no."

Sanders tipped his hat back, looking her up and down. "I'll make it cheaper than what Austin charges at the hotel."

She stiffened. "I already have accommodations."

Sanders shrugged. "Suit yourself."

Wolf stepped up on the platform. "Raymond Wolf, ma'am. May I see to your things?" He figured that was enough of an introduction to have her either admit who she was or turn him away in the same way she had Sanders.

She peered through her hat netting, taking a good long look at him. For a moment, Wolf thought she was going to refuse his help.

"Thank you, Mr. Wolf."

Sanders snorted. "Well, what do you know..."

His tone caused a familiar tension inside. Wolf curled his fingers into fists.

"Guess you got what you came for, ma'am." Sanders didn't bother to tip his hat as he turned and headed back to his saloon.

At that, the woman visibly relaxed. Her shoulders lowered, and she took a breath before focusing again on Wolf. "I don't mean to be rude. I wasn't expecting... I mean... You are Douglas Stewart's friend, aren't you?"

He didn't answer at first. He wondered what kind of assumptions she held about Indians.

This close, he could make out a few observations of his own. She was attractive, even with the dark smudges beneath her eyes. They accentuated the paleness of her skin. Large night-blue eyes with dark lashes stared up at him through the crisscross of black netting.

Her hair was the color of the sun. A few strands that escaped her bonnet floated across her cheek and shimmered, a pale gold. Had it been loose and flowing, instead of knotted up at the back of her head, he figured that sight would bewitch just about any man who had eyes in his head.

The fact that she was dressed all in black swung like a silent weight between them. Nearly a year had passed since Doug's death. She hadn't come to witness her husband being laid to his final rest on the ranch, and that burned inside Wolf. "Cassandra Stewart."

She nodded.

He walked over to her trunk, tipped it slightly and hoisted it onto his shoulder. "I'll take you to the hotel. Tomorrow, when you have rested, we will go to the ranch."

"You misunderstand, Mr. Wolf. I intend to stay on my late husband's property. It is mine now."

Her words echoed inside his mind. *Mine now.* It

didn't seem right. A part of him was angry that for the past year this woman hadn't acknowledged her ties to the ranch and hadn't asked after the men who worked there day after day. Now suddenly she shows up, calling the ranch hers when she hadn't cared one whit about it before.

The entire thing left a sour taste in his mouth. Besides, it was late in the day to head there. That wouldn't stop him if she were a man, but with a woman it was different. A lot was different. Did she really expect to stay with Barker and the rest of the ranch hands? They could be a coarse lot.

"No."

She tilted her head slightly. "No, you won't escort me? Or no, I may not stay there?"

Although she asked politely, he detected a resolve beneath her words. He stood there, the weight of her trunk bearing down on his shoulder, getting heavier and heavier. The ranch was her property now, according to the banker and Mayor Melbourne. Not much sense for him to argue with her. "Are they expecting you?"

"I wrote to Mr. Barker, the foreman, at the same time I wrote to you. You are here."

"Not because you gave me a date and time. I can see the train depot from my shop." He wouldn't admit that he'd been checking to see if she disembarked every time the train pulled through for the past three days.

"Oh. Well then, I'm very glad you noticed my arrival. Shall we go?"

"It'll be dark in an hour."

"I was told it was only an hour's ride."

"On horseback. A wagon with a load takes longer."

He'd had about all he could take of her trunk. He'd drop it in another second. He'd also had about all he could take of her stubbornness. "Look. There are no women out there. And a lot of men." Blunt, but maybe that would explain the situation to her.

She frowned. "I need to stay there. It is at my late husband's request. If you won't take me, I must find someone else who will."

He admired her determination—grudgingly—but that didn't mean he was giving in. "Tomorrow. First thing. You can come with me or stay right where you are until morning. Either way, I'm taking your trunk to the hotel."

Her mouth pinched in disappointment, but this time she picked up her carpetbag and hatbox and followed him.

Chapter Three

The morning sun had barely crested the horizon when Cassandra heard movement downstairs and tiptoed down for a cup of tea and some toast. Usually at night, she was plagued by dreams that robbed her of rest. Her parents' estate was quiet. That's the way her mother and father preferred it. However, the last two nights on the train had been anything but quiet. The gentle rocking of the train car had been soothing, and for the first time in nearly a year, she had slept well. Now, here, in this small town, even the close proximity of the saloon and the occasional shouts coming from within it hadn't bothered her. She found it all rather strange. In an odd way, the noise was comforting. Life went on here, busy and loud, despite the upheaval she had lived through back East.

She pushed the curtain aside and stared out the hotel window at the dusty town, watching as it slowly woke up. Down the road, a portly man stepped from a dark green building. Over his head, a sign spelled out the words *Law Office*. Cassandra took note of it. If that was

Mayor Melbourne, eventually, she would have need of his services.

Nothing looked as she had expected. The way her husband had spoken of Oak Grove, she thought there would be more than framed buildings in the town. She'd expected that at least the bank would be brick or stone—something more substantial than wood. Something permanent. The town wasn't as big as Douglas had led her to believe, but then he had always seen everything as bigger and brighter than it was. She had loved that part of him—the visionary. It drew her to him. He was ever an optimist.

For a man who chased adventure and sought new experiences, Douglas had a soft spot for his homestead. He'd said once that it was the place he considered the center of his life. He'd been anxious to show it to her, anxious to have her love it as much as he did. And anxious for them to make a home and raise a family together there. He'd pulled her right into his dream and now here she was.

She didn't have his history with the land. A home and a family would never happen—at least not here. Even now she missed the breeze off the Potomac and the dogwood trees and the green of the past summer. The trees would start showing their colors now—orange and red and yellow. It was her favorite time of year. Just as soon as she accomplished her duty to Douglas and to his memory, she would be happy to get back home.

For some unknown reason, she had expected Mr. Wolf to be similar to her husband. To be outgoing and personable. The man was the exact opposite. He hadn't even greeted her properly. Although he'd not actually been rude, he'd been distant and quiet. So very different. How had Douglas ever come to be friends with him?

Douglas had not mentioned that Mr. Wolf was Indian. With his skin the color of almonds and his short hair as black as night, it was the first thing she had noticed. The decidedly cool expression in his dark brown eyes was another thing she'd not expected. It was unsettling. And it was obvious he didn't like her on sight. Here they shared a common bond in their feelings for Douglas, but it didn't seem to matter to him. She'd hoped there would be a glimmer of friendship—something so that she would feel less a stranger in a strange place.

He had lifted her trunk with ease and then stood there listening to her for several minutes as if the load he carried was no more than a ten-pound burlap sack of potatoes. Wide shoulders and all, he was a formidable man—a man's man. His jaw square and hard— just like the expression in his eyes.

She was not looking forward to the ride out to Douglas's property. The sheriff might have provided a better escort—or even accompanied her himself. After meeting Mr. Wolf, she was certain that would have been the more comfortable choice.

A sigh of resignation escaped her. There was no getting around it now. He would be here at any moment.

Across the road, a young woman flung open the front door of a cabinetry shop and busily swept the dirt out with a vengeance that spoke of an agitated state. She looked to be near her own age. When she turned, Cassandra stiffened. The young woman was in a family way and close to the date of her confinement. While she watched, a man stepped from the shop door, gently took the broom from the woman's hand

and drew her close. He kissed her tenderly and then picked her up. The woman's head lowered trustingly to his shoulder as he carried her back inside.

Cassandra's throat suddenly thickened with emotion. She pulled away from the window and pressed her fist to her chest as she tried to swallow past the lump that had formed in her throat. It was a good thing that she was going to Douglas's property today. To stay in this room and witness the couple across the street more than once would quickly become unbearable.

A knock came at the door.

"Mrs. Stewart?"

It was Mr. Wolf.

"I'll be right there," she managed to say.

She took two big breaths to regain control of her emotions and then picked up her hat from the bureau. Positioning it on her head, she tied the black ribbon beneath her chin and adjusted the netting over her face. Today her month began. She would get through this. She would stay on the Stewart land for a month to honor Douglas's wishes, then sell the place and return to Alexandria.

Opening her door, she found Mr. Wolf waiting in the hall, his brown Stetson in his hands. He wore dark brown canvas pants and a butternut cotton shirt. His hair was wet and slicked back from his face, with a small wave just over his forehead.

"Are you set on staying out at the ranch?" he asked.

Again, no greeting, but right to the point. And he certainly wasn't a fan of her staying on the property. "I am."

His jaw tensed, the movement so subtle that she could have easily imagined it.

"Are you ready? Packed?"

She nodded, then indicated her trunk sitting where he'd left it, the domed lid closed.

He strode into the room, picked it up easily and carried it down the stairs and outside to the boardwalk. She grabbed her parasol and carpetbag and followed. While he walked to the livery, she found the proprietor—a Mr. Austin—and took care of her bill, then strolled outside to wait by her luggage.

A few moments later, Mr. Wolf drove a one-horse buggy from the livery and pulled it to a stop in front of the hotel. He jumped down and helped her into the rig, deposited her belongings in the boot, then climbed up beside her and snapped the reins. All without a word.

They rode south from town, over the railroad tracks and along the bank of a wide river. On the narrow dirt road, the small buggy seemed to dip into every crevice and small rut, missing none and sending up a small plume of dust behind them as they continued.

"I didn't see this river from the train. Does it have a name?"

He stared straight ahead. "Smoky Hill River. Runs eastward into the Kansas River."

"Does it run through the Stewarts' farm?"

"In places."

"How long did you know my husband?"

"Since he was eleven. I was twelve."

She calculated the arithmetic. "That makes you twenty-seven now."

"Twenty-eight."

When he didn't elaborate or ask anything of her, she stopped trying to hold a conversation. It would be enough just to get to the property. Douglas's cousin—Mr. Barker—would probably be much easier to talk to and answer her questions in a more agreeable manner.

She smoothed her skirt over her knees. Autumn weather could be capricious, and she hoped the October sun would not grow too warm for her in the black gabardine. The shade provided by her parasol was of little use when the material heated up. Twice during the summer, she had fainted because of the heat—although her mother had thought it due more to her indisposition than the humidity and temperature.

"I appreciate you doing this for me," she said, growing tired of the silence and hoping once more to draw the man out. She wanted to know more about the property and his friendship with her late husband. "Do you visit Doug's farm often?"

"When I hunt."

"So, there is good hunting? What sort of animals do you hunt?"

"Quail, turkey, rabbit, deer."

Short answers and still no smile or glance her way. "How did you and my husband meet?"

"At the ranch." He darted a quick glance aside at her. "It's a ranch. Not a farm. Don't call it a farm."

She stiffened. He may have only been correcting her, but it felt like a critical chastisement. "I'm sorry if I offended you. Ranch, then," she said, acknowledging him.

She should be giddy with having drawn such a string of information from him. The sarcastic thought was not like her. What was wrong with her? Why were her emotions on edge with him? Usually, around others she was numb. For nearly a year now she had been numb.

All this traveling must be more wearing on her than she had anticipated.

He didn't elaborate further, and after a few attempts on her part to learn more, she grew quiet. What was the point of trying to drag information out of him when it was obvious he didn't care to talk? She looked over the river to the far bank and the rolling prairie beyond, her thoughts flashing back to the Potomac River that flowed so near her parents' estate. There was no comparison between the two. They were both too different.

The buggy lurched suddenly, and before she could react, Mr. Wolf grabbed her arm. "Hang on!"

Strength pulsed from his steadying grip.

Startled, she met his gaze. "I'm all right."

He let go, but she caught the relief in his eyes before he turned his focus back to the road.

She drew her shawl tighter together at her throat, as if somehow the material could shield her from him. The heat from his touch burned through her sleeve. When he'd thought she might slip off the seat, the look of worry that had flashed in his eyes surprised her. She didn't understand it. Up to now he hadn't shown any concern for her. He had treated her like an obligation— one he carried out with obvious reluctance.

They continued on, the dirt road curving around a few bluffs and then skirting the river again. They forded a shallow creek. Mr. Wolf made no attempt to speak again.

"I imagine this is how it will be at the ranch," she finally said. "No one will appreciate my intrusion. This next month will be an uncomfortable dance between the men there and me."

"You plan to stay a month?"

"That's what my late husband asked of me. Is there a problem with the length of my stay?"

"No. Just figuring things. You'll be around for the fall roundup."

She hadn't heard that term before. "A roundup? Just what does a roundup entail?"

He darted a glance at her, his jaw tightening for a second before he answered. "We gather the herd, brand the new calves and drive a portion of them to the stockyards."

"Oh. Then it is the procedure for taking them to market to sell?"

He shook his head. "Ma'am. You really do know nothing of ranching."

He wasn't condescending. He was simply stating a fact, but still she was irritated. "And obviously you consider that a bad thing. Yet I'm sure you would know nothing of my life back in Alexandria, so perhaps we can call a truce."

He didn't answer immediately but then blew out a breath. "You should know that the men at the ranch are hard workers and loyal to the Rocking S. One has lived on the ranch since Doug's father planted his first fence post back in '63. He and the others helped make it what it is today."

"Meaning that I am an outsider? That I am not welcome?"

"I didn't say that."

Dismay and hurt swirled inside, making her chest tighten. She hadn't expected to arrive with fanfare and a welcome party, but she did expect common courtesy. "Doesn't it mean something that Douglas chose me for his wife?"

Mr. Wolf stared straight ahead.

She huffed out a breath. "Wonderful. So they dislike me already, sight unseen. Even though I married Douglas. Even though I am the new owner of the *ranch*. Thank you for pointing that out."

His jaw ticked. "Most people around here judge someone by their actions. Not by who they marry." He slanted a look at her. "'Course, you jumped at marrying faster than a lot of women would. Five weeks. That's not much time to get to know someone."

So that was what was bothering him so! "Do you think I tricked Douglas into marrying me?"

He pressed his lips together, thinning them into a line. He drew back on the reins, stopping the buggy. When he spoke, his deep voice held tempered frustration. "You didn't come when his body was laid to rest. Why is that? Why did you leave it up to me?"

The full brunt of his animosity startled her. He judged her unfairly. Heat rolled off her as she tried to find the right words. To tell him the full truth would give him the advantage. He would think her a weak woman, and she couldn't let him or anyone think that. "My reasons are no one's business but my own!"

She lifted her chin, unable to believe she faced the same cynicism here as she had in Alexandria. She'd hoped it would be different here. She'd hoped to find a small bit of acceptance, yet if Doug's good friend was suspicious of her motives, how much worse would the men at the ranch be?

He gave a sharp snap to the reins, and the horse and buggy started forward again.

The movement loosened her tongue. "Strange though it may seem to you, where I come from, a woman is judged very much by who she marries. My parents knew nothing of Douglas or his background. They tried to separate us the moment they saw that things were getting serious. They weren't impressed with him or the small amount of property he possessed. But I trusted him, and for the short time we had together, I cared deeply for him. That is why, when he asked me to do this, I promised that I would."

The lump in her throat grew twice as big. Her eyes stung with tears. She would die before she cried in front of this soulless rock of a man. She'd thought… She'd hoped that Mr. Wolf would be an ally. A friend. It was obvious that any regard he had for her husband did not extend past him to her.

Perhaps it was best to speak only of the ranch and the property. After all, her true business in being here— to honor Douglas's request—wasn't anyone's business but her own. Once she had control of her emotions, she tried again, but this time, she made the attempt to see things through his eyes. "I suppose if the men have worked at the ranch as long as you say they have, they must be very good at what they do."

"They are," he said, his words clipped. He paused but then continued in a quieter voice. "What I'm saying, Mrs. Stewart, is they feel a part of the ranch. It is more than a job to them. It is a way of life. If your purpose for coming here is to sell the land, they'll have trouble with it."

She hadn't given the repercussions of selling much thought. Her plan was to spend a month on the ranch and then focus on getting the ranch off her hands and collecting the money. Now this Mr. Wolf brought up an entirely different side. Would new owners bring their own set of men to run the ranch? Would Douglas's men be out of a means to make a living?

"Is that what they think? That I'm here only to sell the property?"

"It makes sense. You are from the East. You are from the city. And you are a woman. You know nothing about ranching." He glanced sideways at her. "You did call it a farm."

She closed her parasol and set it across her lap. "Thank you for your honesty. I appreciate knowing what I am heading into. Truly, I do."

When she'd written to Mr. Barker regarding her intent to sell, he had advised her to hold off telling anyone until after they'd taken the cattle to market. They had to have the full number of hired hands to drive her cattle to the stockyards or there could be difficulty. If the experienced men left to find employment elsewhere before that, she could lose a healthy portion of her profits due to having to hire new, possibly inept cowboys. That had been her only concern—or so she thought.

Now Mr. Wolf had completely upended that. There was much more to consider. By coming here, what was she getting herself into?

Chapter Four

Wolf sat rigid, determined not to let anything the woman said sway him. He'd thought that after a year he had worked through this anger, but apparently it still simmered inside him.

He didn't blame Doug for marrying her. Doug had a big heart—one that had a tendency to jump head-long into things. Over the years, it had gotten him into plenty of trouble—and Wolf right along with him when he jumped in after Doug to pull him out of some of the wilder antics.

He blew out a breath as he thought over the past year. This was something he couldn't fix or cover up. When Doug had headed east to find a better bull to strengthen his beef stock, he'd asked Wolf to go with him and see the sights. But what did the East hold? There was nothing but cities and smoke and people who would cast curious looks his way. He was better off right here in Oak Grove where people knew him.

He missed his friend, but there was more to it than that. The land was a part of him. He'd walked the land that made up the Stewart ranch his entire life—even before it belonged to Doug's family. He'd camped there, hunted there and fished there. And once the Stewarts became a part of his life, he'd helped with roundups. He had thought that he would always have the ranch and the surrounding land as a place to go. Doug's death had thrown everything into confusion. No one connected to the ranch had any idea how long or even if they would continue working there. And he didn't know how much longer he would be welcome.

This woman had not admitted anything, but he knew in his gut that she would sell the ranch. There was nothing to hold her here—nobody that she knew, no inkling of ranching experience. She would never want to keep up a place this size. By the way she dressed, she obviously came from money. She would head right back East with the first snowstorm of the season.

He pulled on the reins, slowing the horse and buggy as they passed a weathered, whitewashed post.

"This is the northern boundary of the Stewarts'— of your property. That post is the marker. It's another mile to the ranch house." He urged the horse on with a sharp whistle of air between his teeth.

They rode the rest of the way in silence. When the outbuildings first came into view, Mrs. Stewart straightened at his side. "This cannot be right," she murmured.

"This is the Rocking S Ranch… The Stewart ranch."

"But it's much bigger than I anticipated. Everything is much bigger. I'm confused."

He looked over the scene, trying to envision it as a newcomer. The main house was a two-story wooden structure with a large wraparound porch, freshly painted white with dark green trim. Wildflowers, overgrown with weeds, edged the porch. A large stable stood across the dirt drive with the bunkhouse—lodging for the ranch hands—and tucked back behind the house was the cookhouse. The place looked the same to him as it had for the past twenty years. The only real change he could see was the small sapling that Mrs. Stewart had planted in the front yard. The oak tree was now twenty feet high and the only tree in sight for miles.

Beside him, the new Mrs. Stewart sniffled. She fumbled with the drawstring on her reticule. "Drat," she mumbled in exasperation, searching for something inside.

He stopped the horse, giving her a chance to find what she was looking for. A second later she withdrew a handkerchief and dabbed at the moisture in her eyes.

Was she crying about a house? He'd never figure out women...

She caught his look and turned away from him.

Guess he hadn't treated her all that well. Whatever was going through her head about the ranch didn't matter. It was none of his business. What did matter was that it wasn't the way to honor his friend's memory. For whatever reason, Doug had chosen this woman to wed, which meant Wolf should at least treat her with respect. "What's wrong?"

She sniffled again and looked back at the house. "I wish my parents were here. They said his house would be a hovel—a dirt hut. And that his cattle were likely mangy. And that his property would be mud and dirt and not nearly enough to survive on. They should see this. It is beautiful."

She turned back to him. "Why would he do that?

Why would he purposely lead them—and me—to believe those things when they weren't true? He even called it a farm."

Her question took him off guard. It painted her in a different light—one that was softer than he had first suspected. A bit more vulnerable...and maybe a bit more innocent. At least he knew for sure that she hadn't married for money now. It was Doug who had tricked her instead of the other way around.

"The joke is on both of us, Mrs. Stewart. You didn't marry Doug for his property."

"Of course not. I didn't know he had much."

"Telling you all those tales was his way of making sure it was him you wanted and not his money."

She sniffled again. "I suppose you are right. He constantly surprised me. That's one of the things I loved about him." She drew in a shaky breath. "How I wish he were here with me now."

"He is here. His spirit is here."

He snapped the reins, urging the horse on. Another few minutes and he pulled the animal to a stop at the front steps. He jumped down and strode around to her side of the rig. After a second's hesitation, she let him assist her to the ground. His hands spanned her waist easily, and when she landed, he felt a slight tremble flow through her.

She darted a glance his way and then stepped quickly back from him, squaring her shoulders.

But that look had revealed a thing or two. She wasn't as sure of herself as she tried to act.

Before he could ponder on it further, Barker strode out onto the porch. His clothes were a cut above what Wolf had seen him wear in the past. Had he taken to wearing his Sunday clothes all the time? Or had he seen them coming down the lane and cleaned up for Mrs. Stewart's arrival?

"This is Mrs. Douglas—" Wolf began.

"I know who she is." Barker interrupted him. An ingratiating smile inched up the older man's face as he came down the front steps. "A pleasure, Mrs. Stewart. We've been busy getting things ready for your arrival. I'm Cleve Barker, the manager here at the Rocking S."

Barker's attitude took Wolf by surprise. Courtesy was not part of the man's makeup, which immediately put Wolf on alert. Yet Mrs. Stewart seemed won over by the foreman, answering his greeting with a relieved smile. Wolf frowned at that. Barker's graciousness was likely insincere, but it sure made his own greeting less than hospitable. Guess he could have been more welcoming.

"Then I suspect I shall have to forgive you for not meeting me at the train," Mrs. Stewart said.

"Oh, I knew Wolf here would see to your transportation. Or the sheriff. Or any number of others in town. We have been preparing for your stay here ever since receiving your letter. I'm sorry for your loss, ma'am. A sad day indeed for all of us here when we learned of Doug's passing. Particularly for me, seeing as how he was my cousin."

Her smile—the first Wolf had seen—revealed dimples. "Douglas mentioned that you are related."

"Second cousins. His mother's side. Which means that you must call me Cleve. We are family now too."

Wolf pressed his lips together, skeptical of this side of the man. Barker oozed an oily kind of charm that put Wolf on edge.

Mrs. Stewart allowed Barker, his hand on the small of her back, to escort her up the steps to the porch. He opened the door for her. "Come right in."

When Wolf would follow, Barker stepped in front of him, blocking his way. "I can take things from here." His hard gaze challenged Wolf to say otherwise.

Wolf didn't like this. Something didn't sit well with him about the entire situation. "I figured I'd carry up her trunk."

Barker looked over Wolf's shoulder to the buggy. "Leave it on the porch. My men can bring it inside later." He didn't budge, still blocking Wolf's path.

His men? Wolf knew Barker wanted the ranch. Once he had learned Doug wasn't coming back, he'd wasted little time changing things around the place to suit him. But the fact remained it was Mrs. Stewart's property. At that thought, an uneasy feeling settled in his bones. Was he leaving her with a snake in a snake pit?

Mrs. Stewart stood at the bottom of the stairs, ready to ascend, her hand on the railing.

"Ma'am? You sure about this?" he called out over Barker's shoulder.

"I'm fine, Mr. Wolf. I do thank you for bringing me here and your help with my luggage."

Guess there wasn't much more he could do, no matter his unease with the situation. He tipped his hat to her and turned back toward the buggy.

As he hoisted the trunk to his shoulder and then deposited it on the porch, he couldn't get his mind off the situation and the vulnerable look he'd seen in her eyes when he'd helped her down from the buggy. It was that look that made him hesitate about leaving her here.

Barker didn't want him around, that much was obvious, but that had always been the way between them. When Barker had arrived looking for work, he hadn't liked that Doug turned to Wolf for advice about the ranch instead of him. Wolf had been a part of this ranch since the beginning, but Barker didn't care about the history between Doug and Wolf. He figured that family came first—no matter how loose the tie. And he knew how to work that connection with Doug. The man might be several years older and rough around the edges, but since Doug had no family around, he wanted Barker to stay.

Barker had worked as a ranch hand before he'd come to find work at the Rocking S. A few decisions he'd made at the beginning made it obvious to both Doug and Wolf that he didn't have the experience to be a foreman. He needed overseeing until he wised up. That's why, when Doug left for the East, he'd asked Wolf to check in on the place every now and then and especially to be there at the stockyards when the cattle were sold. Doug figured that with more experience and instruction, Barker would eventually learn the ropes.

Barker took instruction from Doug, but when it came to Wolf, from day one the man turned a deaf ear. Doug knew it but figured it would eventually work its way out between the two of them. Doug, always the optimist. But once his cousin left for the East, Barker changed—moving into the big house and helping with less of the physical work. By the time everyone learned of Doug's passing, Barker acted as though he owned and ran the entire operation.

In the year that Doug had been gone and knowing Barker like he did now, Wolf wouldn't put it past him to step right in, pretending to comfort Mrs. Stewart in her grief and while he was at it, take what he wanted while she was at her most vulnerable. That could be the ranch. That could be her. Likely it would be both.

He looked out over the ranch, remembering a time before the outbuildings and the main house were there, a time before the few fences had been erected to keep the cattle away from the large garden and out of the corn. Over the years there had been lots of changes, but the land still called to him. It would always call to him. Since they'd learned of Doug's death, all the hired men carried on doing what they knew best— ranching—but knew that sooner or later they would all get word on what would become of the ranch and, by extension, them.

In the corral, Jordan Hughes worked with a horse, getting it used to the feel of a saddle. Wolf walked over and leaned against the railing, watching the young cowhand work with the two-year-old gelding. The kid was entirely too timid, but he'd learn. And being cautious was always better than being foolhardy.

Wolf watched for a few minutes, offering a suggestion once and feeling pleased that Jordan tried it and it worked on the horse. Then he headed over to the cookhouse to say hello to Otis.

As he approached, he heard humming around the back of the building and followed the sound. Otis sat on an old straight-backed chair, a bucket filled with potatoes at his feet as he peeled the one in his hands. He looked up when Wolf appeared and wiped a hand on his dirty apron. His face, swarthy and lined from a life in the sun, managed to rearrange itself into a grin.

"You'll be cooking for more. Mrs. Stewart has arrived."

"Figured that was her in the buggy." Otis tilted his head, squinting into the sun to study Wolf. "You stayin' too?"

"Might. Barker's acting strange."

Otis grinned. "Well, he probably don't know how to act around a proper woman. All he's ever been with is Gertie from the saloon. Nice as she is, he still don't treat her very good."

That didn't do much in the way of reassuring Wolf. "How would you know?"

"Oh, I get into town every now and then."

Wolf grunted. Now that he thought about it, Otis did stop into his parents' dry goods store to get spices that his mother grew and dried. He just hadn't realized the old coot stopped at the saloon too.

"'Course lately, Barker's had Gertie out here for a few days at a time. She's been gettin' real comfortable in the house. Guess things will be different with Mrs. Stewart around. Been ten years since the first Mrs. Stewart. She kept us all on our toes, don't you know."

Wolf remembered. Douglas's mother had had high expectations of everyone and everything, but then she had high expectations for herself too. She had a gentle way with all of it, and the ranch hands respected her. It would be interesting to see how the new Mrs. Stewart fitted in with things.

"When I saw the buggy, I started in on these spuds. Got a special meal planned." He turned over the potato in his hand, critically examining it for any remaining peel. Then he squinted back up at Wolf, studying him. "How long are you fixin' to stay?"

Although Wolf hadn't made up his mind, Otis knew him better than he knew himself. Since Doug had departed with the understanding that Wolf would look after things, Wolf figured a wife was included in that understanding too. Should the situation be reversed, it was no more or less than what he would expect of Doug.

Wolf mentally ran through the work orders waiting on his workbench in town. He had new ones coming in daily. If he stayed here on the ranch more than a day or two, he'd have to bring his tools and supplies here.

"Hmph," Otis said when Wolf didn't answer immediately. "Well, whether you stay or go, it's up to you. All I can say is it's a dang good thing we had a wet spring. The garden's producin' a sight more'n I need what with the comin' of the fall roundup. There'll be a rack of bellies gathered at the table with or without you, though I doubt Mrs. Stewart eats much at all compared to the hands."

Wolf turned a deaf ear. He'd heard Otis's caterwauling ever since he was small and knew the man meant little by it. After years of soldiering with Doug's father, Otis had arrived with him and worked as a ranch hand at whatever needed doing. He'd handled the cattle until his old war injury had gotten the best of him. Since then he had settled into a job that he truly enjoyed. Guess he was more a farmer and cook by nature than a cowboy.

"If I stay, I'll bring in a turkey."

"It'll only set Barker off—you being in the bunkhouse again."

A smile tugged at Wolf's mouth. Didn't bother him a bit. "Barker doesn't own the ranch."

Concern clouded the old man's eyes. "Not yet anyway."

So Otis had concerns about Barker too. That look sealed Wolf's decision. He'd take the rig back to the livery, let his folks know he'd be gone awhile, grab his tools, saddle his own horse and be back. And he would stay as long as it took to see which way the wind blew.

Chapter Five

Cassandra climbed the stairs to the second floor. Four doors—two facing two—lined the short hallway, which was awash in light from a window at the opposite end. The upstairs smelled musty, as if the place needed to be aired out.

She knocked lightly on the first door that she came to. Hearing nothing from within, she swung it open. A small bedroom greeted her—one that hadn't been used in quite some time, considering the dust on the bureau. She walked across the wood flooring, the heels of her shoes making a sharp sound with each step, and cracked open the window.

The next door revealed a man's room in total dis-array. Toiletries and two whiskey bottles littered the small table near the four-poster. A sweat-stained shirt hung from the tall column at the corner of the bed. Crumbs sprinkled across the tousled sheets. A layer of dust coated the lampshade on the table beside the bed. And the odor—oh, my!—like dirty socks.

A framed painting hung on the wall at the head of the bed. She recognized the subject immediately. Douglas as a young boy. He'd said that his mother painted. The thought brought the sting of tears to her eyes. This must have been his room.

Boots sounded on the stairs. She turned as Mr. Barker approached. "Who is staying here?"

"I moved a few things in. It made it easier to do the ledgers late at night in the study." He looked around the room as if seeing it for the first time. "Guess it could use a good cleaning."

The thought of him sharing the house with her was unnerving. Even with the more relaxed standards in the West compared to the East, surely it was not acceptable. It certainly was not acceptable to her. "Your work habits are commendable, but surely you can see my dilemma. I thought I'd be alone in the house."

His bushy brows shot up. "It's a mighty big house for just one person."

Did he think this was his house? He certainly acted that way. Perhaps it was because he was Douglas's relation. "Did my husband ask you to stay here, in what was his room?"

He hesitated.

It was just long enough that she knew Doug had done no such thing. "Really. You must move your things to your regular accommodations while I'm here."

"Are you sure? You might feel safer with a man in the house."

Did he know nothing of propriety? "It isn't... proper."

He frowned. "Guess I could move back to the foreman's room for the time you are here."

"Thank you," she said tightly. "By nightfall, if you don't mind." Sure that the entire room would need to be scrubbed, she was about to ask who cleaned at the house when the front door slammed open.

"Cleve?" a woman called out in a singsong voice.

Cleve sighed. "Be right back. Something I got to take care of. Go ahead and look around."

He strode down the stairs. "Where you been, Gertie?" he demanded. "You were supposed to clean up the place."

A woman? Here at the ranch? Curiosity got the better of Cassandra, and she tiptoed to the top of the stairs. From her vantage point she could see the sliver of a woman through the stairwell. Her dark brown hair was pinned up in a loose knot, with strands falling down her face and sticking to her flushed cheeks. Her dress was simple, but it was the cut and the way she wore it that was quite suggestive.

"Just walking. What else is there to do on this ranch while everybody works and you ignore me? It's plain boring around here."

He lowered his voice. "I told you when Mrs. Stewart came, you had to head back to town. She's here now. Upstairs."

Gertie glanced up the stairs.

Quickly, Cassandra pulled back from view.

"So you are throwin' me out just like that? What about my things?"

Cleve leaned in and whispered something in her ear.

The woman pulled back, giggling behind her hand. "All right then. See that you do. I could use a new hat too."

"Catch a ride with Wolf. He's taking the buggy out front back to the livery."

Her eyes lit up. "Wolf! Oh, now, there's a grand idea."

Cleve pushed her gently but firmly toward the door. It closed, and Cassandra stepped back from the stairwell. A doxy! The man had entertained a prostitute right here in Douglas's house. Probably even in his bed.

A moment later, Cleve came to the top of the stairs. He paused when he saw her standing there in the small hallway. His eyes hardened slightly. "I'll get my things now." He walked into the room he'd been using and began gathering up his clothing.

She stared after him, more than grateful now that Mr. Barker was moving back to the bunkhouse and Gertie was leaving. She didn't want to contemplate whether he would have had the gall to entertain Gertie while she was here. She certainly hoped not.

For all his talk about spending all of his time preparing for her arrival since receiving her letter, she had yet to see even a fragment of that preparation.

Finally, she turned to look at the last two rooms. The first, a smaller room, appeared to have been a lady's sitting room, or perhaps at one time a nursery. Light streamed through the south-facing window, and needlepoint covered the cushions on the chairs. The last room, attached by an adjoining door to the sitting room, opened into a large bedroom. Feminine doilies covered the small bureau and the back of a chair. A pretty pink, white and green braided rug looked as if it had barely been stepped on. A big four-poster stood with the head of the bed against one wall. The colorful quilt covering was a bright Flying Geese design in shades of pinks and greens that matched the rug.

She let out a sigh. What a comfortable, spacious

room. This had to be the bedroom used by Douglas's parents. Here, she felt a welcome that had heretofore eluded her. She could be at ease here. This is the room she would use during her visit.

She walked through the room and peered through the window. The view overlooked the front drive. A short space farther stood the corral and stable. Beyond that were two large pens separated by a wooden fence. One pen held a handful of cows and the other pen had five horses milling about and creating a dust plume. Farther still, cattle foraged lazily through a field of tall grass. And in the distance, water sparkled. Possibly a lake…or perhaps it was the river she had passed on the ride here. It was difficult to tell. With the exception of two windswept bluffs near the water, there was nothing to break the endless prairie and the beige and brown of an earth that was preparing for winter.

It was all so very different from her home. In Alexandria, even this late in the year, pristine sidewalks, cobblestone streets and courtyards overflowing with potted flowers and clematis vines climbing up wrought iron gates provided a feast of color for the eyes.

She turned away from the window, her throat tightening with emotion. The prairie had a beauty all its own, but without Douglas, it was a foreign place. He wanted her to stay here and learn to love the prairie as he did. But this could never be her home. Not without him.

Outside, a door shut, the noise drawing her gaze back to the glass pane. Mr. Wolf strode from one of the smaller buildings, his long, purposeful strides covering the distance to the buggy in the blink of an eye.

He jumped into the conveyance with a catlike grace and grabbed the reins.

"Yoo-hoo!" the woman, Gertie, called out.

Cassandra couldn't see her, but the woman's voice came from below where Casandra stood. A moment later, Gertie ran from the porch to the buggy. After a brief conversation where Gertie did all the talking, Mr. Wolf nodded, then jumped to the ground on her side of the buggy. He assisted her up to the seat and then climbed up beside her and snapped the reins.

The thought of that woman riding back to town next to Mr. Wolf left a sour taste in Cassandra's mouth. He'd done the neighborly thing—no more or less than anyone should have done. The woman certainly couldn't walk all the way back to town. So why this sudden feeling of disappointment? Mr. Wolf didn't owe her anything—no type of allegiance—just because he'd been a friend to her late husband. That would be ridiculous. So, what was the matter with her?

She looked across the yard, and as if to mirror her mood, a cloud scudded across the sky, blocking the sun. Here Mr. Barker—Cleve—had been welcoming and pleasant, yet there was something about him that she didn't trust. He'd not had the sense to keep his personal life separate from his work, and he'd assumed that she'd welcome him staying in the large house with her. Perhaps he felt entitled because he was family, but that excuse sounded weak to her. He was still a stranger.

However, Mr. Wolf had been moody and gruff. Yet even in that moodiness there had been an honesty in what he'd said to her. He'd forced her to consider the other men who lived and worked here on the ranch. And there was something more—he'd acted worried about leaving her here even though, in the end, he'd done as she asked.

A moment later, Cassandra heard Cleve stomp down the stairs and out the front door. On his back he carried a sheet-wrapped bundle and now headed for a low-slung wooden building on the far side of the stable. He had acquiesced to her request, but he was obviously irritated and didn't care if she knew it. He probably considered it a demotion to move from the main house to bunk with the other ranch hands, but he shouldn't. He should have considered her feelings and her reputation to begin with. Her reputation would be in tatters if he stayed in the house—cousin or not.

She walked through the lower level—the parlor, Douglas's office, which was also a library, the dining area and kitchen. She was at odds as to what to do next. It wasn't yet noon. She couldn't unpack until someone carried her trunk up the stairs. Should she explore the outbuildings? Start delving through the business ledgers of the ranch? Eventually, she would have to visit Doug's grave site.

She hadn't expected to feel Doug's presence everywhere. It wrapped around her like the quilt on his parents' bed. Arriving here was enough. Arriving… That was all she could handle for today.

She walked outside and settled onto the porch swing. A cool breeze rustled through the leaves of the large oak tree. The leaves had turned shades of gold and brown, mirroring the color of the tall grasses of the prairie. An old flowerbed, now devoid of anything but weeds and a few spiderwebs, edged the side of the house on each side of the porch steps. While she swung slowly back and forth, a tall, gangly man emerged from the stable and limped toward her. He was followed closely by two other ranch hands and then Mr. Barker.

She stood and walked to the front steps. She'd never been in charge of anything before, much less a ranch. A knot of nerves grew inside her stomach as she waited for the men to stop before her. Was it best to remain on the steps, higher than them? Or step down to level ground? Would they realize immediately that she knew nothing about life on a ranch? Wrapping her hand around the porch post, she leaned against it, relying on its solid strength to steady her.

Surprisingly, the gangly man with the limp arrived ahead of the others.

"Pleasure to meet you, Mrs. Stewart. I'm Otis Klap, the cook and gardener."

"How very nice to meet you, Mr. Klap."

"Just Otis, ma'am. I've been here since the last Mrs. Stewart arrived with your late husband in tow."

She felt the tug of the first genuine smile on her face in over a month. "You knew Doug, then? I'd like to hear your stories of him when he was little."

Otis grinned up at her from the bottom of the steps. "He was all of eleven years old and full of vinegar, if you don't mind my sayin' so. I'm sure I can think of a story or two."

The other ranch hands arrived then. One man whipped off his hat and murmured a polite welcome as Cleve introduced him. He was simply called Fitch— a stocky, bowlegged and, by the heavy sprinkling of gray in his beard, a good twenty years older than she. Beside him was Jordan Hughes, who was quite young—"barely into his whiskers" as her father would have said.

"I'm puzzled. I thought a ranch this size would take more workers."

"Two of the hands are helping with the roundup at the Circle P, and another is riding the range here, keeping an eye on Rocking S cattle," Cleve said. "They'll stop in when they get a chance. I'll make sure to introduce you when they do. Did you pick out a room?" he asked, changing the subject.

"The one with pink and green."

"Figured you'd want that one, seeing as how it is the biggest. Jordan? Fitch? Carry Mrs. Stewart's trunk up to the south room."

The two men did as he'd instructed. When they returned, she thanked them.

"Ma'am?" Otis said. "We're all real sorry to lose Mr. Doug. And…maybe this ain't the best time to be askin', but it's been nigh onto a year now…" He hesitated.

"Go on," she prompted.

"Well, what we want to know is if you are sellin' the ranch and if we will be out of a job."

Cleve stepped up to stand beside her. "Nobody has said anything about selling the ranch. Now, give the lady a chance to settle in before you pester her with your questions." He moved to take her elbow.

But Mr. Wolf's words had settled inside her, and she was suddenly thankful that she'd had time to consider the ranch hands' point of view, if only briefly. These men were worried about their livelihood—something she had never had to address in her own life. They had a right to some sort of reassurance. "As long as you are content here, I…don't intend for there to be changes for any of you."

Cleve rubbed the three-day-old stubble on his chin.

He was the only one who knew she planned to sell. He was also the one who had told her not to say anything to the rest of the hands until after the sale of the cattle.

"May I see the rest of the property? Perhaps after the noon meal?" she asked.

"Today is not the best day for it, ma'am," Cleve said.

She glanced up at the sky. Clear. Blue. Only one small cloud. "I...I don't understand..."

"I got a few things to take care of first."

She hadn't thought of that. Of course, he had ranch business to attend to. "Perhaps someone else could escort me?"

He didn't look happy. "You are going to want to know a few facts about the place, and I'm the one who knows them, so it will be me accompanying you. But we'll go tomorrow morning."

It was obvious that he wasn't going to budge. "Then if not the property, perhaps the outbuildings?" she asked.

"I could show you around, ma'am," Otis said, stepping forward and glancing at Mr. Barker. "If'n you're interested in the garden or the smokehouse, that is."

"That would be perfect. Thank you, Otis."

She turned to address the men. "Very nice meeting all of you. My husband thought highly of each of you, and I thank you for all your hard work, especially since he has been gone."

She was finished, as far as she knew, but the men continued to stand there, waiting. Finally, she turned and entered the house, feeling their gazes following her. She climbed the stairs as Cleve continued speaking with the men. Last-minute orders, she supposed.

* * *

Otis called her down to dinner two hours later and rang the triangle iron by the kitchen door. She was famished. She sat down at the table to a steaming bowl of onion soup and a plateful of mashed potatoes and steak. Mr. Barker seated himself at the foot of the table.

For a ranch foreman, he had made himself quite at home—dining at the main table, sleeping in the house... Perhaps that was how things were done here, but it felt odd to her. At home, her parents had a maid and a cook. The maid had a room in the downstairs part of the house, but the cook went to her own home at the end of the day. There were no men living in the house but her father and the butler. The coachman had quarters over the carriage house. Still, all the help ate at the kitchen table—not in the formal dining room.

No matter, really. She would adjust. Perhaps it would bode well. At breakfast she and Mr. Barker could discuss the plans allocated for each day. For the time she was here, she would make a place for herself, a routine.

She glanced up to see Otis waiting for her to take her first mouthful. As craggy and wizened as he might be, did he care about her opinion on his cooking? She found it endearing and quickly cut off a small square of the meat and took a bite. A bit tougher than what she was used to, but flavorful. A spoonful of soup followed.

"It's very good, Otis," she said honestly. "Thank you."

"Wasn't sure it'd be to your likin'. Mrs. Stewart—Douglas's ma—she paid attention to details about everythin'. But Doug...he weren't picky about his meals. Could be I got sloppy over time."

"Well, this is fine. What about Jordan and Fitch? Surely they are hungry too."

"Oh, they don't miss a meal—especially that young Jordan. He's got a hollow leg that's as long as Kansas is wide. They're both out here in the kitchen with me." He nodded and then slipped back into the kitchen.

That eased her mind a bit about being alone with Mr. Barker. She took a few more sips of soup. "Mr. Barker, I want you to know that I appreciate all you have done in Douglas's absence. It couldn't have been easy to manage a place this size."

"I'm glad to see that you are aware of that."

"With your obvious expertise in all things related to this farm, I am going to draw on your knowledge frequently. I need your help. You see, I know nothing about farming or cattle."

His chest puffed up a bit as he cut off a generous portion of steak and stuffed it into his mouth. "Then I'd say the first thing you need to do is to quit calling me Mr. Barker. My name is Cleve. And the second thing is, this is a ranch, not a farm."

She grimaced, her reaction a mixture of watching him talk and chew at the same time as well as realizing she'd heard that comment before and not too long ago. "I've already been so informed. There are no ranches near Alexandria. I'm used to farms."

"I can understand your confusion. You passed a few of the fields we planted in wheat and a few in oats. That's all winter feed for the cattle." He leaned forward and covered her hand with his own. "I'm family now, Cassandra. You can count on me just as Douglas did. I care about this place."

She was so shocked at his gesture that she froze.

His gray eyes glittered. "There are several improvements I am making to the place. I'll call them to your attention as I show you the property. Anything to bring in more profit, right?"

She pulled away, uncomfortable with his touch. "My husband didn't mention any improvements, but it certainly sounds like him."

"No? Well, I can't blame him there. A woman as pretty as you? I'm sure he had better things to talk about than cattle prices and fertilizer." He chuckled lightly at his own quip. "Don't worry your pretty little head about it. I'll fill you in on our ride tomorrow."

She didn't care for his condescension. No longer hungry, she stood. "I believe I'll finish unpacking. Please thank Otis for the dinner."

Chapter Six

Wolf rode in just after dusk. A talkative customer, his father's request to watch the dry goods store and an injured pup in Wally Brown's livery had all conspired to keep him from returning quickly to the ranch.

As he dismounted, a golden light flared and caught in the upstairs bedroom of the main house. So, Mrs. Stewart had chosen that room as hers. It would suit her. He remembered seeing the feminine touches the first Mrs. Stewart had sprinkled about the room. He'd been young then and thought such things unnecessary and impractical—a waste of precious time that could better be spent hunting or fishing or setting a trap. What did a cushion decorated with colorful ribbons have to do with a ranch? But it had brought her joy. And in a hard land like the prairie, joy was a precious gift.

He stabled his horse and carried his gear to the bunkhouse. He shook out his bedroll and smoothed it over the first available straw mattress. In the bed next to his, Otis snored away. As the cook, the old man had to be the earliest to rise and get a large breakfast ready.

Cleve Barker strode through the door and stopped short at seeing him. "What are you doing back?"

"Thought I'd stay a few days. Maybe do a little hunting. See how Mrs. Stewart settles in."

"I can manage things."

Wolf remained silent, but his eyes narrowed. He wasn't going to budge. The sooner Barker realized it, the better things would be.

Finally, the man continued on to a room at the back of the building and shut the door.

So he'd moved back into the foreman's quarters. Good.

There had been a few rough patches that sparked the animosity between him and Barker when Douglas first hired him on, but eventually Barker figured out where they both stood in the scheme of things at the ranch. Looked like Mrs. Stewart was figuring it out too and insisting on her place. His opinion of her rose a notch.

Seemed like ever since Doug left, Barker had taken on more liberty with his position, to the point of making decisions that changed the vision of what Doug had for the ranch. Wolf figured as long as they could be easily reversed, most could wait until Doug came home and saw to things himself. Trouble was, Doug wasn't coming home now and Barker acted like he owned the place.

What was going through the man's head now that Mrs. Stewart had arrived? If she planned to sell the property, could Barker afford to buy the ranch himself? A foreman didn't make that kind of money. Did he hope to prove to her that he could take care of the place and she should keep it as an investment? That

might not be a bad thing at all for the men here—
except where did that leave him and his promise to
Doug? Watching over things for a short while was one
thing, but that had already stretched to a year. How
could he continue for an indefinite time, especially
since any respect between him and Barker continued to erode?

Wolf lay back on the bed, laced his fingers together
under his head and stared up at the long wooden beam
over his head. If only he could buy the land. He had
a little saved up, and he knew how to run cattle. He'd
worked the land with Doug for years whenever his own
parents didn't need him at the store.

He'd still need a loan to cover the difference between what he had and what he needed. Would the
bank work with him? It always came back to the fact
that he had Indian blood. Some people couldn't see
past that, and the banker, Micha Swift, was one of
those people. Guess for now it didn't matter. Cassandra Stewart hadn't said a thing about selling.

The important thing was to see to Doug's last
wishes. In the same way that Doug had a motive when
he tricked Cassandra into believing him poor before
marrying her, he had motives for everything he did. He
was smart and, more often than not, one step ahead of
most people. Of the two of them, Wolf was more cautious, having to think through each part of a plan and
the consequences before acting, where Doug plowed
right on ahead.

This month that Cassandra had agreed to stay wasn't
an idle request on his best friend's part. Doug had probably expected her to come much sooner than this. Until
he understood it all, he'd hang around. He'd make sure

that Cassandra stayed safe from any harm while she was here. Harm could come in any number of forms— a snake in the grass, an ornery steer or a two-legged varmint named Cleve Barker.

Chapter Seven

The next morning, Cassandra waited on the porch for Mr. Barker to appear from the bunkhouse. He had been absent the rest of yesterday after their dinner—an occurrence of which she was most appreciative. When he still hadn't appeared after ten minutes, she walked to the stable and found Jordan, pitchfork in hand, scattering fresh straw in a stall.

"Hello, Jordan. Is there a horse that I can use while I am here? Mr. Barker is taking me to see the property today."

He leaned the pitchfork against the wall. "Sure 'nough, ma'am. Got the perfect mount." He strode to the back of the stable and came back with a small gray mare. "She's our most gentle. Her name is Patsy."

"Hello, Patsy." The animal's ears flicked toward her. Cassandra stroked the horse's neck as she eyed the saddle Jordan threw on its back and cinched it. At home, she used an English saddle—one made for a woman.

The hinges on the large wooden door squeaked, and more light poured into the large interior of the stable. Mr. Wolf strode through the entryway.

"I thought you went back to town!" she said, surprised.

"I did. Turned in the buggy and came back."

"Whatever for?"

An almost imperceptible raise of his brows occurred. "Figured I'd make sure you got settled in." He upended a nearby barrel and set the large bulky sack he held on it. "Everyone has a job here that they have to do. They won't have time to show you all that goes on with the day-to-day workings of the ranch."

"Aren't you in the same situation?"

"I can spare a few days." He eyed the horse. "Leaving so soon?"

She stiffened. "No."

A spare smile tilted his mouth. He had tried to get a reaction from her, and he'd succeeded.

She huffed out an irritated breath. "Mr. Barker agreed to show me the property this morning. However, I have not seen him today."

"Patsy is a good choice," he said. He walked over to the horse and smoothed his hand down the foreleg as if checking it for soundness. He straightened, which brought him face-to-face with her. "I could take you around."

Her pulse, in reaction to his nearness, quickened—a rather disconcerting response. It irritated her. She was still in her official mourning period for goodness' sake. Her black garb should alert him to be considerate of that.

"You would do that?" she said, suspicious of his motives. He hadn't been friendly yesterday. Things had been a bit rough between the two of them. Would today be better? Yet she was anxious to see the ranch, he was offering his services and Mr. Barker wasn't anywhere to be found. And for some reason, she felt she could trust him.

He gave a brief nod, his expression serious.

"Very well, then. Another problem is that I have never ridden astride."

"We don't have a lady's saddle here." Jordan said, his ears turning pink as he spoke. He looked to Mr. Wolf as if the man could verify his words. Why would Mr. Wolf know anything about the saddles available?

She eyed the saddle on Patsy. She loved riding and used to be quite good at it. That was before losing Douglas. Since then, and her extended illness, often the simple task of rising from bed in the morning had required more strength than she possessed.

However, oddly enough, not this morning. She'd been up with the rooster crowing.

She patted the mare's warm neck. Perhaps her strength was returning. Just how hard could it be to ride astride compared to sidesaddle? The challenge of learning a new ability stirred something inside. How long had it been since she'd looked forward to anything? "If Douglas's mother was able to do without one," she said gamely, "I suppose I can learn also."

A look of approval flashed across Mr. Wolf's face. Then he walked up to her and laced his hands together for her to use as a step.

She put her foot in his hands and suddenly, she was flying up and was deposited in the saddle. "Oh!"

Disoriented and dizzy for a moment, she clung to the horn. It was a strange sensation, seated like a man on a horse. Wolf watched her quietly. He hadn't completely let go of her but steadied her with his hand on her thigh. She should be shocked. She was shocked. Yet, the moment she focused on him, no longer dizzy, he moved her leg forward and swatted the folds of her skirt out of his way to shorten the stirrup.

"How is that?" he asked as he placed her boot into the stirrup.

"Better." She adjusted her skirt while he walked around to the other side and repeated his efforts with the right stirrup.

He took the reins from Jordan and led the mare from the stable. When he stopped her mount by the corral, he handed her the reins. Even through her riding gloves, the touch of his fingers sent a reassuring flash of strength up her arm.

He mounted his own horse, a larger black that had been drinking at the water trough. It took him one effortless jump.

The front door of the ranch house slammed shut, and Cleve strode across the dirt drive from the house. Seeing Wolf, he stopped short.

Jordan led another horse out from the stable. Cleve mounted and reined the animal over to Wolf, pulling up aggressively close to the black. "No need for you to tag along."

"Just the same, I'm coming."

Cleve drew his mouth into a flat line.

Mr. Wolf replied easily enough, but Cassandra sensed more beneath his words. It was quickly becoming obvious that the two men did not see eye to eye.

Cleve had been the boss here for over a year and was used to controlling all aspects of the day-to-day happenings at the ranch. In most things, she felt she should acquiesce to his expertise. But despite that, she was still the owner of the property and she realized that she wanted Mr. Wolf to accompany her. He may have suspicions about her, but of the two men, he was the one that she trusted.

She urged her horse forward. "Shall we go, gentlemen?"

Cleve skimmed over her riding habit with an appreciative gleam in his gaze. "If that's how you want it, Mrs. Stewart. This way."

He took the lead. She followed. And then Mr. Wolf followed her. Using a dirt trail, they traveled in the opposite direction from the road she'd arrived on, through a gate and out onto the prairie.

Tall golden grass brushed against her stirrups as her horse plodded along on the trail. A few hardy bees skimmed the petals of the remaining flowers and buzzed around her in a curious manner.

"Mr. Barker…" It still didn't seem right to call him Cleve, whether he asked her to or not. "Is the rifle you carry for protection or is it for hunting?"

He patted the wooden stock of his rifle, which protruded from its leather scabbard. "Out here a man doesn't go anywhere without being armed."

Her heart beat a little faster at the thought of seeing a wild animal. Even the birds in Alexandria seemed quite tame if she offered them bread crumbs. "What should I watch for when I am out riding on my own?"

"You won't be alone. Ever."

The words came from behind her. She turned and met Mr. Wolf's gaze. "Why not? What have you seen that would be a danger?"

"Wolves. Rattlers. Once a cougar."

It was as much what he said as the timbre of his

voice that sent shivers through her. His voice was deep and smooth and commanding. She had noticed it yesterday when he first spoke and again now as they skirted the perimeter of a small herd of grazing cattle. "And do they bother the cattle?"

"If a heifer is separated from the herd. Yes."

The cattle standing a short distance from them were completely black in color and on closer inspection had no horns. "I thought all cattle out this way had those massively long horns and were quite deadly in a fight. That's what Douglas led me to believe. How can these even defend themselves? Except for their color, they look like the milking cows back in Virginia."

Cleve chuckled. "You need to learn your cattle, Mrs. Stewart. The ones with the horns you describe are the Texas longhorns, and yes, they can be cantankerous."

"What kind of cattle are these?"

"Black and red Angus. Although we also have a few longhorns that mingle in with the Angus. Your late husband was interested in breeding them before he headed east."

Mr. Barker's words spurred memories she'd forgotten. "I remember him saying something about that. He found a good bull back East and was making the arrangements to purchase it when his accident occurred. Why do the Stewarts raise Angus? Is Angus meat tastier? And how many animals are here on the ranch?"

Cleve pulled his horse to a stop at the edge of what looked like a shallow, dry creek bed. "You sure are full of questions."

He was right. She didn't need to know everything about the cattle. All she needed to know were the facts that would help her sell the property—the general lay of the land, the number of animals and the number of acres for grazing and for farming. But she loved learning new things...or had when she was younger.

She glanced quickly at Mr. Wolf. He was already suspicious that she would sell the land, and Cleve's words probably hadn't helped. What bothered her was that Cleve was the one who had warned her not to reveal anything, yet he seemed to be taunting Mr. Wolf. "I'm simply gathering all the facts so that I can make an informed decision with this property."

"Sounds like my cousin married a smart woman." Cleve indicated a three-foot post. "This marks the eastern edge of the property."

The prairie stretched forever, broken only by a few small bluffs and the sparkling water of the wide river far in the distance. Here, the taller grasses had given way to a short purplish vegetation. In the distance, a man appeared from around the nearest bluff. He rode toward them at a fast speed.

"Wait here," Cleve instructed sharply. He rode ahead to meet the man.

Wait here? Wasn't it her place to know what was going on?

She glanced at Mr. Wolf. "I'm sure Mr. Barker will let us know what is going on."

He didn't answer but sat his horse with his hands folded loosely over his saddle horn. His relaxed posture belied the intense way he watched the two men.

"Is that a ranch hand from here at the Rocking S?" she asked.

Mr. Wolf nodded. "Barker hired him a while back, along with another cowboy. Said he knew them from a previous job they'd all worked on together."

"I thought my late husband did the hiring."

He met her gaze. "He did."

Cleve had taken it upon himself to hire an extra man? Or was he replacing someone who had left? "I'm sure Mr. Barker must have had good reason," she said.

"Maybe."

"Well, I certainly would have deferred to his judgment had he contacted me while I was in Virginia."

"You still need to find out about it."

"I…I will. Thank you, Mr. Wolf."

"Ma'am? Call me Wolf. Everyone else does." He trained his gaze back on the two men.

Then he went by his surname—Wolf. She'd heard both Otis and Cleve call him that. In the letter she had addressed a few weeks ago, she had used his first initial— R—but she hadn't known the rest of his given name at the time.

Tiny lines fanned out from the corner of his eyes, and again Cassandra was struck by the squareness of his jaw. Everything about him was solid and steady and strong. She was beginning to see what her late husband saw in him as a friend.

The urge to let him to call her Cassandra surfaced, but something held her back. It was too soon, too familiar and too friendly. And they barely knew each other.

"You don't like Mr. Barker, do you?"

He snorted softly. "He doesn't much like me."

"Why is that?"

He looked over at her. "It's between him and me."

Was it a woman? Could it be Gertie? The twinge of discontent with his evasive answer shouldn't bother her so. "Fair enough," she said, raising her chin. "But he is Douglas's cousin, and Douglas chose him as the foreman here."

"Don't worry, Mrs. Stewart. I'll make sure he doesn't run your ranch into the ground."

"*You'll* make sure?" In her shock, it came out as half a question. Her horse shied to the right, away from Wolf and his mount.

"That's what Doug asked me to do."

"You?" she repeated, unable to keep the surprise from her voice. "But why?"

"That's what brothers do."

"Brothers!" What in the world was he talking about?

His mouth tightened. "Seems we both have promises to keep."

Her head was spinning with his revelation when Cleve's voice rose in a sharp oath.

The sound drew her gaze, and for a moment she was caught between delving more into Wolf's place in her husband's life or moving closer to the other men to find out what was going on. She really should know what was happening, especially if it was related to the ranch.

She kneed her mare forward, aware that Wolf followed closely behind. The moment the stranger noticed her approach, he stopped talking and gave Cleve a chin nod in her direction.

"Mrs. Stewart," Cleve said. "This is Tom Roth. He's been working the roundup with another hand, Jarvis."

He was a large man, rough-looking with a scraggly, mud-colored beard. He tipped his hat, his eyes expressionless.

"Hello, Mr. Roth," she said. "Do you mind telling me what is going on?"

"Nothing for you to worry about," Cleve answered for him. "Fence is down on the other side of the corn. Tom here noticed and wanted to report it."

It seemed as though they had been embroiled in conversation for a much longer time than just talking about a fence being down.

"Where are they in the roundup?" Wolf asked.

Mr. Roth ignored him.

"What's the word, Roth?" Cleve prompted.

"Ten days out," he answered. Then with a brief nod to Cleve, he reined his horse around and trotted away.

Surely, Mr. Wolf recognized the slight. Perhaps there was a history between Mr. Roth and Wolf also. She turned to Cleve. "What did he mean by 'ten days out'?"

"That's a guess on when they'll get to the Rocking S. There are five ranches involved in the roundup with men from each ranch pitching in to help out. The men are finishing up at the De Bois place now. Then they'll cross to Patterson's on this side of the river. This ranch is the farthest out. They will come here last."

A quiver of excitement flashed through her—something she hadn't felt in ever so long. "I'm looking forward to seeing it." She paused, remembering his words from yesterday. "I thought you said some of the men were at the Circle P?"

"A slight miscalculation on my part. Which reminds me that there are a few things I need to take care of before they arrive. Guess it's a good thing that Wolf tagged along today. Now he can make himself useful and take you back." Without giving her time to say more, he spurred his horse and galloped away.

* * *

She sat back in her saddle, surprised at how fast everything had changed. "I hope you don't mind, Mr. Wolf."

"No, ma'am. And it's Wolf."

"That's right. Shall we go back, then?"

"Thought you wanted to see the ranch."

"I did. But I had hoped Mr. Barker would answer more of my questions."

Wolf let out a soft, derisive snort. He reined his horse away from the fence, striking out through the meadow.

She kneed her mare, urging Patsy up beside Wolf's larger black gelding. Would he be able to answer her questions? Apparently, he had lived in this area all his life. "Is the river part of the ranch?"

"The Stewarts—you—own this side. The opposite bank and lands south of it are open for homesteading."

She shielded the sun from her eyes. "I don't see any homes."

"That side of the river floods. Last spring was the worst in fifty years. There was so much rain that several families had to move to safety north of the river. It took two weeks before they could get back to their land and some of them, on seeing all they owned destroyed, gave up and moved out."

Looking at the land now, she had a hard time imagining it flooded. "That had to be difficult for them."

"It was. More so for the farmers. Through the summer, they had an extra crop of weeds to contend with from the seeds the river water deposited on their land."

She blew out a breath as she surveyed the river and the land beyond it. "I am still in awe of the acreage the

Stewarts own. I don't suppose you know how many cattle are here?"

"A thousand or so."

"A thousand! Just imagine!"

She followed as Wolf circled around the small bluff. The land sloped to the river where the cattle were gathered. They lined the bank, their heads lowered to drink. To Cassandra's right, a large fenced field was covered, not with prairie grass, but with stubble from cornstalks.

"It's so backward here," she mused. "In Virginia, we fence the cattle in and not the crops. Here it is the exact opposite."

"You gotta have range enough to feed the cattle. It's too large an area to fence in. Roundups separate the different brands so that part can be sold and part can be used for breeding."

They rode parallel to the river for a while. As her horse followed his, he'd point out a certain bird or the trail of a fox or rabbit through the grass, and he relaxed more and more. He seemed so at-home here— a different man than the one who'd greeted her at the train station.

"You do know the land," she said quietly. "How many acres are part of the ranch?"

"Twenty-five hundred. Mrs. Stewart—the first Mrs. Stewart—had a map made. It might still be somewhere in the new house."

"New house?"

"Guess you haven't seen the old one."

"There are two?"

"The first house was a soddie. It's not too far from the other buildings."

She'd seen a couple of the earth homes through the

window of the train as it raced through the countryside. Humble beginnings. A new appreciation rose inside her of where Douglas's family had started and how far they had come with the new house and all the outbuildings on the property. But then her thoughts turned back to the man beside her. He knew so much about the area, and that made her curious.

"You live in town. How is it you know so much about the ranch?"

"I spent a lot of time here with Doug. Before that, my father would take me hunting and fishing along the river." He met her gaze. "My mother is Wichita. My father, English. He owns the dry goods store in town."

"That explains much," she said. His looks must come from his mother.

"You were curious," he said. "Most people are. My father made certain that I went to the school in town, but I escaped more than he knew to come out here. The Stewarts always had something going on that was much more exciting than schoolwork."

She smiled at that. "I imagine so. How can numbers and letters hold a young boy's interest when there are fish to catch and horses to break?"

Looking at him now as he sat tall and straight on his horse, there was no hint of the boy he had once been. He was all hard lines and confident strength. And handsome—very handsome. At the errant thought, her cheeks warmed. She shouldn't be noticing such things.

Wolf urged his horse to the top of a small grass-covered hill and stopped several yards from its crest. "We've been riding an hour. This is a good place to stretch our legs and see the entire ranch. It's the highest point."

She didn't want him stopping because of her. He might think her weak. "We don't have to stop."

He slid to the ground anyway, and then, surprising her, walked over to grasp her mount's bridle. "We will stop. This is where Doug is buried."

Her gaze flew to the top of the knoll. She wasn't sure that she was ready. Yet, this is what she'd come here for. While her doctor and parents acted as if her marriage to Douglas had never existed, she knew that it had. By coming here and walking on his land, she felt closer to him. But was she ready for this?

"I'm not sure…"

Wolf waited quietly beside her horse.

She was grateful that he neither hurried her nor remounted to lead her away from the hill. He just waited for her to decide.

It was past time. She had to do this. This was required of her…she felt it in her heart. "All right. I'm ready."

He moved closer, still waiting and watching her with his dark brown eyes. She saw no condemnation in them now.

Finally, she placed her hands on his shoulders and let him help her down. He was a tree—stiff and sturdy. As her feet touched the ground, her knees buckled slightly.

He grasped her waist tighter.

She gripped his forearms. Through his coarse cotton sleeves, his muscles tensed rock hard beneath her fingers. She needed his strength right now and was grateful he hadn't backed away. Her heart raced—and she wasn't entirely sure that it was from her stumbling. His nearness did things to her…inside her. Heat suffused her cheeks. He was so close, and so very strong. The scent of horse and leather and something else subtler filled her lungs.

"You are right. I do need to build up my tolerance in the saddle. I haven't ridden a horse in over a year, and then it was with a sidesaddle."

He probably realized there was more to her shakiness than simply unused muscles, but he remained silent.

Slowly, she released his arms. "Thank you. If you don't mind, may I keep hold of your arm? Just until my legs are steady."

He nodded, offering his arm once again.

Slowly he led her over the bumpy ground to the top of the hill. Just beyond the crest, with a full view of the sloping land all the way to the river and beyond, a small area had been portioned off from the rest of the prairie by a picket fence. He opened the gate for her. "I'll wait here."

She was to continue by herself, she realized. He was offering her privacy.

The small cemetery held four graves—all Stewarts—and was large enough to encompass more. Headstones marked the graves of Douglas's parents, and beside them, an infant daughter.

No wonder he had asked to have his body transported back. He would rest easier here, on his own land and with his family. It was much better for him than in the church cemetery back in Alexandria.

His grave was sparsely covered with prairie grass. No doubt one more growing season would see it completely covered. A wooden cross had been pounded into the earth at the head of the grave. On a braided leather cord hung an oak plaque with his name, date of birth and date of death burned deep into the wood.

She sank to her knees and stretched her fingers over the raised mound before her. The heat of the sun-warmed earth slowly permeated through her soft leather gloves. An aching emptiness had filled her ever since his death. She'd hoped that with this journey she would feel closer to Douglas, that the gaping hole of what could have been—what *should* have been— would close a little.

Her throat thickened with emotion, and she couldn't pretend that her heart wasn't breaking all over again. This time, however, there was a sense of rightness to it all. As if something inside had waited for this precise moment to start healing. She knelt there, feeling bits and pieces of her soul come back to her.

Slowly she began to notice her surroundings—the sweet scent of autumn on the breeze and the warmth of the sun on her shoulders. Wolf stood beside her. She hadn't heard his footsteps or sensed his presence until just then. She stared at the cross as she spoke.

"Douglas was brash and bigger than life itself. I think he lived more in his twenty-six years than most people live in a lifetime. To him, life was a great adventure and to my surprise, he wanted to share it with me. My parents had other plans for me with the son of one of their friends. They asked me once, 'How can you be sure he's telling the truth? What if his money comes from gambling?' But I never doubted him. Not once. I loved him."

She glanced up. Wolf watched her quietly, his dark brown gaze assessing.

"It was the way he spoke of this place. It grounded him. Gave him roots that grew deep and solid. I knew that a man who was that committed to his family and their legacy had to be a good man. He spoke so often of this place. He was anxious to show it to me," she murmured. Her eyes burned with the sting of tears.

"I miss him too," Wolf said in his deep voice.

With that one brief admission, she felt a softening of the brittleness that had engulfed her since Doug's death. Wolf didn't know the gift that he'd just given her. Finally, someone else on this earth truly shared her pain. Overwhelmed by his admission and the feelings that surged to the surface, she could no longer hold back her tears. She had held them in for so very long.

Tears trickled down her cheeks, washing away months of anguish and hurt. Embarrassed that Wolf should witness such a display, she tried to turn away, only to feel him grasp her arms and lift her to her feet. She turned into his arms then, crying until her tears were spent. "Oh, Wolf. He really is gone, isn't he? It's real now. Seeing his grave makes it all real."

Finally, she pulled back from him and wiped her face with her gloves. "Please forgive me. I don't mean to make you uncomfortable."

"You're not."

She swallowed, gaining more control of her emotions. "Doug had so many plans for making the ranch bigger, for making it better than it already was. What will happen to those plans now?"

"His father was the same way," Wolf said. "He was always thinking of improvements for the cattle. After the grasshoppers came and destroyed the crops a few years ago, he took Doug halfway to Kansas City to buy a new type of wheat he'd heard about—Russian wheat. It was supposed to be hardier. There is a field of it planted there." He pointed to a large section of flat land where the soil was turned over. He spoke of a few more plans Doug had that she had not known. Wolf's quiet voice soothed the rawness inside, and after a while, she realized he was talking to give her time to compose herself.

His earlier admission had endeared him to her. Now, listening to him go on when he was more comfortable with silence, her heart softened toward him completely. She touched his forearm, stopping him. "I'm sorry I couldn't come sooner," she said. "I should have."

He nodded once in acknowledgment.

"The cross is lovely, but perhaps…while I'm here, I could arrange for a headstone. Something more permanent." She looked up into his dark eyes. "I'm ready to see more of the ranch now. I want to see all of it. I want to know all that you know."

A slow smile inched up his face.

Cassandra might want to see the entire ranch that day, but he knew that would take much more than a morning, and she wasn't used to riding astride. Her enthusiasm was catching, even if it was larger than her common sense. He took her down to the river's edge and let the horses drink. They dismounted and walked for a while, stretching their legs, as the sun reached its zenith. He offered her a sip from his canteen and a piece of jerky.

She teared up two more times. The call of a meadowlark did it the first time. He hadn't wanted to notice—hadn't wanted to care. But he did. It'd been almost a year since Doug was laid to rest. He thought she would be past such raw feelings, but the moment at Doug's grave told him otherwise. There was a frailty to her that she struggled hard to hide. And those shadows under her eyes gave a haunted look to her pale skin. He wanted to comfort her each time he saw her eyes glisten with tears.

Was it right to take her to Doug's grave so soon after her arrival? He wasn't sure. One part of him had wanted to wait until she asked, but the other part won out—the part that wanted her to confront what was real, what was here and now. A person had to do that before moving on with their life.

On the way back to the ranch, he asked the one question that the man who transported Doug's coffin to Oak Grove couldn't answer. "How did Douglas die?"

She looked over at him. "You don't know?"

He shook his head.

"It was a boating accident. A new acquaintance of his had a sailboat and had been challenged to a competition on the bay. He invited Doug along. They rounded a buoy for the last leg of the race and a gust of wind blew them into another boat. Doug lost his balance and fell between the two vessels. When the doctor examined him, he said several ribs were broken and internal organs crushed. The doctor gave him something to help with the pain. He lasted two days before he succumbed."

The thought that Doug had suffered sickened him. "I'm glad he didn't die alone. It is good you were there to ease his passing."

"It was hard." She closed her eyes a moment. "But I'm glad I was there too."

They headed back to the ranch, and he helped her dismount. This time she was better at keeping her balance.

"I'll see to the horses," he said. "You go on in. Likely, Otis held the noon meal for you."

Her relieved nod made him glad that he had returned even when she said she wanted to see more. He watched her for a moment as she headed into the house.

She should have been with her husband while seeing the ranch for the first time. Instead, she rode on a horse next to a man who was a stranger. He was as foreign to her as the land was. And yet he had held her while she cried. He had only wanted to comfort her. He hadn't expected to be comforted himself. It had been hard to hear what had happened to his brother, yet in not knowing, he had imagined worse circumstances. Knowing the truth set his mind to rest.

He prided himself on being able to read people. One thing he knew for sure after today's ride—he'd been wrong about Cassandra Stewart. She hadn't schemed to marry Doug. Her own parents had tried to talk her out of it. She'd fallen hard and fast, just as Doug had. Wolf accepted that now. What had once been a reluctant attempt to help her for Doug's sake, he now committed to fully.

Chapter Eight

The next morning, Wolf rose early. After a breakfast of bacon and eggs, he rode his mustang out toward the eastern pasture. If he was going to find a turkey for Otis as he'd promised, that area of the ranch was his best bet. Yesterday during his ride he'd seen at least nine of them wandering through the harvested cornfield. About this time of the morning, they'd likely be down by the creek.

After an hour he dismounted and tied his horse to a small cedar sapling that clung to the bank of the creek. Turkeys tended to stick together and wander over the same land again and again. All he had to do was to be quiet and wait them out. He crouched down in the tall grass and listened for their distinctive sound.

The sun had shifted in the sky, shortening Wolf's shadow a few inches, when he heard the familiar gobble of a big bird. It came into view a moment later, followed by two smaller hens. He put his rifle to his shoulder. Aimed…

The shot rang out, and the large bird flapped its wings once and then crumpled to the ground. The other two birds panicked and scattered, making a mad dash, half running and half flying, back to the safety of the taller grass. He stepped from his hiding place and checked to make sure he'd gotten a clean shot and the bird was dead.

He gutted it, leaving the entrails for the buzzards. He had crouched down to rinse off his hands in the creek water when the weak bawling of a calf caught his attention. The sound came from a short distance away, across the small creek and around the sheared-off face of a hill.

Quickly, he tied the bird's feet together and hung the carcass from his saddle. He mounted, urging his horse to move forward, down through the water and up the other bank. As he rounded the bluff, the calf—a heifer—came into view. She jerked her head up and stared at him, her eyes so large and frightened that the whites showed.

"Easy, girl…" he murmured, slowly closing the distance between them.

She backed up, tugging against a rope that hobbled her leg.

"Easy, girl…" he said again and swung his rope over his head in a big loop. One, two, three times, whipping the cord through the air. Then he let it sail.

It slipped over her head and tightened around her neck. She jerked against it and let out a feeble bawl. He wrapped his end of the rope twice around his saddle horn, securing it. He didn't want her so frightened that in trying to get away, she fought the hobbling rope and hurt herself. He only wanted to be able to control her.

But she was weak and obviously half-starved. She gave a half-hearted tug but then stopped.

He dismounted and walked up to her slowly. Speaking softly, he gently removed the rope from her leg and examined her for injuries. A few areas on her lower leg had been rubbed raw, but other than that and the fact that she was hungry, she looked sound.

"Who did this to ya, girl?" he murmured. It was an age-old way of rustling. Stealing a calf was easier than stealing a full-grown cow or steer. At least the thief hadn't gotten around to branding her. He'd like to wait for whoever had done this to return so that he could identify him. There might be more calves in the same predicament. One calf didn't make a herd, and a dishonest man would want more than one. He'd like to know who it was.

It was more important, however, to get the little heifer back to her mother. She needed to eat.

Wolf mounted his horse with one arm around the calf and laid it across his lap. She struggled for a second and then settled down, too weak to continue fighting him. They headed back to the ranch. As he rode, he watched for signs of a cow, her udders bulging, that had no calf at her side.

The main herd of cattle had gathered in the pasture behind the stable. He only hoped the calf's mother was somewhere in that herd. A maverick—a calf without a mother—would have a hard time surviving. He knew of only one way to encourage the cow to stop grazing and come for her calf.

He rode into the stable, dismounted and laid the calf on a pile of straw in one of the empty stalls. Poor little thing was all tuckered out from the stress she'd been through.

Jordan sat on a three-legged stool near the tack wall.

Upon seeing Wolf and the calf, he stopped rubbing saddle soap into a saddle. "Where'd you find that 'un?"

"A way out. Lost its mama."

"Don't look too good."

Wolf walked back to his horse and loosened the ties that held the turkey. "I'll be back for it just as soon as I take this bird over to Otis."

He turned and found Cassandra watching him from the open doorway. Again, she was completely dressed in black, but this time she did not wear a bonnet. When she stepped back to let him pass, moving into the sunlight, her hair gleamed a pale gold. It was a treasure—that hair of hers—and he wondered if it felt as smooth and soft to the touch as it looked.

Her blue eyes widened as she noticed the large turkey he held.

He tipped the brim of his hat.

She smiled hesitantly. "I see we are having turkey in the near future."

"Otis will fix it right up."

Her light brows drew together for a second. "Where did you find the calf?"

"Over by the creek."

"So far away? What was it doing there?"

He didn't want to say anything to her about the fact that the calf was tied up. He'd like to find out who did it first. Whoever it was, Wolf didn't want him alerted to the fact that he was aware of his game.

Cassandra fell into step beside him. "Was it alone? I remember you also said that predators hunt those that are separated from the rest of the herd."

He nodded.

She let out a sigh. "I'm so glad you brought it back."

He found Otis hoeing weeds in the large garden that spread out behind the cookhouse. "Got a bird for you."

A big grin lit the old man's face as he straightened from his task. "Just like you promised. That'll cook up nicely for everybody." He leaned his hoe against the cookhouse and pulled a faded red rag from his dungarees, then proceeded to wipe the sweat from his face and neck with it before stuffing it back in his pocket.

"All right then. Give it here." He held it up by its feet. "Looks like a young one. Should be nice and tender for you, Mrs. Stewart."

Cassandra followed him as he carried it over to a large table at the back of the cookhouse and stretched it out. Otis reached for his meat cleaver.

"You might want to stand back a little more than that," Wolf said, wondering how many birds she'd seen butchered.

The cleaver came down, severing the neck of the bird and a small amount of blood splattered Otis's hands.

Cassandra paled. She backed up as Otis severed the wing at the first joint and then glanced up to see Wolf watching her. "Our cook, Mrs. Mulligan, walked daily to the grocer and the butcher to get our meat. It came to the house wrapped in brown waxed paper." Her voice was a bit shaky.

"Not as fresh as this one?" he asked, although he knew the answer already.

She shook her head, still looking pale. "Not nearly as fresh."

Otis hung the bird on an iron hook that protruded from the side of the cookhouse and began pulling out the feathers. He tucked them into a burlap sack at his feet.

"What are you doing with those?" she asked him.

"Once I get these washed and dried, I'll have enough for a pillow," Otis said and kept on working. "Nothin' goes to waste around here if I have a say."

Wolf needed to get to that calf he'd left in the stable. "I could use a few hot coals."

Otis tilted his head toward the door to the cook-house. "Can't say how hot they'll be since I been weeding awhile, but you can help yourself."

Wolf ducked inside. Using a small shovel, he scooped some of the coals from the stove into an old kettle. He covered the pot with a lid and headed for the stable.

When Cassandra followed, he shortened his steps. "Still checking out the ranch?"

"You are very busy for someone who is not hired on."

"Lots to do on a ranch."

"I'm finding that out. You don't mind if I tag along, do you? You did say that all the other men had their own work to do."

He had said that, he realized. And it wasn't that he minded having her around. He wanted to keep an eye on her and make sure she was treated right by Barker and the other men. Douglas would expect that. It was just…being around her stirred up memories, and if he was honest with himself…other things too. She was a pretty woman. A man would have to be blind not to feel more than a twinge of interest toward her.

But she might not care for what he was about to do.

* * *

Cassandra considered herself tall for a woman, but Wolf's legs were that much longer than hers. She still had to hurry to keep up with his steps. He walked with a sureness of stride and a sense of purpose—a quality that had drawn her to Douglas. Such different men and yet similar in that one way.

Last evening, after Otis had finished cleaning up the kitchen, the house had grown quiet and her thoughts had wandered often to the way Wolf had seen to her comfort during the ride over the property. He'd removed his hat at the grave site. It was a small ordinary show of respect. Then he'd spoken those words—*I miss him too.* They still echoed inside her. She sensed that the simple admission hadn't been easy for him.

He stopped at his horse and removed the saddle. Then he let the mustang loose inside the corral. He carried the saddle and horse blanket inside the stable and deposited them on a railing between two of the stalls.

He certainly seemed right at home here.

He handed the kettle filled with hot coals to Jordan and then strode over to the stall with the calf, going down on one knee to gather the calf into his arms. He aimed his words at Jordan. "Grab the branding iron and a rope and then come with me."

Alarmed, Cassandra quickly followed him out of the stable. "Branding iron! What are you going to do? That's just a baby! Surely you don't mean to brand it now?"

He didn't answer but kept walking. At the gate to the pasture he turned to her. "Open the gate. Then stay back if you don't want to watch."

Where had the wonderful man from yesterday disappeared to? She unlatched the wire over the post and swung the gate wide. Should she follow? Wolf continued through the gate with Jordan at his side, and she realized that they both expected her to stay behind and latch the gate. She quickly did so but then hurried to catch up with him.

"Can't this wait until the calf is older?"

"It's the only way to bring on its mother."

She still didn't understand. They were a short stone's throw from the herd now, the closest she'd ever been to the cattle. She was nervous to be without a fence between her and the large beasts—particularly the ones with the long horns. On horseback, as they'd been yesterday, was one thing. On horseback she could race away. But standing on the ground was another thing entirely. She would never be able to outrun a steer.

She moved nearer to Wolf, relying on his confident air. Jordan didn't seem worried either. They knew what they were doing, and she had to trust that.

"This looks close enough." Wolf stopped and laid the calf in the grass, reaching up to take the rope from Jordan. "Get the fire going."

Wolf kept hold of the calf while Jordan pulled a tin of matches from his shirt pocket. In a bare spot, he piled up a mound of dried grasses, a dried cow chip and the coals from the cookhouse. When the fire sparked and caught and then burned steadily, he pushed the end of the branding iron into it.

As the flame flared up, the calf struggled against Wolf's hold. It couldn't get away, and when it gave up and settled down, Cassandra felt sorry for it. "I still don't understand. How can what you are doing help?"

Wolf met her gaze. "A mother knows her baby's cry."

She drew in a sharp breath. "You mean to hurt it… so it will cry out? That's barbaric! There must be another way." A gentler way.

He ignored her.

Upset, she took a step back. She didn't want to see this. Something inside her cried out to the poor, defenseless calf.

"Iron's ready," he told Jordan. Then he bound the calf's legs with the rope.

She looked from the calf to the iron warming in the small fire.

"Go back to the house." Wolf watched her with a steadiness in his gaze. He meant what he said. He wasn't giving her a choice.

She bristled. "I don't like being ordered about."

"You look white. Like you are about to faint."

She swallowed. She did feel nauseous, but apparently this was a part of ranch life. Doug would have teased her if she shied away. She should see all that happened. And this being her ranch now, she had to accept it. She took a deep breath and lifted her chin. "Please. Continue with your task."

Wolf took firm hold of the calf. "Go ahead," he said, speaking to Jordan. "Keep the pressure steady, even if the calf fights it. A good three seconds. You've got to make it deep enough to scar. I'll tell you when to let up."

Jordan pulled the hot iron from the fire and pressed it against the hindquarters of the small calf. The animal immediately bucked against Wolf's arms. It bawled out a shocked and then scared sound—a sound Cassandra had never heard before. The whites of its eyes showed as it struggled to get away from the pain. Her heart went out to the defenseless and frightened baby

gathering eggs. Wolf headed to the main house and knocked on the door.

No one answered.

He knocked again.

Finally, Cassandra appeared at the door and stepped out onto the porch.

"I wanted to make sure you are all right."

She gave a tight nod.

She didn't look all right. "This is a ranch, Mrs. Stewart. Your ranch. That calf was half-starved. It needed to eat, which meant we had to find its mother. Few calves survive at that age without their mothers. Branding it today saved it from being a maverick at the roundup and possibly getting another ranch's brand."

She crossed her arms over her chest. "So hurting it now served two purposes—marking it for the ranch and finding its mother?"

He nodded. "It'll be fine now. Grow up fat and happy."

"I...I see. Then all is well. Forgive me for being so critical and so...overly sensitive."

She was taking the whole thing sensibly. Still, something seemed off about her quick acceptance. "Nothing to forgive. You have a right to question whatever you want. This is your place."

A small smile—one that encompassed little of her face—tilted the corners of her mouth. "That may be, but I do need to respect the training and experience of my hands."

He didn't want her thinking he was one of her workers. What he wanted was to be her friend. "I'm not your hand."

"Again, forgive me." She stared at him, her gaze un-readable. Then she blinked and leaned across the rail-ing, looking out over the yard. "Do you have time to show me the rest of the ranch now? I'd like to see the buildings, and I certainly don't want to surprise any-body in the bunkhouse."

"I've got time."

"I'll just get my shawl."

He waited as she ducked back into the house. When she returned, they descended the steps and headed to-ward the stable.

"You should know—and keep to yourself until I know more—that the calf was tied up when I found it. Someone meant to separate it from its mother."

"Why in the world would someone do that?"

"So they could brand it as theirs…if it lived."

"But it belongs to this ranch!"

"Not everyone is honest, ma'am. It's become a tradi-tion among rustlers to start their own herd by stealing from someone else's. A calf, being smaller, is easier to steal away and hide than a full-grown steer."

She rubbed her forehead. "Mr. Barker should be made aware of it. He'll know what to do. He has prob-ably handled this situation before."

He didn't want her doing that. "The less people who know that we know, the better. I don't want them cov-ering their tracks just yet."

She frowned. "You are saying I shouldn't tell Mr. Barker?"

"I'll leave that up to you, but I wouldn't. Not yet anyway."

"Very well. I'll do as you suggest. For now." She stared at the ground for moment and then back at him.

"What would have happened if the mother cow hadn't appeared?"

He grimaced, not liking the thought of playing nursemaid to a calf. "I would have come up with something else. There is nothing as good as the calf's own mother."

She had many questions as he showed her the rest of the ranch. Most showed her lack of knowledge about anything related to ranching, but that didn't deter her from asking. She was like the earth, soaking up information like it was rain after a drought. What he figured would take half an hour—just going through the outbuildings and the old homestead—ended up taking the better part of two hours as he explained the different jobs each of the men did that kept the ranch going and answered all of her questions.

By the time they walked around the bend and came to the soddie, the building farthest from the main house, he couldn't recall a time he'd talked so much. He also couldn't recall a time that he'd felt so at ease with a woman. Talking about the ranch came easy for him. The fact that she was truly interested surprised him. For someone who would be leaving at the end of a month, it didn't make sense to him. What would she do with all the information she was gathering? Why would a woman like her care?

"This is the original house the Stewarts built," he said, wondering what a woman of means from the East would think of the humble life that would be rendered in such a home.

With her hand, she shielded the sun from her eyes and studied the sod bricks, worn from the constant wind and the weather but still sturdy. She stepped forward and peered through the open doorway into the one room. Long ago the wooden door had been removed and used on the bunkhouse. "It's small! Did Douglas grow up here?"

Wolf nodded. "They built this for a quick shelter but straightaway ordered wood and started building the stable and then the bunkhouse for the hired hands. For a while the hired hands had it better than the Stewarts did until they could get the main house up."

"I cannot imagine my parents doing something like that," she murmured. "Is it safe to enter?"

He nodded and then followed her inside.

"A dirt floor and only one window... My mother would have scurried right back to her own parents and waited until everything was in perfect order for her to move in."

"Given a choice, I guess most women would do that. It takes courage for someone who is used to comfort and ease to give it all up for the unknown. Mrs. Stewart had courage. And she didn't want to be separated from her husband. She'd had enough of that with the war. She pitched in and worked right alongside him doing what needed to be done to build their dream."

Cassandra pulled back, her shoulders flush against the wall to look up at him. "She must have been an interesting woman. I wish I'd known her."

He looked down at her, captured by her wistful expression. A slight flush perfused her skin as if the walk to the soddie had exerted her more than usual. This close he could see green flecks in the pools of her blue eyes. The smudges beneath had lessened. Maybe she was sleeping better. Maybe the ride yesterday and the fresh air had helped.

His gaze dropped to her lips. Were they as soft as they looked? He itched to find out, to sweep his thumb across her full lower lip. Would he be able to stop with that? If she allowed his touch, would he then press further, replacing his thumb with his mouth?

It had been a long time since he had felt the urge to kiss a woman. A long time since he'd wanted to know a woman more than as a passing acquaintance. He had never been one to dally with the Gerties of the world although he'd had his chances. Watching Cassandra now, he wanted to lift her chin and kiss her.

Only one thing stood in his way—his conscience. He meant to look out for her for his best friend. If yesterday at Doug's grave was any indication, she was still sorting through her grief. She was still vulnerable.

Her gaze clouded over, and she lowered her gaze to the dirt floor.

He blew out a breath. What was he doing? Had he made her uncomfortable? He corralled his thoughts and stepped back from her.

"Do you think Doug's mother would have liked me?"

"She admired anybody with gumption," he said. "So yes, she would have liked you."

He wasn't one to hand out compliments. Heck, he wasn't one to talk much at all.

Her smile grew. "You think I have gumption?"

He hadn't thought so before, but after all her questions today, his opinion was changing. There was more to her than he'd first expected. He could see what had captured

Doug's interest. Beyond her attractive exterior beat the heart of a compassionate and intelligent woman. "I think you've got the makings of a decent ranch owner."

Her eyes widened in surprise. "Even though I cannot stand a branding?"

"You didn't shy away. You stayed, even though it was difficult. I get the feeling that you're a strong woman."

She drew closer. He could smell the perfumed scent of the soap she'd used that morning. It was a heady combination. It made him want to drag in a long, slow breath and fill his lungs with the sweetness of it.

"Thank you for saying that. I needed to hear something good about myself." She sighed. "I've heard many disparaging things of late. My parents didn't want me to come here at all."

She couldn't know that her nearness caused havoc within him. He tamped down on the urge to close the distance between them and instead tried to concentrate on what she said. "It's unusual for a woman to travel so far alone. Maybe that's another instance of your gumption."

"I suppose it could be. Although my best friend would say it was only my impulsiveness."

The sound of a horse thundering down the lane toward them made him step farther away from her and walk outside.

A second later, Jordan rounded the curve in the trail and pulled his horse to a stop in front of them. "Ma'am? Mr. Barker asked me to fetch you. Mayor Melbourne is waiting at the big house to talk to you."

"I'll be right there." She turned back to Wolf, a questioning look filling her eyes...along with confusion. "Thank you for the tour." Then she hurried down the path toward the ranch house.

He waited, letting her get ahead of him, then followed at a slower pace. He was shaken by his response to her. It wasn't anything he wanted to feel. He had to make sure it didn't happen again. When she wasn't guarding her every word and move, Cassandra had a quality about her that drew him. In spite of all he'd said about her being strong, it was also obvious that she was still fragile—still healing. He wanted to protect her. Not make things worse.

He rounded the curve in the trail and caught sight of her talking with the mayor and Barker and some other man half-hidden behind the mayor. Josiah Melbourne carried his work satchel and had a folder tucked under his arm. He pulled that out and handed it to Cassandra.

Wolf's gut tightened. Now he recognized the third man—Micah Swift, the banker. Whatever was happening was official, and he'd bet anything that it had to do with the property.

Cassandra nodded at something the men said, and then she indicated the door. The four of them disappeared into the big house.

Something ominous swirled in the pit of his stomach. These were the men who would be needed to sell the ranch. The thought of strangers living here made his gut curl into itself. How could he abide having people he didn't know own the place?

He knew one thing: if she sold the land, it would be lost to him for good. A stranger wouldn't welcome him walking the property.

What could he do to stop it from happening? If he

had more time, maybe he could convince Cassandra to... To what? What were his options? Was it even possible to convince her to stay?

Chapter Ten

Another night of undisturbed sleep! That made seven in a row since she'd arrived at the ranch. Even after the early crowing of the rooster, she'd managed to doze a bit longer. And what's more, she felt refreshed. Quite the miracle.

Cassandra flung the quilt off her legs and rose from the soft bed. Light streamed in the windows, and at her movement, dust motes swirled through the air. She glanced about; from her bureau to the windowsill, there was dust everywhere. Well, what did she expect? With only men at the ranch, things like dusting the furniture would be a last priority.

She started to dress in her usual black garments and paused halfway through putting on her fitted blouse. The end of this month marked a full year since Douglas's passing. She'd had enough of the black, and yet she knew propriety demanded she wear it for at least a year. That was in the East, however, and she was heartily sick of the color black.

She unbuttoned the few buttons she'd fastened and threw her blouse onto the bed. Then she tugged her white blouse from her trunk. It was slightly wrinkled, but she didn't care. Anything was better than the black. She would give a nod to her mother and propriety by wearing her black skirt, but the blouse would be this one. Wolf had said she had gumption. Well, this was a part of it—dressing to suit herself, not everyone else. Besides, the ranch hands probably wouldn't even notice. Things were more relaxed this far from town.

Once dressed, she headed to the kitchen. Pans clattered and bacon sizzled, the aroma wafting up to her as she descended the stairs. She peeked through the doorway and inhaled the aroma, hoping that this time her stomach would not rebel if she ate a small amount. The doctor in Alexandria had said there was hope that as time went on, she would find her nervous indigestion easing. She longed to be her old self. Sometimes— more often since coming to the ranch—she ran into the woman she had once been.

She caught sight of Otis standing at the stove. "Good morning. Nothing for me but a bit of toast this morning."

He scowled. "You sure about that? You ain't eatin' enough to keep a flea alive, Miss Cassandra. I got flapjacks here all ready to pour."

He'd gone to so much trouble that she hated to disappoint him. "All right. Just one."

Otis mumbled something but ladled the batter onto the pan.

She walked to the dining room and sat down at the big empty table. Mr. Barker had said he had to go into town early and wouldn't be at breakfast. It seemed the man was gone more than overseeing things at the ranch.

Chapter Ten

Another night of undisturbed sleep! That made seven in a row since she'd arrived at the ranch. Even after the early crowing of the rooster, she'd managed to doze a bit longer. And what's more, she felt refreshed. Quite the miracle.

Cassandra flung the quilt off her legs and rose from the soft bed. Light streamed in the windows, and at her movement, dust motes swirled through the air. She glanced about; from her bureau to the windowsill, there was dust everywhere. Well, what did she expect? With only men at the ranch, things like dusting the furniture would be a last priority.

She started to dress in her usual black garments and paused halfway through putting on her fitted blouse. The end of this month marked a full year since Douglas's passing. She'd had enough of the black, and yet she knew propriety demanded she wear it for at least a year. That was in the East, however, and she was heartily sick of the color black.

She unbuttoned the few buttons she'd fastened and threw her blouse onto the bed. Then she tugged her white blouse from her trunk. It was slightly wrinkled, but she didn't care. Anything was better than the black. She would give a nod to her mother and propriety by wearing her black skirt, but the blouse would be this one. Wolf had said she had gumption. Well, this was a part of it—dressing to suit herself, not everyone else. Besides, the ranch hands probably wouldn't even notice. Things were more relaxed this far from town.

Once dressed, she headed to the kitchen. Pans clattered and bacon sizzled, the aroma wafting up to her as she descended the stairs. She peeked through the doorway and inhaled the aroma, hoping that this time her stomach would not rebel if she ate a small amount. The doctor in Alexandria had said there was hope that as time went on, she would find her nervous indigestion easing. She longed to be her old self. Sometimes—more often since coming to the ranch—she ran into the woman she had once been.

She caught sight of Otis standing at the stove. "Good morning. Nothing for me but a bit of toast this morning."

He scowled. "You sure about that? You ain't eatin' enough to keep a flea alive, Miss Cassandra. I got flapjacks here all ready to pour."

He'd gone to so much trouble that she hated to disappoint him. "All right. Just one."

Otis mumbled something but ladled the batter onto the pan.

She walked to the dining room and sat down at the big empty table. Mr. Barker had said he had to go into town early and wouldn't be at breakfast. It seemed the man was gone more than overseeing things at the ranch.

Cousin to Doug or not, the trust she'd felt for him before coming here was sorely tested.

Otis started whistling a happy tune in the kitchen.

She heard the back door open. Immediately, she strained to hear who it was, hoping it might be Wolf. She wanted to see him, wanted to prove to herself that the strange awareness between them at the old homestead was nothing—due only to her active imagination. She had to make sure. She'd thought of little else the rest of that day and the three days since. She had seen him daily, but he was always busy with one thing or another. One day he was helping Jordan work with the horses, another day he and Otis put a new roof on the cookhouse, and yet another day he secreted himself in the stable, working on rifle and gun orders that he had to get done. Was the man avoiding her on purpose?

But it was Jordan's voice she heard as he entered the kitchen along with someone else. Oh, yes… Fitch was his name. The scrape of chairs told her that they were sitting down. A moment later, Otis came through the door separating the dining room from the kitchen, bringing her a plate and hot tea.

"Ahem," she said, looking from the plate-sized pancake to Otis. "There is no way I can eat so much."

"Couldn't be helped, ma'am. I'm used to cooking for the men. Could say you are lucky there ain't three or four stacked there." He hurried from the room. A moment later, he was back and placed butter and a crock of sorghum molasses in front of her.

The scent wafted up to her, making her stomach rumble. She prepared her pancake and, to her surprise, ate the entire thing. Between bites she half listened to the banter in the next room as Jordan, Fitch and Otis teased each other.

The back door opened and shut once more. She knew... She just knew that it was Wolf. The creak of a chair told her that he sat down.

She gathered up her empty plate and teacup and carried them into the kitchen.

The conversation at the table stopped. "Mornin', ma'am," everyone said in disjointed unison.

She didn't hear Wolf's deep voice.

"Good morning, men," she said, a bit self-conscious with all of them staring at her. Fitch nodded politely. Jordan grinned, his face flushing at her use of the word *men*. All except Wolf, who tended to his breakfast.

She motioned for Otis to keep his seat and slipped her dishes into the large pan of water he had warming on the stove. "What will you all be doing today?"

"Getting ready for the fall roundup and the harvest," Fitch said. "Won't be long before the men from the Circle P will be showing up. Barker left word to start getting things ready. Said he was going to check up on Roth and Jarvis and find out when everyone would likely be here."

"He said he'd back by tonight," she said, hoping the news would be helpful to them.

Fitch snorted. "Don't count on it. He'll probably spend the night in town."

"Town?" Mr. Barker hadn't said anything about town to her. "Is it on the same road as the Circle P?"

Otis shook his head, a warning frown directed at Fitch. "Not polite to discuss such things with a lady present. Ma'am," he said, directing his next words to her. "We've handled the roundup for a long time. We'll be fine getting things a-goin'."

The way they spoke, she had an inkling of what they implied when they said Mr. Barker wouldn't be back—and she wore a purple silk dress and a matching glass necklace. Gertie.

"I'd like to help." She noticed a slight rise in Wolf's brows at her statement. Hadn't he said that Mrs. Stewart joined right in and rolled up her sleeves to help when it was needed? Everyone had to do their part. Well, she might not have regained all of her strength since her illness, but surely there was something she could do to help.

"And you, Mr. Wolf? I haven't seen you around lately. What are your plans for the day?"

He looked up from his plate, his brown eyes meeting hers. There was something unreadable in them. "I'll ride east to the far pasture and see how Winston is doing. With the other men helping at the roundup, someone should check on him and see if he needs any help with the cattle."

"You don't have to do that. You aren't actually employed by the Rocking S."

"Just the same. It needs to be done and I'm available."

Disappointment landed heavy on her shoulders. "I had hoped you would be free to accompany me on a horseback ride. I've studied the ranch ledgers until my eyes are blurry. A ride would be inviting."

"Jordan can accompany you," he said.

"I sure can, Mrs. Stewart. Be happy to once my chores are done."

"Thank you, Jordan," she said. A ride with Jordan

would be nice, but it was an afternoon with Wolf that she really wanted.

With the size of the ranch, he would be gone a day or two. She wanted to suggest that Jordan or Fitch go, but something in his eyes had her keeping her thoughts to herself. He wanted to go. He'd promised Douglas to watch out for his ranch, and this was his way of keeping his promise.

Wolf pushed back from the table. "Fine breakfast, Otis." He slipped on his hat, and with a nod to her, he headed outside, quickly followed by the other two.

She stared at the back door as he closed it after leaving, listening to the sound of his footsteps fade away. He was staying away from her on purpose. She was sure of it now. That moment of awareness hadn't been imagined. It had been real. For him as well as her. They'd stood so close she could hear his heart beating.

Or was it hers?

Seven days ago, she hadn't even known him and yet been upset when he hadn't shown her deference as Doug's widow. Now she was upset because he had.

Wolf grabbed his rifle from his bunk and headed out on his horse. It wasn't just to check on the cattle and Winston as he'd told Cassandra. He had to get away, put some distance between the two of them and clear his head.

When she had first arrived, he'd been set to watch out for her, doing what he thought right as Doug's friend. But that day in the soddie had unsettled him. His motives had become all jumbled up in his head. Here he'd thought Barker was interested in using Cassandra's situation for his own goals—either buying or marrying into the ranch property—and yet maybe he was no better.

Oak Grove didn't have many unattached women, and he'd made his peace with the fact that he'd likely remain a bachelor. Once the few eligible women found out he carried Indian blood, they shied away, but Cassandra hadn't let that bother her. She'd seen him first as a friend of her husband's, even with his gruff treatment of her at the start. And now she seemed to consider him her friend too.

Those first days with a beautiful, guileless woman had changed something inside him. He'd enjoyed her company. Probably too much. He wasn't used to a woman's interest. Cassandra thought of him as a source of information and knowledge. Few people in town sought his expertise unless it had to do with firearms. And on the ranch, there wasn't much he could say to Otis and Fitch. They'd been here since the start of the place, just as he had. But Cassandra hung on his every word as if she really cared about the place…and maybe him. He'd let it go to his head.

She'd made him feel alive for the first time. That's probably why in the soddie he'd thought about kissing her. He wasn't surprised by the urge, but he was glad he hadn't followed up on it. It was a poor way to honor his friend and a poor way to look out for his friend's wife. That thought alone had made him step back from doing anything with her the past three days. He still made sure of what she was up to and watched out for her. He simply did it from afar.

He'd reached the far pasture by late morning. He'd passed one small herd of cattle but kept going, intent on making the far side of the pasture by noon. Ever since coming across that calf the other morning, he'd wondered if there were more and he aimed to find out. Eventually, he'd have a talk with Barker that included Cassandra, but only after he had all the facts.

He'd spent that day and the next checking the herds pocketed farthest away from the ranch house. With free grazing, some of the cattle carried the brands of other ranches. That was to be expected. The cattle from every ranch around intermingled until roundup time, when they were herded back to their own spreads. Then some were portioned off to go to the holding yards near Oak Grove and on to markets in the East or to Denver.

He'd spent a few hours the second afternoon with Winston. The man was twenty years into the life of riding herd and used to being alone. He enjoyed hearing the news from Oak Grove and what was happening at the ranch. When they parted, Wolf handed him five hard-boiled eggs from Otis, four cans of beans and the latest issue of the *Oak Grove Gazette*.

Wolf was halfway through the morning of the last day, riding the crest of a small hill that separated the Stewart property from the Patterson ranch, when he heard men shouting and cussing. Following the noise, he came across Roth and Jarvis struggling to free a bull from a buffalo wallow. The animal had sunk to its knees in the muck.

Both men stopped working when they saw him. Jarvis darted a furtive glance at Roth, who rode up to Wolf. Roth sat rigidly and claimed ownership of the situation. "What are you doing here?"

"I could ask you the same thing," Wolf said. "Thought you were helping with the roundup."

"Don't it look like we are? Started on Patterson's

place this morning. This young bull is a maverick. Heard it bawling from over yonder and came to see what the ruckus was."

"'Course that pretty woman will appreciate it when I get this bull into her count," he continued. "Barker too. No need to let Patterson or Putnam know a thing." Roth's eyes narrowed, challenging Wolf to keep his thoughts to himself.

He didn't like the way the man spoke of Cassandra. It made him glad that, so far, these two new riders had not had much contact with her. He couldn't see what Barker saw in either of the men.

"So, Putnam was voted roundup boss again this year," he said, choosing to dwell on that rather than talk about Cassandra. Putnam ran a tight operation. Well, except for these two trail bits. Wolf wondered if Putnam was aware they'd ditched the other workers.

Somehow, the young bull had been missed at the roundup last spring. He should have been branded then. Since the bull was on Patterson land, it should be taken back to Putnam, who would decide as to which brand it would wear. What Roth suggested would make enemies if it was found out. Wolf also wondered, if he turned his back, would Jarvis use the Rocking S branding iron or another one of his own making. Either way, it was considered rustling at this point.

Roth raised his chin to Jarvis. "Get on in there."

"Why can't he do the dirty work?" Jarvis said, indicating Wolf. "I been at it for weeks."

"You're the one getting paid," Wolf said.

Jarvis didn't budge, apparently waiting for Roth to back him up.

"Just do it," Roth answered.

Jarvis scowled. "If I get kicked, I expect you to shoot the stupid beef!" he grumbled. He dismounted and grabbed his bullwhip and then waded into the muck behind the bull.

Wolf whipped his rope overhead in a circle and threw it easily over the bull's horns and head. He and Roth pulled hard, but even with the two of them pulling, the longhorn remained mired in the mud.

Jarvis sneaked up behind the animal and snapped the end of his bullwhip, stinging the bull's hindquarters. At the same time he yelled, Roth and Wolf yanked hard on their ropes.

With a loud bawl, the bull snorted and lunged forward. Another snap of the whip and the beast scrambled from the wallow. It took a few unsteady steps, disoriented and tossing its head.

Before the bull could get his bearings, Wolf jumped from his horse and strode up to retrieve the ropes. He removed the three ropes from the animal's neck. A moment later, the bull tossed his head once more and dashed off into the brush.

Roth rode up to him on his horse and took his rope from Wolf. His expression simmered with anger. "Stupid to remove my rope. Now I'll just have to catch him all over again."

"Catching him won't be the problem. Branding him will." Wolf got a bad feeling in his gut about Roth. This was a man he wouldn't turn his back on.

Jarvis waded from the buffalo wallow and stomped his feet to free the mud and muck from his boots. Then he walked up to Wolf.

Wolf tossed him his rope.

"What are you doing way out here?" An oily confidence coated Roth's tone. "Hunting again? Funny, I don't see any evidence. Maybe you're gathering cattle of your own?"

Ignoring the verbal jab, Wolf walked over to his horse and unhooked his canteen. He wiped off the rim with his sleeve and drank half the water that was left while still keeping an eye on Roth. He stowed his canteen and mounted his horse.

"I figure three to four days with Patterson's ranch will be all it takes. His herd is smaller than the Rocking S's. I'll let the boys at the ranch know you're headed their way."

Wolf reined his horse away, his shoulders tense. Honesty was something Doug and his father had insisted upon with their ranch hands. Honesty and loyalty to the brand. Roth and Jarvis might be doing the job they'd hired on for, but their loyalty sat square either with Barker or with themselves.

If Doug were here, Wolf would be quick to say something to him, but Cassandra was new to this type of thing. Still, she needed to know. He'd talk to Otis first and see what he knew about the two new ranch hands before saying anything to Cassandra. He would mention it to Barker too—as much for the man's reaction as anything. Forewarned was forearmed.

Chapter Eleven

Wind blew the rain in sheets that battered the house. The squall had slowed down their preparations for the roundup for the past twenty-four hours, but Otis clattered around the kitchen, doggedly making pies and muffins a day ahead of the start of the roundup. Cassandra enjoyed the wonderful scents that drifted into the study, but after a few hours of reading the few books on farming and cattle, she was ready to seek out some company.

She'd watched for Wolf to return to the ranch for the past two days and finally saw him ride in shortly after sundown yesterday. From where she stood at the parlor window, he'd looked wet and tired, hunched over against the onslaught of rain. He hadn't come to the house—not even for a hot cup of coffee. It had bothered her. Was he purposely avoiding her? He'd said he would stay until she settled in. Well, maybe she had a small amount, but she would still like to see him.

She rose from her seat and walked into the kitchen. The aroma of Otis's latest sweet concoction tempted her. A tray of cinnamon muffins sat cooling on the table. Otis stood at the large washbasin, cleaning dishes.

"Do you know what Jordan and Fitch are doing?" she asked.

"Not sure, ma'am, but if their chores in the stable are done, they most likely are playin' poker in the bunkhouse."

She would have liked to ask about Wolf but didn't, maybe because to call attention to him would show her interest. She shouldn't be asking after him. Cleve Barker was a more appropriate query. "And Mr. Barker?"

"Oh, he lit out with Roth and Jarvis before the storm. Said he had a few things to get ready before tomorrow."

After two days with Mr. Barker constantly around the ranch, she was glad to learn he wasn't there. He had shared every meal with her and grown more solicitous with each one, yet it put her on edge rather than reassure her. When it came down to it, she might trust the foreman with the ranch, but she didn't quite trust him with her.

There were two oilcloths folded on the table, ready for use on makeshift tables they would set up outside tomorrow. She grabbed one. "I think I'll just peek in on Jordan. He was sniffling a lot yesterday."

Otis grinned. "Young whippersnapper would probably like that. I imagine his ears will turn red if you make over him."

She giggled, surprising herself, and then slapped her hand over her mouth. "I thought I was the only one who noticed that!"

"Well, we don't mention it much, but it happens to

him just about any time he gets around a pretty gal. Seems a shame not to tease him a little. It'll toughen him up some."

She lowered her hand.

"'Bout time you relaxed enough to laugh. You been through a hardship and it ain't been easy, but like the good book says, there's a time for grief and a time to move on. Mr. Douglas wouldn't have wanted you sad."

"Thank you, Otis. That's kind of you to say."

He dried his hands on a towel. "We all go through such a time in our own way. There's no right or wrong or up or down to it."

He indicated the plate of muffins on the table. "Take Jordan a muffin, if you want. Take one for Fitch and Wolf too. And don't you dare tell 'em I offered them or I'll never hear the end of it."

On impulse, she rose to her toes and kissed his weathered cheek. "Thank you. I won't say a word."

She wrapped herself in her shawl and then threw the oilcloth over her head, making sure to protect the muffins, and hurried out the back door. Big drops of rain drummed the oilcloth in a steady rhythm as she carefully picked her way across the muddy yard toward the bunkhouse. As she passed the stable, a light flared from within. Curious, she changed her course. At the stable door, she pounded twice to warn anyone within that she was entering. In the process, the protective oilcloth slid sideways and the muffin plate dipped precariously. She struggled to keep herself and the treats dry as the door swung open.

Wolf stood there. A light jumped into his eyes the moment he realized it was her. It helped to ease the jittery feeling inside her stomach. He'd been so distant, she wondered if he would appreciate her barging in.

He grabbed the plate of muffins and then backed up to allow her entry.

Swinging the cloth down from overhead, she shook it gently to release the excess water. As she adjusted to the changed temperature from outside, a shiver ran through her. Or was it her nerves? Inside, the stable was dry and cozy, a considerable contrast to the cold, wet and windy weather outside. She walked to a nearby sawhorse and laid out the cloth to drip-dry.

Wolf watched her every move, waiting for her to speak first. He looked relaxed and comfortable standing there. He wore a leather vest with the two buttons undone over his coarse cotton shirt. From a leather cord around his neck, a small blue-and-black-speckled stone dangled at the hollow of his throat. It sat askew against his skin, and she had the crazy urge to reach out and straighten it. Did the stone hold special meaning?

She scanned the interior of the stable, searching for the other ranch hands. Apparently, she was alone with Wolf. A large barrel, upended so that it could be used as a table, contained an oil lamp and all sorts of metal pieces. On closer examination, she realized it was parts of a gun...or rifle.

"I came to check on Jordan. He looked so miserable at breakfast that I wanted to see how he was doing."

"He and Fitch finished their chores and are in the bunkhouse." He selected the biggest muffin and took a bite. "Hmm... Let's not tell either of them about these."

His brown eyes held a glint of devilment. It so surprised her to see a bit of levity in him that she blurted out, "You have a sweet tooth!"

He finished off his treat. "Is the extra one yours?"

"I might share. After all, all you've done since coming here is work, and you haven't demanded any payment. A muffin is the least I can offer you." She broke it down the middle and held out half for him.

His fingers brushed her palm as he took it from her, tickling her skin unexpectedly and sending new shivers up her arm. Suddenly she was aware of how close she stood to him and how her nose came to the level of his shoulder. Warmth flushed her cheeks. She stepped back. She should keep her thoughts and questions related to the ranch. She broke off a small portion of her muffin and popped it into her mouth.

He walked a few steps away and set the plate on the post corner of an empty stall.

"What are you up to in here?" she asked, indicating the makeshift table and tools.

He walked over to the small table. "I am fixing Fitch's Winchester. The trigger was sticking and giving him trouble."

"Do you like this sort of work?"

"Been doing it a long time."

She noticed how he skirted answering her question. "Then you must be quite good at it."

"A man has to have a decent rifle. Fixing them is a necessary skill. But given a choice, I'd rather be outside on the back of a horse." His gaze lingered on her, causing her to flush again and look away, searching for words to fill the silence.

"My mother gave up on trying to keep me inside doing embroidery and sewing cushions. I loved to garden and go boating and riding. Anything that was active and outside. Douglas was the same."

"He took risks."

It was unnerving how Wolf dug beneath the surface of what she said. She couldn't hide anything from him. "How...?"

"You forget. I knew him much longer than you."

"I told him not to go that day on the boat. The wind was fierce and had changed directions from when they had last sailed. He wouldn't listen."

"Sounds like my brother."

Brother. He didn't look like Doug's brother—not with his dark eyes and hair. Yet, she realized now, that the bond he felt was deeper than looks and stronger than friendship.

She swallowed, meeting his gaze. "I'm glad you are back. It hasn't been the same around the ranch with you gone. Why didn't you come up to the main house when you returned?"

"Mrs. Stewart—" he blew out a breath "—Cassandra. There is something that I need to say. About...what happened the other day at the old homestead."

Nothing happened, she wanted to say quickly. Because to talk about it would make it so. And to make it so would make her feel a traitor to her late husband.

"There was a moment..."

She tightened her grip on her shawl, holding herself rigid. "Nothing happened that we need to feel uncomfortable about."

He studied her quietly. "I don't feel uncomfortable. You are a beautiful woman. I'm sure other men have... reacted to that in you. But you were Doug's wife and he was my blood brother. You don't need to worry. I won't betray his or your trust. I won't let myself."

By the time he was finished talking, her insides

were a jumble of mixed feelings and jagged edges. He was at once admitting his attraction to her and at the same time promising to keep his distance. What kind of man did that? He must know himself and his own limits well. She drew in a shaky breath and let it out before speaking carefully. "I loved Douglas."

"I know."

It was a simple statement, but his calm acceptance, his belief in her, meant everything. "I can see why he considered you his friend. I didn't understand that when I first met you. You are so very different from him. But you know that, don't you?"

"Just trying to do the right thing."

She strolled along the tack wall, pretending to evaluate the equipment hung there so that, for a moment, she could escape his penetrating gaze. "Did you find Winston?"

"I did. He's looking forward to some company during the roundup."

"I imagine it can get lonely watching over cattle. Can you think of anything more that needs to be done? I want to be as ready as possible for everything tomorrow. I hope this rain stops before then."

"We're set."

"And your mother? Will she help this year too?"

He looked at her in surprise. "Otis told you about her?"

"While you were gone. He explained that your mother has been a big help every year during the round up, helping him with the cooking. I look forward to meeting her." She wondered about the woman. Did Wolf get his beautiful brown eyes from her or his father?

"I'll leave late today to get her and won't be back

until tomorrow. Will you… Do you feel comfortable here?"

"With Otis and Jordan and Fitch? Of course." She answered quickly although his question shouldn't surprise her. He'd said he would stay make sure she settled in, and she was coming to understand that Wolf did not say things idly in passing. His words held weight. He felt responsible for her.

"Barker?"

She glanced up. Did Wolf know the way Barker had been acting lately? "He isn't around much. Which I find odd. But when he is here, he has been a gentleman. And the others are still at the roundup." A fact she was thankful for. Although she still hadn't met Jarvis, her introduction to Roth unsettled her.

"About those two… Be careful around them."

She sank to a nearby three-legged stool. "You don't trust them?"

He shook his head. "I'm not sure where they place their loyalty—or if they have any." He hiked his hip on the barrel. "Just…be careful while I'm busy with the cattle the next few days. Don't go riding alone. Stay close to the house."

How had he found out that she'd been riding while he was gone? She didn't go far, staying in view of the ranch all the time. "I enjoy riding. Patsy is a sweet mare. But I will take care and not go far." She looked forward to the rides. She would hate to give them up.

She paced a few steps away. He was being honest with her…about his feelings, about his watchfulness over her because of Douglas. The least she could do would be to give him the same courtesy. "When Mr.

Swift and Mayor Melbourne were here, we talked about selling the ranch."

"I figured as much," he said flatly.

"How can I make sure that the new owners will allow you access to the property?"

He hesitated before answering. "Don't worry about me. I can hunt farther out."

Even though she had become used to his spare way of speaking, the pause before he replied revealed his concern. The situation bothered him. It bothered her too. She remembered the way he had looked, riding in from the prairie with the calf slung over his saddle. He was at home here, and yet it wasn't his home. Not anymore.

"It's Otis and Fitch I'm worried for," he said. "At their ages, they'll have trouble finding someone else to hire them on."

For the first time, she wished Douglas would have thought of his friend and those loyal to him and this ranch. He'd left her with a burden—one that was not easily removed without causing hurt. What was she to do? "The money from the sale of this place will see me back to Virginia. It will help me make my way for a good many years." It would make it possible for her to live on her own and not under her parents' roof—a future she'd only just started to envision.

"And then what?"

"I suppose I would marry. If not, I would have to live very frugally."

"Wouldn't you go back to your folks'?"

She walked to the corner, considering her words. "I told you that my parents didn't want me to marry Douglas. They also didn't want me to come here. I had disregarded their wishes so often—the first time with letting Douglas court me and second time with marrying him. When I told them that I intended to honor my promise to him, they gave me an ultimatum. When I return home, I must live by their rules."

His brows knit. "Then why go back at all?"

"My life is there. My friends are there," she answered quickly but then wondered, What life? What friends? She'd been in bed for six months and refused to see anyone. The thought of hearing of her friends' lives and how perfect they were when she was struggling to save the small one growing inside her had been unbearable. In the end it had all been for naught. Her friends had deserted her, and the baby had not survived. As things now stood, she had no hard and fast plans for what she would do when she returned East. She knew only that she didn't belong here either.

"The words they spoke were born of their frustration at me and their desire to keep me safe. I understand that now. I am their only child. But obeying their rules has come harder since my marriage to Douglas and being out on my own." She smiled ruefully. "Actually, it was difficult before I married. I have never been very good at following rules."

He listened, quietly watching her.

"They will expect me to marry eventually—a man of their choosing this time."

"You have friends here now. Stay. Learn to run the ranch."

She shook her head tightly. "I would make a mess of things. I know it."

"You could learn. There are people who would help."

She was afraid to consider it. It was a crazy idea.

"No. I couldn't. You were right from the start when you said it all makes perfect sense for me to sell."

His jaw tensed. "I wish I hadn't said that."

"Well, it was the truth. The best I can do is try to find someone who will keep everyone on so that nothing changes for those who work here. And for you. I really do want you to be able to continue hunting on the property, no matter who owns it."

"Guess I wouldn't say no to that, but Doug married you. He'd want you to keep it. Even if keeping it means living back East and letting Barker handle things here."

"No, Wolf. Douglas wanted me to see the place...to stay here for a month because *he* loved it. He wanted to share it with me, and when he knew that he couldn't accompany me here, it gave him peace at the end to know I would do as he asked. He didn't expect me to remain here without him."

As she contradicted him, Wolf's countenance closed off to her second by second. He moved to his makeshift workbench, sat down and picked up the rifle. "Can't hear the rain anymore. It's probably stopped."

"Wolf. Please try to understand."

"I do." He met her gaze. "You're scared."

The sudden shift in his mood, his shutting her out, hurt. But what had she expected? That he would be thrilled she planned to sell?

"That's not true. Change happens whether we are ready for it or not," she said with a frown. "I know that more than anybody after this last year that I've had. People adjust. They have to. We all will..."

She wished he would understand her position. She left him there, picked up the plate of muffins, threw the oilcloth over her head and stepped out into the drizzle.

Chapter Twelve

Wolf paced a groove in the floor of Micah Swift's office. This was taking too long. He needed to get back to the ranch. The roundup would start with or without him, but he wanted to be there.

The banker had been late this morning to open the bank, and when he'd arrived, he'd ushered Wolf into his office and then promptly rushed back out to ask his teller to get him breakfast from the restaurant. There was no question why Micah was late—rumpled clothing, his tie askew and no hat. His marriage was still in the honeymoon stage, and it showed.

His wife, Rebecca, had been on the first trainload of women brought out by the Betterment Committee from the East. Rebecca ran the roost, and she ran it well. Even had a good head for figures. Wolf was glad that Micah was the banker, and not her. He would never have a chance at a loan if she were the one making the final decision. She'd take one look at his assets and refuse to take a chance on him. Micah, on the other hand, could sometimes be swayed.

They were opposites, yet Micah was giving his all trying to adjust to a demanding woman in the house and Rebecca, perfect and rigid as she was, had her moments of genuine softness. They seemed to be happy together.

Opposites… He could say the same thing about Cassandra and himself. She'd come from wealth and, from the sound of it, wanted to get back to it. He had slept little last night as he mulled over all she'd said about her family and about her decision to sell. He'd expected it, but hearing her come right out and say it had been the prod he needed to try for a loan one more time. It was his only hope to buy the ranch.

Micah stepped back into his office. "Sit down, Wolf." He took a seat on a chair behind his desk, drew out his watch fob and placed it on his desk. It was Micah's subtle way of announcing he had only so much time to listen to Wolf's request. Wolf wondered if others got the same treatment. It was demeaning…as if his situation was less important than that of anyone else who walked into the bank looking for a loan.

Unfortunately, it was a familiar occurrence. Many people treated him that way. Cleve for one. But not Otis. Not Jordan or Fitch. And surprisingly, since she came from the East, not Cassandra.

Micah steepled his fingers over his waist. "Well? What is it you want from me?"

"Reconsider the loan. Mrs. Stewart is looking to sell."

He looked surprised. "She told you that?"

"No one else knows."

"Has she signed the papers?"

"No. It's not official yet. I just want to be prepared with an offer."

"I suspected that might be the way of it from the

questions she asked when I rode out there. At the time, she hadn't made up her mind. It sounds like she has now."

"Like I said. Nothing is official yet." But he was glad to hear that Cassandra had been truthful with him…and with the other men who wondered about their futures at the ranch.

"You are the second man to come in here about a loan for that property."

"Cleve Barker?" It didn't surprise him.

"I can't divulge names, but he had collateral. Which is more than I can say for you."

Wolf frowned. "I can put up my business."

"I wouldn't call that a business. Your shop is a table and a few tools in your parents' store. That's not much. Not for collateral on a property that big and that rich."

"The reason I use my parents' place is so that I am there to help them when they need it. I have orders from as far away as Kansas City and Denver. My name is getting out there…and my ability. People like my work. Some even prefer it." He hated touting his own work. Yes, he was proud of what he could do with a gun or a rifle, but a person's product should speak for itself.

"There is no doubt that you are good at what you do. Your…background…hasn't crippled you."

"If he's smart, a man doesn't care about background when he buys a gun. All he cares about is that it shoots true and straight and slips out of his holster easy."

Micha paused. "You should know…a man from Denver is also looking at the property. Mrs. Stewart has been putting him off for two months now."

That got Wolf's attention. He hadn't realized news of the prime property had spread that far.

Trying to convince this man was like trying to turn the wind around. Micah held all the cards. It had been the same when he'd been here five months ago, the first time he'd set out to buy the Stewart property. He'd learned then that it hadn't been put up for sale.

"I'm good for the amount," he said urgently, standing and leaning over the desk between them. "And you would get a good return on your money."

Micah sat back in his chair. "Tell you what. Seeing as how you were Douglas's friend and all... If you can talk Mrs. Stewart into signing an exclusive contract with the bank so that the only place a person would be able to get financing for her property is through me, I'll reconsider your situation."

Wolf straightened. He'd heard of the tactic and knew that other banks got away with it. He didn't like it. What Micah suggested could easily run up the cost of the loan. "I won't do that."

"Then I can't go forward and loan you the money. I'm sorry, Wolf. It's not personal. The bank just can't take on the risk."

Wolf stuffed his hat on his head. "Right."

Micah stood and walked around his desk to Wolf. "I wouldn't want this to come between us. I don't want to make enemies here in Oak Grove. Your father is an upstanding citizen. Even keeps his money here in the bank."

Wolf had heard enough. He wasn't going to change Micah's attitude about the loan, and any further talk wouldn't help. He nodded sharply. "Thank you for your time. I need to get back to the ranch. We're starting roundup."

Micah raised his brow. "You are helping them out, the same as other years?"

"I promised Doug."

"He's gone."

"Doesn't change anything. My word is good. I keep my promises...and pay my debts."

Micah pressed his mouth into a thin line, his eyes hardening.

Wolf didn't bother extending his hand to shake. He was sure Micah wouldn't take it anyway. He turned and strode from the room.

Cassandra watched from the porch as, just after daybreak, cowboys rode in from four neighboring ranches, each group followed by a chuck wagon. Cleve Barker stood at her side, and as each crew arrived, he directed them where to set up their chuck wagons and tents just beyond the stable.

A man from the last outfit broke away, riding up to the house and dismounting. He was a formidable-looking man, about ten years older than she, tall and muscular. He dismounted and strode up to the porch.

He reached for Cleve's hand. "Barker," he said, shaking it. Then he stepped back and tipped his hat at her. "Ma'am. Steve Putnam from the Circle P."

"He's the roundup boss," Cleve said.

She nodded. "Mr. Putnam. I appreciate your help this week."

He removed his hat. "Good to meet you, ma'am, and sorry for your loss. Your husband was a good friend."

She was touched that in all the hustle and bustle of

the morning, he'd thought to say something of Douglas. "Thank you."

"How is Hughes working out?" He directed this at Cleve.

It took her a moment to realize he meant young Jordan.

"He's pulling his weight," Cleve answered, shrugging at the same time.

"Good. I wouldn't want to saddle you with a slacker."

"Jordan worked for you?" Cassandra asked.

"For a few months." Mr. Putnam chuckled, looking down at his boots as if drawing on a memory. "He was a bit too enamored with my new bride—in a puppy-dog kind of way. I thought a change of scenery might remedy the situation and get him back on track."

She remembered Jordan's ears turning red every time he'd ridden with her over the past few days. He'd been nothing but respectful. "He's doing well here. He fits right in."

"Good to know."

"What, may I ask, does a roundup boss do, Mr. Putnam?"

He resettled his hat on his head. "Oh, a bit of everything. I make sure the men know what they are doing for the day and work hard, and that the right calves go to the right brand." He remounted his horse. "Nice meeting you, ma'am."

He followed the caravan of cowboys out to the field and pens behind the stable.

"I'd best be moving too," Cleve said. He furrowed his bushy brows. "Now, don't take this the wrong way, ma'am. About today and the rest of the week… You need to stay near the house. I don't want to see you out there with the men and cattle. You'll only slow them down. They'll be looking at you instead of concentrating on their jobs, and that could cause accidents. You wouldn't want that now, would you? Besides, they are a rough lot. Their kind of talk ain't for genteel ears."

"Surely there is no harm in watching."

"It's for the best if you stay inside."

Was she or was she not the owner here? "Is there anything I can do to help? Other than keep out of everyone's way?"

He thought for a moment. "Otis might have something to keep you occupied. But you make yourself scarce around the stable and pens."

She watched him stride down the steps and over to the stable, her mood souring by the minute. He spoke as if she needed a nanny!

Her annoyance quickly dissipated as she spotted Wolf on horseback, coming down the lane toward the house. Beside him, riding a smaller horse, was an older woman. Their horses were laden with several large cloth sacks stuffed to the breaking point and tied to the saddles. Wolf's mother carried a large rectangular basket on her lap. They rode into the yard and dismounted at the corral, where Wolf tied the horses to the railing.

So, this was his mother. Cassandra descended the front steps and walked over to her, looking forward to meeting another woman and especially the woman who had raised Wolf.

The way Otis had spoken of Mrs. Wolf had created an image in Cassandra's mind of someone small who liked to cook and was a bit outspoken in her own domain. The woman who stood beside her son was fine boned and slender and as tall as herself. She was beautiful in a proud, self-possessed way. The large basket she carried was filled with food and wedged on her hip. When she looked up, Cassandra saw that she did indeed have the same expressive brown eyes as her son.

Wolf came around his mother's side of the horse. "Mother, I'd like to introduce Mrs. Douglas Stewart." He looked at her. "This is my mother, Lily Wolf."

"I am delighted to meet you," Cassandra said, smiling. "Thank you for helping with the roundup."

Lily handed the basket to Wolf. "Take this inside to Otis, son." When he'd gone into the house, she took Cassandra's hand in her cool and slightly roughened ones. "My heart is heavy for you and for the loss of young Doug. He was a son to me. The world is less because he is gone."

Cassandra hadn't expected to be so touched, but suddenly her eyes brimmed with tears that threatened to fall. "Thank you," she whispered. "It means so much to me to hear you say that. My family…didn't know him well."

Understanding filled Lily's eyes. It was unnecessary for Cassandra to explain that her family had not accepted Douglas. She squeezed Cassandra's hands before releasing them. "We will talk. For now, I must find Otis."

"Yes. Of course." Cassandra blinked away her tears as Lily hurried inside the house. Although her chest was tight with emotion, it seemed a small fracture in her heart fused together and began to heal. Here was someone who understood.

Wolf stepped out of the house and walked over to her. They hadn't spoken since yesterday in the stable when their words to each other had turned terse. He took in her tears without comment. His mouth tightened. Then he turned to his horse and began untying the sacks.

"Here. Let me help," she said, removing the two from Lily's horse. "Everything goes to the kitchen?"

"The small one goes upstairs. My mother usually stays in the guest room during roundup time."

"I'll take it up. I'm glad she's here. I look forward to talking with her."

He stopped untying the second sack. "I brought something from town for you."

A gift? Surprised, she set the sacks down at her feet.

He dug in his saddlebag and withdrew a new Stetson—a light tan one. "You need a hat that works out here on the ranch."

"What is wrong with the one I've been wearing?"

He shook his head. "It is too fancy—a Sunday hat. And I like to see a person's eyes when I'm talking to them."

"You don't like the netting?" she asked seriously, but then a fit of fun filled her. "It's all the rage back East. I'm supposed to look mysterious."

His smile came reluctantly. "This is Kansas. The brim on that hat isn't wide enough to protect you from the weather."

"My nose has become pink," she admitted. Of course, it might be because she had stopped wearing the hat altogether around the ranch. If she should go back into town, she would, of course, don it. She took the hat from his outstretched hand and put it on to check the fit, delighted that he hadn't purchased a black one. "Thank you. And I like the color."

"Thought you might want something different."

His smile widened as he assessed her critically. "Should do."

A second later he looked into her eyes. His demeanor changed. "I meant what I said yesterday."

His words about her staying and learning to run the ranch filled her thoughts. The Stetson… Was it his way of a nudge in that direction?

He gathered the rest of the bundles and carried them into the house.

She stood at the corral, wanting to go after him, but knowing it would do no good. Nothing she could say would change anything. The hat—a lovely gift in her mind—had been nothing but practical in his. Perhaps he'd bought it for her in the hope that by dressing like a rancher, she would turn into one. If only it were that easy.

He was her friend, and she hated that they were now at odds. Once, she might have been tempted to try running a ranch on her own. That was before all that had happened over the past year. She was wiser now. That impetuous girl, so full of life, was gone. He believed that she could stay here and make a home, and she knew she couldn't. It was senseless to entertain the idea.

Wasn't it?

Chapter Thirteen

Heeding Cleve Barker's orders, Cassandra stayed clear of everyone that morning. The stable blocked her view of much of what was happening, but from the front porch she could catch glimpses of the men herding cattle down from the rise to the east. The entire operation moved at a steady pace. When their horses would tire, the men changed their mounts for fresh ones from a makeshift enclosure. Otis had called it a remuda. Although she watched for Wolf, she did not see him the rest of the morning.

An hour before noon, tired of keeping out of the way, she marched into the kitchen and demanded a task. Both Otis and Lily looked up from their work at the table, surprised.

"I ain't about to refuse good help," Otis said. "If you're willin', take up that parin' knife there and get to peelin' that pile of potatoes."

She settled to her task, listening to Otis and Lily talk about the food preparation, spices and gardening as they worked. It was amazing all that she absorbed, sitting there. She learned that Steve Putnam had held the honor of being roundup boss for three years. He was a natural for the job, Otis said and then described what the job entailed.

That first morning, he had met with the boss of each brand and told them which direction to send their men out onto the open range, making sure a cowboy from each ranch was involved with every group. Doing that helped to control any wayward inclination among the cowhands to mark a maverick calf—one separated from its mother—with their own brand. Over the past weeks when the operation had been at the other ranches, the maverick calves that had been rounded up there had received the brand of the nearest ranch. It was the Rocking S's turn now.

When the ranch hands came in for the noon meal, the men washed up at the water pump outside and sat down at tables that she and Otis had arranged in the yard. Rocking S hands could all fit around the table in the large kitchen on a regular day, but at roundup, Otis and Lily were known for setting a spread with extra food for those other cowboys tired of their chuck wagon meals. As the last ranch involved in the roundup, it was something special the Stewarts had started doing when they'd first moved to the area. It made the last week of roundup a bit more tolerable to the men who were tired of the saddle and ready to head back to their own ranches.

Cassandra met many of the ranch hands from the neighboring ranches as she and Lily helped serve the food and replenish drinks. The men were polite and watched their language in the women's presence. Even Tom Roth was subdued. She met, for the first time, Bill Jarvis. His perusal of her, and the predatory look in his eyes, immediately set her on edge. Wolf had warned her not to be caught alone with either of the two men. Thankfully, many other ranch hands surrounded her.

Wolf arrived at the table last.

"Lost your way?" Fitch chided him, making room for him to sit beside him. Other men followed suit, teasing Wolf. There was an air of camaraderie to it, and Cassandra realized it was all in fun, a release from the day's tension.

Steve Putnam stood. "I'd like to thank Otis, Lily Wolf and Mrs. Stewart for a putting out a spread that beats all."

A chorus of thanks rose from the men around the table.

"I'd like to take a moment to welcome Mrs. Stewart to the area. Ma'am? I hope you enjoy our beautiful state and plan to stay here a good long time. You won't find a better place or better neighbors—" he grinned "—anywhere."

"Thank you," she said. "Please go ahead and start in. I know you are hungry after watching all your hard work this morning."

Steve nodded to her and sat back down. He turned to Wolf, who sat across the table from him. "You were just in town. What do you hear on the markets?"

"Two dollars per head higher than in spring."

"That's what I like to hear. Now, what do you think about…" Putnam went on talking costs and expenses and profit ratios.

She drew closer, interested in what he was saying. She wanted the ranch to do well. It was important to her because it was Douglas's dream. As she listened to Mr. Putnam and Wolf talk business and noticed the other cowhands joining in with suggestions and observations, she realized something else. They all had a stake in the business that was more than just monetary. It wasn't just a job to them. It was a way of life that they loved, and their happiness depended on whether their ranches did well. By the way they spoke, banding together helped each of them build on the past mistakes or successes of their neighbors.

Wolf caught her watching and listening. Their gazes held for a moment, but then Jordan said something to him and he turned to answer.

After the meal, as the men left the table, they stopped by to slap a hand on Wolf's shoulder or say something to him. A few also came up to her and offered their sincere condolences and again thanked her for the meal.

Back in the kitchen, Otis and Lily cleaned up the dishes. Cassandra grabbed a towel and helped dry them while she listened to the small talk between the two old friends. Lily had a quiet, competent way about her that reminded her of Wolf. It was pleasant to be around her. Every so often she would mention something about Wolf or Douglas when they were younger. Otis added his own embellishments to the story. Cassandra found herself wishing she'd known the two men as boys.

Once the dishes were stacked away, she helped Lily make five shoofly pies for the men. While the pies were baking, she wrote down the ingredients and spices that Lily had brought from town, and mused out loud whether she could plant a few of them in the garden and get them to grow.

"Dag nab it!" Otis said. "Yer figurin' how to make more work for me, and I got enough now as it is!" He grabbed her new Stetson from the wall peg, pushed it at her and shooed her from the kitchen into the dining room.

"But I'll take care of them!" she protested, speaking of the herbs and spices. Then was struck with the realization that she wouldn't be around to make good on such a claim. Swiftly, she closed her mouth.

She marched outside, crossed her arms over her chest and paced the length of the porch, having a good self-imposed pout. How dare they exile her from any part of the ranch! It was her ranch, was it not?

A shout drew her attention and then the bawling of an animal. In the farthest pen, a small herd of cows with their calves milled about while men stoked a fire in an old fire pit. The branding must be starting. Over the last three days, Jordan and Fitch had gathered what they called prairie wood—dried cow dung. The cow chips burned well and would be used as fuel to keep the fire going through each day's marking of the calves.

If she stayed out of their way, she could at least watch what was going on. They were so busy, they wouldn't even know she was around. She marched across the drive and, staying this side of the stable, circumvented the small corral and the bunkhouse, and came to the close side of the cattle pen. As reluctant as she was to see the actual branding, she was curious about everything that went on and didn't want to miss a thing.

A group of men stood around a fire pit that had been built near the cattle pen. They smoked and talked and spit while they threw chips on the fires and watched the flames. She recognized Fitch, Jordan, Roth and

Steve Putnam among them. Every so often Mr. Putnam would pick up an iron, checking the glowing red end, then rotate it and set it back into the embers, apparently waiting for them to heat up more. There were several irons in the fire, and she imagined that along with the three shaped in the form of the Rocking S brand, there were ones that represented the other ranches.

She was glad that, during her tour of the buildings, Wolf had explained what to expect at roundup. Since the prairie was open range, without fences, cattle foraged for food, mingling with the cattle from neighboring ranches. Twice a year, at roundups in the spring and fall, they would be sorted out by brands. Any new calves would then take on the brand of their mothers. After that, a number of cattle would be separated out and driven to the stockyards for sale, leaving the best breeders on the ranch to replenish the herd.

In the large cattle pen, pairs of cows and calves milled about. These cows all wore the Rocking S brand and so would their calves. A line of cowboys shooed them all toward the gate. The cows were eager to escape back to the prairie and hurried through, but as their calves tried to follow, the ranch hands turned them back into the corral. They were the group to be branded.

A second smaller pen held the cows that sported a different brand. There weren't as many of those, so they'd stay together until it came time to brand them individually. It was all a lot of milling about and coordinated confusion, with cows mooing and stomping their hooves and bellowing their unease at the change in their routine. Cassandra found it fascinating.

Movement far across the flat landscape caught her attention. A man on horseback raced after a runaway steer as the animal dashed for freedom. It was a longhorn—too light in color and quick to be otherwise. Angus cattle, she had noticed, were heavier and slower.

The cowboy kneed his horse, dashing first this way and then that way, as he chased down the animal. He was one with his horse, in breathtakingly fluid and graceful movements, leaning with his mount and flying across the prairie.

She couldn't take her gaze away. And in that moment realized the rider was Wolf. Moving closer to the gate, she stood transfixed, holding on to the wooden post. It was thrilling to watch him fly across the prairie. Her pulse galloped in unison with the horse.

The steer was no match for his agile horse as Wolf closed in on the animal and tried to turn it back toward the others. Another twenty yards, and he whipped his rope overhead once, twice, and then the third time he used the momentum to throw it in a wide, arcing motion over the steer's horns and head.

Winded from the chase, the steer used his remaining energy to fight against the rope's insistent tug. It tossed its massive head and dashed this way and that, kicking up dust and rocks. Wolf let it have its way, feeding out just enough rope to keep it from an all-out turn and run again. A few more minutes passed with a lot of caterwauling on the steer's part before it finally settled down and Wolf led it back toward the ranch.

It was then that Cassandra realized she'd been holding her breath, caught up in the excitement.

When Wolf arrived with the steer in tow, Jarvis

rode behind it and called out the brand. Wolf led it to the correct herd.

A shout drew her attention back to the large pen where Mr. Putnam had his fist in the air and circled it, indicating the irons were ready and it was time to start. With an ease that spoke of long experience, Fitch mounted a horse and readied the coils of his rope. A calf was released from the large pen, and as it ran toward its mother, Fitch threw a rope over its head and pulled the slipknot taut. Then he dragged it toward the fire pit. The calf's eyes rolled with fright as it fought the rope. Once Fitch had positioned the animal close enough to the fire, two men descended on it and wrestled it to the ground.

They bound the animal's legs. Quickly, Winston grabbed a Rocking S iron from the fire and held it against the calf's hindquarter. Cassandra counted to three slowly and it was over—the iron pulled away. The men removed their ropes and released the calf. It sprang up and ran toward its mother.

Cassandra breathed a sigh of relief.

Before she could relax, another calf was released from the pen and the process repeated. This time, however, a wild kick from the calf before it was completely subdued caught Tom Roth unaware. He cried out and then cussed at the frightened animal.

Foreboding filled Cassandra as Roth stormed to the fire pit, grabbed the Rocking S branding iron, glowing red-hot, from the fire and shoved it hard against the animal's hindquarter. "I'll teach you to kick me!" he snarled at the calf. The calf bawled and squirmed and pitched, trying to get away from the pain.

The mother cow drew close to the outer railing, agitated and mooing. The look on the cow's face seemed to say, *What are you doing to my baby?*

Cassandra watched in horror as Roth pressed harder, putting his shoulders into it. She remembered Wolf's instructions to Jordan when they had branded the calf a few days ago. The iron was only supposed to be against the hide for three seconds. Three seconds! Roth had already passed that amount of time!

"Enough!" a cowboy called out from the other side of the fire pit. "That's enough, Roth!"

Cassandra clutched the post in front of her. What was wrong with that man? He was purposely hurting the small innocent calf.

Suddenly, Wolf appeared, reining his horse to a quick stop. In one motion, he slid to the ground and kicked the iron away from the calf. "What's your problem?"

Roth, caught off guard, still managed to hold on to his end of the iron. He regained his balance and stood with his feet spread, brandishing the iron in the air and glaring at Wolf, who clenched his hands into fists, prepared to defend himself.

Cassandra's heart pounded. Surely, they wouldn't fight!

"Well?" Wolf said, challenging Roth.

The man stiffened, his chin coming up. He glanced at Fitch and the other men, who now watched. "No problem at all. Just making sure the mark sticks."

"You were doing more than that. Take over as wrestler. If we lose a calf because of your foul temper, it will come out of your pay."

"You ain't my boss," Roth said.

"Go get Barker if you have a problem with my orders."

Roth glanced over at Barker and Putnam. They watched the entire scene from Putnam's chuck wagon. Neither man stepped forward to challenge Wolf's words. Roth gave him a surly look, stormed over to the fire pit and threw down the iron.

Wolf turned to Fitch. "You handle the branding. When you need to be spelled, Jordan can take over."

Fitch gave a quick nod and began coiling his rope.

Cassandra closed her eyes as the image of Roth delighting in hurting the calf played through her mind again. It sickened her. The cool breeze blew toward her, filling her lungs with the odor of charred flesh. She couldn't get the bawling of the little defenseless calf to stop ringing in her ears.

Then she understood. It wasn't her imagination. The men had continued with their work, and it was happening again and again as they wrestled each calf down and branded it.

Her knees buckled, and she sank to the ground. Her forehead pressed against the fence post as she relived the memories she thought she'd banished—memories of another defenseless baby. Jumbled into the sounds of the bawling calves and the bellowing mother cows, she heard her own whimper.

She pressed a hand against her lower abdomen. She had tried so hard to keep Doug's baby, doing all that the doctor said, but was there something she'd missed? Had ignorance on her part undone everything? Or were the things her great-aunts said true? Was her prideful, willful nature the cause of punishment from above? Was it her fault? All her fault that she'd lost the baby?

"Cassandra!"

The shout permeated the fog of her thoughts, and she looked up to see Wolf jumping from his horse. Behind him, the other ranch hands had stopped their branding and stared at her. Wolf dashed toward her, climbed through the barbed wire fencing and dropped to his knees in front of her.

Chapter Fourteen

He'd seen her go down, crumpling in a heap. She pulled back from the post, looking disoriented, her blue eyes too big for her face—a face that was white.

"What are you doing here?" he asked, angry with himself. If she couldn't handle the branding with the calf he'd rescued a few days ago, why had she hung around to watch this time? And this time had been brutal. Roth had been brutal. She had been so still that he hadn't known she was watching until he saw her sink to the ground. She was a strong woman. The fact that she'd traveled to Kansas on her own proved that. But she'd been through a lot over the past year, and a person could only take so much.

"Here, let me help you up." He grasped her and helped her to her feet. She wobbled a little. She couldn't walk like this. She was still in shock. He swept her up into his arms.

"I can walk!" she protested, pushing weakly against his chest.

"I know," he said in a tone that also said it didn't matter. He wasn't about to put her down. She'd only drop to a heap on the ground again.

He started for the house. The faint scent of soap on her skin caught his attention, and he marveled at its presence in the midst of the overpowering stink of cow and leather and sweat that carried on the breeze.

Slowly, she slipped her arms around his neck and relaxed against him.

"What were you thinking?" he murmured as he strode past the stable. He didn't expect an answer. He climbed the steps and deposited her gently on the porch swing. "I'll get you some water."

"No. Don't go..." She reached out, a hand to his forearm, stopping him. "Wolf? Why must you hurt them so? They are just babies. Isn't there another way to separate them?"

She sounded so innocent, so very fragile, as if one more cry from a calf would undo her completely. At least the color was coming back to her face. "It's how things are done. How they've always been done. It's a part of ranching."

"It...it's barbaric." A tear slipped down her cheek.

He wanted to hold her again—for no other reason than to comfort her. Would she accept it from someone like him? There was a world of difference between them, and it came down to money and privilege and position in this world.

He sat beside her and set the swing into a gentle, slow rock. "You think of a better way, and I'll get it done."

She wiped away her tear. "I believe you would."

Then she surprised him by leaning her head against his shoulder.

"Cassandra," he said, noticing again that she rubbed

her abdomen. She didn't seem to realize she was doing it. "What's really going on here?"

"I don't know. Suddenly, I just couldn't bear the bawling of the calves and the smell of burning hair." She raised her head slightly. "I suppose I've ruined everything. The men will think they have an emotional female for a boss." She sniffled. "And I'm afraid it's true."

"You are being hard on yourself. You haven't had an easy year. I think most of the men realize that. Besides, I'd fight anybody who said anything."

He kept the swing moving gently, wondering what else he could say to calm her down. "So tell me. What is going on?"

She let out a big sigh and then straightened on the swing.

He made certain to continue with the gentle rocking.

"I'm better now. I'm…healing. I'm sleeping well for the first time in months. The fresh air and getting away from the city has helped."

What was she talking about? "Have you been sick?" Then another thought. "Is that what kept you from coming to Doug's funeral?"

She nodded tightly.

He started connecting the situation—the calf, the cow, the pain, her holding her stomach. And he stopped the swing. "You were with child."

She squeezed her eyes shut. Tears leaked from the corners. "I'm sorry. I thought I was finished with all these episodes." She dabbed at her eyes with her sleeve.

"I lost the baby. I did everything I could…everything the doctor said…but in the end, nothing helped.

It didn't make it." She closed her eyes again and began sobbing.

It was downright painful to see her hurting so much. He put his arm around her and drew her to him. If she wanted to pull away, so be it, but he couldn't sit there and do nothing.

She leaned into him and cried, her shoulders shaking with gut-wrenching sobs. A dark stain from her tears grew on his leather vest.

He could kick himself. No wonder the bawling of the calves had unhinged her. He'd been angry because she missed the funeral. He wished he could call back the words he'd thrown at her that first day on the ride to the ranch. Here she'd been doing all she could to help her baby. She had mentioned that her parents didn't approve of her marriage. What had been their reaction when they'd learned their daughter was expecting a baby? Had she had any help to get through such a dark time?

When the tide of her tears had lessened, he had one more thing to ask her. He waited while she straightened and dabbed at her eyes again. Belatedly, he whipped off his neckerchief and offered it to her.

She took it and finished drying her eyes. "I've made a mess of your clothes."

"That's not important," he said, half-irritated that she mentioned it. He was relieved to see that her outburst was over and that the color had slowly returned to her cheeks.

"Thank you, Wolf," she said, looking slightly embarrassed.

"Did Doug know?"

"He was so happy with the news—a complete fool

about it. I told him it was much too early to mention my condition to anyone." A delicate furrow formed between her brows, even as her eyes clouded over. "Why did he have to go boating that day? I begged him not to go. There were gale-force winds from the southeast. He knew it was risky!"

He could envision his friend's excitement about the weather. "Doug never could say no to a challenge. Which made some of the things he did bigger than life and some..."

"Utterly foolhardy."

"He probably thought going nose to nose with a storm was a test the boat could handle, and one he needed to conquer."

"It happened all at once—the boating accident and then the stomach pains that told me something wasn't right. The doctor put me to bed immediately. I remained there for the next six months, but in the end, it didn't matter." She let out a shaky breath. "It was a girl."

He swallowed. There was nothing he could say that would make any of it better. "I am more sorry than I can say."

She met his gaze, her blue eyes softening. "Me too."

Something between them shifted in that moment. He couldn't put a name to it; he only knew that he wanted to see Cassandra happy again, and he'd do just about anything to make it happen.

She spread his neckerchief over her lap. Her breathing evened out as she composed herself.

"You said it yourself," he said. "You are feeling better here. Healing. That should tell you that you belong here." *Stay*, he wanted to say, but they'd already been down that trail and come to a T with both of them going opposite ways. Letting her cry on his shoulder was one thing. Expecting her to change the course of her plans wouldn't happen.

She folded the cloth and handed it back to him, a tremulous smile on her face. "I'm better. Thank you. And I've kept you from your work long enough today."

She was dismissing him. He should return to the cattle, but he was more worried about leaving her.

"I won't forget your kindness."

He stood. "You will stay away from the branding?"

A contrite smile formed. "I believe I will."

That evening, as twilight descended and the men finished their work for the day, they gathered around the campfires near their own ranch's chuck wagon. Cassandra was glad the night would be dry and clear. From the porch, she could hear them talking and at times laughing.

Otis set a place for her at the long dining-room table. He'd done this every evening since she'd first arrived on the ranch. She'd gone along with it. Her parents never sat with the servants, and that's all she knew. But now, it only seemed lonely after all the activity of the day.

"Yer lookin' at me like you got somethin' on your mind," Otis said, pausing in his duties.

"I don't like eating alone."

Otis grinned. "You want company?"

"Yes. Absolutely."

"Just had to say something. When your late husband was here, he always had Putnam, Lily, Wolf and me eat with him. Said it was more like family, and he looked forward to it after a hard day's work in the saddle. 'Course, that was before Barker came around. He'd probably have Barker here too if he was here now." He set a few more places.

That evening, Mr. Putnam, Cleve, Lily, Otis and Wolf joined her. They carefully avoided any talk of her collapse until Mr. Putnam mentioned that she was looking recovered.

"Recovered from what?" Otis asked, looking at her sharply.

"It was just a moment," she said, trying to make light of it. She didn't want everyone worrying about her. "I think the noise and dust and sun overwhelmed me. I'm fine now."

"Good to know, ma'am," Steve Putnam said.

Cleve Barker was not so easily appeased.

"I told you to stay away from the pens and the cattle," he said, a frown on his face. "Thought I made myself real clear this morning. See that you heed my words the rest of the week. Branding time is a man's business and the men don't have time to watch out for you."

Side conversations quieted. Cleve had exceeded his place as her foreman. Back in Alexandria, her father or Douglas would have stepped in to address this type of situation. Now, looking around the table, it was obvious that the others waited to see what she would do.

She set her teacup back on its saucer. "I understand the wisdom of leaving the men to do their work, Mr. Barker. What I don't appreciate is a dressing-down in front of everyone."

He pressed his mouth closed for a moment. "Guess I

worry about you. After all, you are my kin. Can't have anything happening to you."

It was an excuse—not an apology. He realized he'd gone too far.

Cleve stood. "Guess I'll get back to work. Got a few things to attend to," he said sullenly, and then headed outside.

Cassandra rose from the table and followed him to the porch. "Mr. Barker."

He stopped, but didn't turn to meet her gaze.

"I won't keep you long. I wanted to say that I do appreciate all you've done for the ranch and for my late husband. It couldn't have been easy to manage things here. And…I hope, after what happened at the table, things are settled and we can put this behind us."

He nodded.

"About Mr. Roth and Mr. Jarvis. They don't seem to join in with the others. Where did they come from?"

He finally turned back to her. "I worked with them on a ranch down near Dodge before coming here. They make a good team. Just not joiners, if you know what I mean. I knew they were hard workers, so I hired them when they came needing work."

"Mr. Roth certainly has poor control of his temper."

"Like most men, he don't like to be crossed. I saw what happened today. Ma'am—it was just a cow. Can't get too worked up about that. The animal will still bring good money at the market once it is growed." He shrugged. "'Fraid what happened today was your fault. I told you to stay near the house."

She bristled at his reply. *Her fault!* "Whose ranch?" she asked evenly.

His gaze narrowed slightly. "You wouldn't know of it. It's way south of here."

Steve Putnam stepped onto the porch. "Thank you for the fine meal, Mrs. Stewart."

"You're welcome. However, you don't need to leave so quickly."

He settled his hat on his head. "I'm pretty tuckered out. Going in search of a poker game before I call it a night." He turned to Cleve. "You in, Barker?"

"Guess we are done here." The hard look on Cleve's face challenged her to say otherwise. "Right, ma'am?"

She wasn't done, but she also felt this needed to remain between the two of them. She nodded once. "We'll talk again later."

As they sauntered away, she stared after Cleve. He seemed different now than the first few days she'd spoken with him. He'd been solicitous then, although that side of him had made her slightly uncomfortable. His words tonight bothered her. She didn't expect a man to treat a calf as a person, but she certainly thought that an animal deserved more consideration than she had witnessed. Roth had been a beast. And Cleve had just now defended him!

Mulling over their conversation, she walked back inside.

In the kitchen, Otis was busy cleaning up the dishes and pans and in the parlor, Lily had settled onto a chair near the fireplace and was darning socks. Wolf was crouched before the hearth, preparing a fire. Once it was glowing steadily, he stood. "That should keep you both warm until you turn in." He gave his mother a hug, nodded to Cassandra and then headed for the door.

Cassandra quickly followed him out to the porch. Stars twinkled overhead. "You're leaving too?"

He stopped. "I have work in the stable. One of the men from Patterson's ranch needs a new hammer on his rifle. And tomorrow's another early day."

His warm breath turned to vapor between them. The crisp night air circled around and created goose bumps on her arms.

"Was there something else?"

"No. Not really. I guess… What happened earlier has been on my mind."

His shoulders relaxed. "You seem better now."

"I am. Thank you again. I appreciate that you didn't mention it at supper."

"It still came up."

She shrugged. "It couldn't be helped. The men were curious."

A moment passed and when he spoke, his voice held a hesitancy she'd never heard before. "I…wasn't sure how to help."

"You were perfect."

They stood there, staring at each other. She wanted to say that she understood now why Douglas had chosen him as a friend, but she didn't want to bring up Doug. This wasn't about him at all. Wolf had been there constantly ever since she'd arrived on the train. He'd been a tremendous support. And after today there was no doubt in her mind that she trusted him and depended on him completely. More than that, she was coming to care for him deeply.

An owl hooted somewhere to the west. A shiver ran through her. She rubbed her arms.

"You're cold. Better get back inside."

"I should." But still she didn't move. She didn't want the evening to end. Something had changed between them and she wanted to understand it…wanted to understand him. He made her feel cared for. Being with him…near him…felt right.

"I'll see you in the morning." Wolf nodded again, then turned and strode down the steps and toward the stable.

Chapter Fifteen

Wolf didn't let himself dwell on all that had happened yesterday—not that crying bout of Cassandra's or the talk they'd had on the porch last night. He had work to do. It was better to keep his mind occupied with the job rather than try to figure out what was happening between the two of them.

He was up early the next morning seeing to the horses along with Jordan. Then, after a word with Putnam, he and Jordan headed along the river to pick up stray cattle. By afternoon, they'd gathered up six pairs—cow and calf—and started their drive back to the ranch.

"I gotta thank you for getting me this job," Jordan said, pulling his horse up beside him as they settled in behind the six pairs they'd gathered.

"Putnam thought you'd do well, and so far you are proving him right."

"I aim to. One day I'll have a ranch of my own. Gotta learn as much as I can first."

"Longhorns or Angus?" Wolf asked and then half listened to the reply. The boy could talk till the cows reached the ranch with little more than a wink of encouragement.

As they neared the rise, he spotted a dash of black up near the old cemetery. "Can you make that out?" He pointed with his chin toward the hill.

Jordan squinted. "A lone calf?"

"Maybe. Think I'll check it out. Take 'em slow. I'll catch up with you."

He reined his horse toward the hill. He was halfway there when he realized it wasn't a calf at all half-hidden in the tall grass, but Cassandra, sitting at her husband's grave. He pulled his mount to a stop, checking the surrounding countryside at the same time. She was alone.

Should he disturb her? After yesterday, maybe she wanted to have a minute alone. Still, he'd talked about this with her on her first day. She shouldn't be this far from the house without some kind of protection.

On that thought, he kneed his horse into a gentle lope and headed farther up the slope.

As he approached, she rose to her feet, swinging her new Stetson against her leg. The day had warmed with the afternoon sun, and she used the hat now to fan her face. "Hello, Wolf."

He looked around. "Where is your horse?" The words came out sharper than he'd meant them to.

"I walked."

"Thought you understood that you're not to be away from the house by yourself."

"But it's not so far. I can see the house from here."

Just like that first day when he met her at the train, her stubbornness was showing. How could he look out for her if she wouldn't look out for herself? "Cassandra…"

"I know. I should have asked for an escort. It's just…

Everybody has a job to do. The first week I was here, you had time to humor me, but now with the roundup even you are busy. That's not a criticism. It's simply a fact. And I am a grown woman. I should be able to take a walk on what is my own property."

No argument there. She was very much a grown woman. But there were snakes and coyotes and possibly wolves. It didn't make sense for her to risk it. "Your walk couldn't have waited?"

"No. I…I wanted a moment alone with Doug. Especially after what happened yesterday." She grimaced slightly at the memory, but then her blue eyes began to clear. She brushed back a tendril of golden hair from her face. "Truthfully, I didn't think I would get caught. I should have known better. You know what happens on this ranch more than anyone."

"I have to. I told Doug that I'd keep an eye on things."

"I remember." She paused and then looked back up at him. "By *things*, you also meant me, didn't you?"

He nodded.

"I've seen the way the others talk to you—with respect, even admiration. They look to you as a leader."

He didn't know how to take her compliment. He wasn't in the habit of getting them. "Someone has to take the position."

"Meaning Mr. Barker's lead isn't adequate."

He figured she could see that for herself. "Are you ready to go back now? Jordan is waiting on me, but I'm not leaving without you."

She glanced down the hillside, shielding her eyes with her hand as she looked for the boy. Then she remembered her hat and put it on, tightening the string beneath her chin. "I suppose I am ready. I have strict instructions from Mr. Barker that I am not to be a nuisance and slow down the entire roundup operation."

"He said that?"

"Not in those exact words, but the message was clear."

He jumped down and helped her onto his horse behind the saddle, then he mounted in front of her. "We'll catch up to Jordan."

She slipped her arms around his waist, surprising him when she leaned her cheek between his shoulder blades.

He forgot to breathe for a moment. At her touch, tingles raced through his center. He'd promised her she was safe with him and he meant it, but having her arms around him—even this innocently—played havoc with his senses. This ride might just be impossible... and a slice of heaven at the same time. He smoothed his gloved hand over hers, wishing it was her skin he touched. "Hang on."

He reined his horse down the hill. They caught up to Jordan and the cattle, and drove them on to the cattle pen. Leaving Jordan to finish up, Wolf delivered Cassandra to the drive in front of the stable.

He offered his arm, easing her slowly to the ground. "Doug had a small derringer that belonged to his mother. It should be in the house somewhere. If you are going to take any more of these walks, I want you to have it with you."

"I'll look for it."

"Let me know if you don't find it."

"I will."

She looked up at him from under her hat brim.

Her eyes were so blue that they mirrored the sky. He thought he might drown in them.

"You'll be at the table for supper tonight?" she asked.

He nodded, wondering what he was getting himself into.

"Good." She spun around and walked across the yard, disappearing into the house.

The bunkhouse door creaked behind him. "I see you're making a habit of cozyin' up at the big house," Jarvis said, stepping out of the bunkhouse and slipping his suspenders over his shoulders. "Nice situation for a man such as you."

Wolf didn't care for his insinuation, but ignored it this time.

"She's a widow woman. Probably has needs like the rest of us. You think you are man enough for her?"

He hated hearing talk of this sort, especially hearing it about Cassandra. "Why aren't you out with your crew?"

Jarvis smiled like the weasel he was and answered smoothly. "Had to fill my canteen. Thirsty work and all." Then he sauntered over to his horse, mounted and rode away.

That evening, Cassandra brought down Mrs. Stewart's sewing basket from the sitting room upstairs and sat down beside Lily. "I thought you might be able to use something from here," she said, pulling out several colors of thread and floss, and a pair of small scissors.

Beneath the notions, Lily discovered a half-finished cross-stitch sampler. "This needs to be completed. Perhaps...?" She held up the cloth to Cassandra.

"I'm not very good at sewing. I never took the time

to learn it well. There was always someplace to go, something to do that caught my interest more, much to my mother's chagrin."

Lily smiled. "You were a girl then. It is a different season in your life. Perhaps now you would like to try? I am happy to help if you have questions."

Cassandra took the cloth and settled back onto the settee, studying the stitches. She snipped a length of moss green floss, threaded a needle and began, continuing the delicate leaf pattern that bordered the edge.

She'd sewn five leaves and was starting on her sixth when she looked up and realized that Wolf had taken the seat across from her and stretched out his legs toward the fire. In his lap, he held a book from the study, but he wasn't reading. His head nodded, his eyes already closed. The firelight flickered over his face, creating shadows of darkness and light over his straight nose and cheekbones and the soft curve of his lips.

She glanced at Lily and saw that she too had noticed her son. They shared a smile.

"How are you doing there?" Lily asked softly, indicating her stitching.

Cassandra glanced at the sampler in her lap. "It's comforting, isn't it? I mean… I get so completely involved in what I'm doing that everything else fades away."

"It can be like that—soothing. It can also be frustrating when stitches need to be pulled out and started over. Do not get discouraged if that happens a time or two."

"I won't."

"When you are finished, my son can make you a frame."

Something stirred in her…a memory. "He works with wood? My husband tried a few things."

"They both went through a 'season' where they whittled and sawed and taught themselves to make things. They were always trying to outdo the other, although much of what they made was very rough. If you want a fancy frame, Jackson Miller at the carpentry shop in town would be the better choice."

"I'll remember that." However, she didn't think she would be finished with the sampler before leaving for home. "Douglas never told me how he and Wolf met. Do you know?"

"That is his story to tell," Lily said, looking at her son.

On hearing his name spoken, Wolf had roused and yawned.

"I tried to ask him once," she said. It had been in the carriage ride from town the day he'd brought her to the ranch. Wolf hadn't wanted to talk about it. It had made her nervous to ask him again. "I'm still curious."

"I didn't know you well. Not enough…" Wolf shifted in his chair.

"You were angry. You thought I married Doug for his money."

Wolf's deep brown gaze steadied on her.

"Son!" Lily said, shocked. "Is that true?"

He nodded.

"And now?" Cassandra asked, challenging him.

He watched her in warm amusement. "Now I think it was the other way around. Doug tricked you."

"I believe you are right, Mr. Wolf." She shared a smile with him. "Do you feel you know me well enough now to tell me?"

"Yes. Well enough." His gaze lowered to the fire in the hearth. "The Stewarts moved here in '63. Doug's father, along with Otis, had sustained injuries fighting for the Union in the war, and they both mustered out. Douglas Senior wanted a fresh start for his family, away from the memory of the war."

"He was an officer," she said quickly.

"Yes. Because of his service, the government gave him enough money to make a good start here. He used it to buy this property. Doug was eleven."

"And you?"

"I was twelve. I had hunted here with my father from when I was very young. By twelve, I was hunting on my own—all over. I didn't know where the Stewarts' land ended and the open prairie began, but sometimes I would watch Doug and his parents from far off, building this house and moving the cattle.

"One day in the middle of summer I followed the tracks of a deer—a very intelligent big buck I'd hunted many times before with little success. It always got away. The day that I met Doug, I was hunting down by the river when I came upon the buck. Crouching with my bow and arrow ready, I suddenly saw Doug squatting only a few yards away with his rifle ready. We stared at each other while the deer dipped its head and drank. Later, Doug told me he was scared as could be, seeing an Indian for the first time in his life."

"What happened then?"

"Suddenly Doug jumped up, yelling and dancing like a crazy person. Then I saw wasps fly up from the ground, mad as could be. He'd stepped into a nest of diggers. They swarmed all around while he waved his arms and swatted at them. The buck raced away."

Kathryn Albright   *169*

"Smart deer," Cassandra murmured.

Wolf grinned. "I dropped my rifle and dived at him, knocking him into the river. He thought I was trying to drown him and fought back. It didn't help that he was bigger than me. We both got our share of stings with him trying to get away from me, and me trying to keep him beneath the water's surface and away from the wasps. He thought he was a goner. I thought I was. Finally, he quieted down and we both made our way upstream.

"When the sky was clear of any wasps, we dragged ourselves up on the bank. We both laid there for a moment and then he started laughing. Crazy-sounding laughing with hoots and cawing. Then I started laughing too."

Cassandra smiled. "I can just imagine it…"

"We were so relieved to escape those tiny buzzards that we went a little nuts. We slapped on mud everywhere we got stung. Then we started slinging mud at each other—just having fun. That's when my throat started closing up. I fell down gasping for breath. Two wasps had stung my neck. Doug slapped mud on the stings and then said he was going for help.

"I couldn't admit I was afraid, but I was. I didn't want to be alone if I was gonna die."

"What did Doug do?"

"He stood there looking down at me and slowly sat back down. 'I can't leave,' he said. 'You saved my life. Besides, all Ma would do is put mud on you the same as I'm doin'.' He sat by me the entire night. Every time the mud would dry, he'd wash it off and slap new mud on. He was a mess himself. A wasp had stung him over one eye, and it had swelled shut. His other eye wasn't so bad, but it was still swollen.

"By early morning, I was breathing better. He could barely see, so we helped each other go back to get his rifle and my bow. Then we headed for the soddie. His mother had one of her ranch hands ride into town and tell my father what had happened."

"My!" Cassandra said. "That's quite a story. Is that when you became blood brothers?"

"No. That was a few years later." Wolf inhaled deeply and let it out as if the entire story he'd just told them had taken something from him.

"They were inseparable after that," Lily said, smiling at her son. "It is good to remember."

"Yes," Wolf said simply.

Before heading to his bed that night, Wolf leaned against the outer wall of the bunkhouse, thinking over his mother's words and watching the lamplight in Cassandra's window. Something had shifted as he spoke of Doug tonight—shifted and lightened inside him. It was good to remember, as his mother had said. He only hoped that by putting together the pieces of Doug's life that Cassandra had not known, it would help her too.

He wanted her to feel connected to this place. So much so, that in the end she would choose to stay. She was stronger than she gave herself credit. With a better foreman than Cleve and a little help, she could run this place. She just had to believe she could do it.

The roundup would be done in two more days, and then they'd take the cattle allocated for the stockyards to Oak Grove. After things settled down and she saw the profit she made by selling the beef, maybe he could convince her to stay on a little longer. That would mean the rest of the hands would feel more secure. He didn't want to see them, especially Otis, looking for a new job with winter coming on.

When the lamp in her room sputtered once and went out, he turned toward the bunkhouse door and a solid night's sleep.

Chapter Sixteen

After a brief search the next day, Cassandra came across Mrs. Stewart's derringer. When Wolf came in with the other men for the noon meal, she met him at the corral as he tied up his horse and showed it to him.

"Are you going walking or riding this afternoon?" he asked.

"I'd like to."

"Then I want to check this out. Make sure it is ready for use. Come with me. This won't take long."

He entered the stable and sat down at his make-shift workbench. Quickly, he took the small pistol completely apart, cleaned it, oiled it and then put it back together. "Were there any bullets?"

She held out a small green box, nearly full of caps.

"How much do you know about guns?"

"Next to nothing. It wasn't necessary in Alexandria."

His brows rose. "You didn't need protection there?"

"The men in the household handled that."

"Men?"

"My father, when he was home. Otherwise, we depended on our butler. He had a room in the servants' quarters. And there was Freddie, our coachman and gardener, who lived above the carriage house."

Wolf's brows rose further. "Impressive, Mrs. Stewart, but all those men aren't here. So you've never shot a gun before." He stood and moved closer. "First you need to get used to how it feels in your hand and how the trigger action works." He handed the gun to her, in doing so brushing her hand with his fingers.

Tingles raced up her arm. The odor of the cleaning oil, leather and something completely male filled her senses. She tried to concentrate on his instructions, tried to follow them. Had he felt anything? He continued teaching her how to load the pistol's two-barrel chambers, apparently unaffected.

She could feel his warmth radiating off him in the quiet interior of the stable. He reached around her from her back and his hands closed over hers to adjust her hold on the weapon. The gun was cold against her skin, but his hands were warm—the skin of his palms calloused from hard work. His breath on her neck did crazy things to her senses. Everywhere they touched—hands, arms, shoulders—was on fire. Her heart raced in her chest.

She looked up at his familiar face, so close to hers. He stopped talking. He might have stopped breathing.

He'd held her while she cried two days ago and offered her his comfort. He'd shared his childhood with her last evening. And now...now she wanted him to kiss her. His lips were so close, she had only to rise to her toes and he had only to dip his head slightly. He'd said he cared for her... It couldn't all be because of Douglas, as if it were a duty, could it? Surely there was something more that she sensed.

Overhead, two mourning doves cooed from somewhere in the rafters and then suddenly swooped down through the stable and flew out the open door.

Startled, she jumped, the spell between them broken. Wolf let out a breath, and then they both chuckled—the sound nervous and awkward.

He swallowed and released her. "Most likely you would only need this to scare off snakes or coyotes," he said. "Probably the noise from the men and the cattle will keep most of the big animals away."

"I hope I won't need it while I'm here."

The light went out of his eyes. He stepped away.

The unspoken message that skirted behind her words dampened the moment. She would be leaving soon. Two weeks had already gone by. Her time at the ranch was half-over.

"With the roundup, I can't take the time to teach you to shoot today, but you have the basics. Don't practice near the cattle. It could start a stampede."

"I understand. It's only for an emergency."

"Right." He looked as if he wanted to say more, hesitating for a moment. Then he slipped on his Stetson and headed outside.

With the men otherwise occupied and the roundup moving along at a busy pace, Cassandra fell into a comfortable routine. Every morning, she helped Otis and Lily with the preparations for the noon meal. Then, after the dishes had been cleared and they were busy with the cleanup, she would take Patsy out for a leisurely ride, always remembering to take her derringer with her.

The evenings, with the table full at suppertime, were her favorite time. She learned so much listening to Wolf and Cleve and Putnam as they discussed cattle prices and bantered around ideas to increase profits. Then afterward, when everyone scattered, she enjoyed sitting with Lily and Wolf in the parlor. Sometimes, Cleve joined them. Unfortunately, when he did, the general tension in the room increased, putting everyone on edge.

Tonight, Wolf was not anywhere to be seen and yet he'd been at the supper table. She wandered through the house, searching for him and found him in the study.

The room had a fireplace on one wall and a large desk near another wall. Two large comfortable chairs sat facing the fireplace and behind them stood a large bookcase. On the last wall hung a huge map of the entire Stewart Rocking S Ranch.

He glanced at her and then went back to studying the map. "I was looking for a book on breeding that Doug once mentioned. I thought he might have it in here."

She'd moved that book just that morning when she'd organized the shelf. She fetched it from the bookshelf and then joined him, staring up at the map. The date it had been finished was etched in the corner—1866. "This isn't the bookshelf," she teased.

"It's been a while since I really looked at this. Mrs. Stewart had a cartographer from Denver make it as a present for her husband. I was fifteen. After seeing his work, I took up drawing for a few months—birds, small animals, horses. I wasn't very good."

"Hence the reason you became a gunsmith?"

He grinned slightly. "Guess so."

He didn't speak of himself much. The other evening

when he'd told her of meeting Douglas was the exception. It made this moment somewhat magical. Cassandra studied him as he turned back to the map. It seemed that every day something happened to make her more aware of his good qualities. He had a quiet strength that permeated everything he did—reassuring and surprisingly fascinating to her.

"It's changed some." He pointed to an island in the river. "That washed away with last spring's flooding." With his finger, he circled a large area off to the east. "And they added on more land for grazing here." He lowered his arm. "They had big dreams."

"And you?" she asked, seeing again in her mind's eye how he'd ridden across the prairie, chasing after that steer. "What about your dreams?"

"Now, there's a crazy question." His voice, his look and the way he pulled back, shutting out the openness that had just been between them, spoke volumes.

She wanted to know. "Everyone has dreams."

"Not everyone."

"Because it's too impractical?"

Did her attempt at probing amuse him? His eyes twinkled, but his words pushed her away again. "Aren't all dreams on the impractical side?"

"No. And don't change the subject."

"I didn't think I did."

"I asked about your dreams," she said, persisting.

"I don't have any. It takes vision to dream. I tend to be practical. I deal with the here and now."

"I see. So you don't have any visions or dreams or hopes for the future?"

He turned to her, serious now. "What are you getting at?"

He was uncomfortable. He kept skirting her question instead of answering, but she wouldn't be put off. She held out the book he'd requested, the one on animal husbandry. "Like trying to interbreed Angus cattle with longhorns?"

He looked at the book and then met her gaze. "Yeah. Like that."

He tugged the book from her hands and smoothed his hand over the embossed letters. "I've always liked ranching. I figure the more I know, the better. Someday I might have a small herd." He walked over to the desk and set the book there. "You really want to know what I want right now?" He stared at the map again and slid his gaze to her. "To kiss you."

Butterflies started a frenzied dance inside her.

Slowly, deliberately, he strode to her, suddenly the one in control. He reached out and caressed her cheek with the back of his fingers and then cupped her chin in his palm. "I've wanted to kiss you ever since the day in the old homestead. I told you once that you could trust me. You can. But it doesn't change the fact I can't stop thinking about you, Cassandra. That I want more between us than friendship."

Her mouth went dry. She was back in the soddie, feeling the heat of his gaze on her face. Longing and desire curled out from him and circled around her, creating tingles everywhere his gaze touched as he looked from her eyes to her lips. Had it been there all along during these past weeks and tamped down? That meant the moment in the stable when she'd thought it all her imagination, he had felt something too.

She should step back, but couldn't find the strength of will to do so. What would it feel like to be in his arms, held close enough to feel his heat? She wanted to know what his lips would feel like against hers— soft and gentle or firm and demanding? "How much more?" she asked, barely breathing, knowing as she asked that she'd breached some invisible line and done so willingly.

He slipped his hand behind her neck, his fingers cool against her warm skin. Fire raced to the hairs on her head and down her back. He drew her gently toward him, the pressure of his hand ever so slow and unrelenting. His gaze never left hers, but darkened as she neared. There was time to escape if she truly wanted to. She could pull back, and he would honor her will.

She didn't want to. She did care about him, and she wanted this kiss—had wanted it, she realized, ever since he'd held her close while she cried over the calf. She moved her hands to his chest, splaying her fingers over his vest. Then she closed her eyes and turned her face to his.

His lips brushed over hers, lightly, tenderly—a whisper of a kiss. He kissed her as though she were something precious that he didn't want to scare away. She tilted her head, and with that smallest of encouragements, he deepened the pressure.

Chapter Seventeen

The last morning, she stood on the porch and watched the cowboys saddling up and preparing to drive their own cattle to their respective ranches. After they left, the Rocking S cattle that were marked for the stock-yards would be driven to Oak Grove. The roundup had been an exciting time, although she still wished there were a kinder way to brand the calves. When Steve Putnam said his goodbye, he mentioned there would be another roundup in the spring. As much as she was ready for the men to move on and for life at the Rocking S to get back to normal, she knew if she were in Virginia come spring, she would miss being here for that roundup.

More and more she longed to stay on the ranch, and Wolf had much to do with that desire. What would she do when the time came for her to make a firm decision? The time would come quickly—only two weeks away now—that Douglas's terms would be fulfilled. Would she sign the papers at Mayor Melbourne's office to officially put the ranch up for sale? Still? After the kiss she'd shared with Wolf?

His plea to her to stay and learn how to manage the ranch was heavy on her thoughts. The kiss had turned her future upside down. It had been so gentle, so tentative at first that when he pulled back slightly, she'd leaned into him, drawn by an invisible ribbon of desire to be closer and to have more of him. That's when, deepening the kiss, he'd claimed her and quite possibly her heart all at once. It held a promise. It could change everything if she let it, if she wanted it to.

No words had passed between them since that moment. Cleve had entered the study in search of the ledgers. They'd both broken apart, but not before Cleve had witnessed what had happened.

The kiss shook her to the core.

She glanced out to the branding pen, looking for Wolf. He was standing near a small cook fire while the other men from the outlying ranches were eating a breakfast and drinking coffee. Tall, strong and handsome. Once she'd spotted him, she had trouble looking away. She wanted to drink in everything about him— the way he stood, the way he spoke, his careful, but easygoing manner. It looked like he was saying his goodbyes as he shook hands with each of them and looked them in the eye.

Over the past week he'd gone about doing whatever was necessary to help with the roundup. He never completely joined in with the other men, but they often looked to him for direction, even after Cleve had given them their instructions. They obviously respected him—especially Mr. Putnam, who deferred to a few of his suggestions.

The more she witnessed, the more she wondered what he was doing in town as a gunsmith. This was what he loved doing. Had he ever considered it? Had Douglas ever asked him?

One of the men said something, and Wolf threw his head back, laughing. He slapped his hat against his thigh. She wished that she could see his face better. She'd never seen him so at ease, never heard him laugh.

At that moment, he glanced over and saw her. A moment passed, then he wiped his brow with his forearm and replaced his hat on his head. Another pause as he looked at her again and then, as if coming to a decision, he said goodbye to the men and turned toward her.

A thrill of anticipation dashed through her. He meant to speak to her.

She descended the porch steps. Cleve stepped out onto the porch behind her. He stuffed the leather packet containing the ranch's ledger into the saddlebag under his arm. "Things are wrapping up," he said. "All that remains is to drive your cattle to the stockyards in town. It'll take most of the day to get there. The sale is tomorrow. Don't expect us back until sometime Sunday afternoon. It's traditional to peel off some of the cattle money so the hands can have a Saturday night on the town."

She tried to keep track of what Cleve was saying, but my, oh, my, Wolf cut a fine tall figure as he strode toward her. The rest of the cowboys were dispersing, each to their own brand to head back to their ranches.

Suddenly, Cleve's word registered. "Don't expect them back? I thought I would go too."

His brows shot up. "For a night on the town?"

Her cheeks warmed as she realized he'd mistaken her intent. "Of course not. I mean that shouldn't I be there to negotiate a price for the cattle? Isn't my signature needed?"

Cleve dragged in a long breath as he threw his saddlebag over his shoulder and pushed up his hat brim. "We've made do at the last two roundups. I realize your intentions are good, but two weeks doesn't make you all that knowledgeable about this business. You've been reading up, checking the books and all, but there's more to it than figures on paper."

"Such as?"

"You've got to look the buyers in the eye and know when they are paying fair price. Being a woman, those men at the yards would take one look at you and figure you were a pushover. And believe you me, I'll get a better price for each head without a woman next to me."

She didn't like hearing that. She wanted to be there, but she also wanted the best price possible for the cattle. Frustrated with hitting a wall, she focused on her other concerns. "With all that money, things might get a little reckless. How will you safeguard the money while everyone is enjoying themselves?"

"Right after I divvy out the men's pay, I'll get the rest to the bank." He dropped his head slightly, focusing on her. "You don't need to worry, ma'am. I've done this a time or two. I'll bring back the books with a stamp and receipt that'll let you know the price per head I got, and the number of cattle." He pulled back. "I would think Wolf would have explained it last evening. You were pretty friendly."

It was a jab at the way he'd come across them in the study. Her cheeks flamed.

It was obvious that he didn't want her along. She was disappointed. She had looked forward to a trip to town. But, what would she do? Eat alone at the restaurant while her ranch hands whooped it up down the street at the saloon? That did not sound appealing. And she certainly didn't want to stay in town for the next two nights. She wanted to be back here, on her ranch.

Her shoulders lowered. "Very well, Mr. Barker. Get a good price for me—for all of us."

A satisfied smirk appeared as he stroked his whiskers. "You can count on it."

"I still worry that the men will spend all their money in one huge party. You know what may happen soon with the ranch. They need to be aware that their pay will have to stretch until they are either rehired with the new owners or hired somewhere else."

"Aw, don't worry about them. They'll be all right. You're taking too much on yourself. Once a man's paid, it's his place to figure out where to spend it."

"Perhaps you are taking on too little."

His expression hardened. He descended the steps, tipping his hat at the bottom. Then he strode toward his horse at the corral, ignoring Wolf when he passed him.

When Wolf stopped at the steps, the intimate look in his eyes brought back the kiss. Her pulse quickened.

"Good morning," he said as he looked up at her. "What's that sour expression for?"

"Mr. Barker was much too enthusiastic about getting away to do the negotiating for the cattle on his own."

"And you thought you would negotiate?"

"I did. At least stand by his side and be a part of it."

His eyes twinkled. "Bet he talked you out of that real fast."

She frowned. "They are Doug's cattle. I should know what's going on."

"Cassandra. Women don't negotiate."

"Most women don't own a ranch."

"Can't argue there, but it's a man's business, a man's job."

She sighed. "Will you go with him? Make sure he gets a good price?"

He grew serious. "Already had that in my plans." He moved to the bottom step, removing his Stetson and holding it in front of him. "I don't think you need to worry. The better the price he can get, the more he will take home in his pocket too."

"I know."

"Then what is it?"

"Just…him. He said he was going to pay the men their wages right there in town. All of them. But, Wolf…they should know to hold some back in case they need it soon. I'm afraid…especially for Jordan."

She saw the moment he understood. His entire demeanor changed.

"You mean when you leave?" His face shuttered down.

She hadn't considered her words before speaking. She should explain—at least let him know of her confusion now over things. "Wolf…" she began. "Last night—"

"If something happens, Jordan will land on his feet," he said, interrupting her. "He's young. Likable."

He didn't want to hear any explanations. Her chest tightened with hurt. "And Otis? Oddly, I feel closer to him than I ever did with my mother's cook. He is very…personable. More a friend than a hired hand. I couldn't bear it if he was suddenly cast out."

"Last night didn't mean anything," he said flatly.

"Of course it did! But…it confused me."

His lips pressed together.

"I'm sorry." She hated to disappoint him. Caring

about him was one thing. For her to stay and run the ranch was another.

He didn't speak for a moment. "Be up-front. Tell everyone what you have in mind. Let them know you are going to sell out so that they can prepare."

"Mr. Edelman told me not to. I'm to wait until the last minute to protect my assets."

"Who is Edelman?"

"My attorney back in Virginia. Mr. Barker said the same thing."

"Edelman is looking out for your interests. Barker is looking out for his own. The trouble is, now you are worried about the people here—Otis, Jordan, Fitch and Winston. That should tell you something."

He was right. She'd come to care for them. And because of that, she was in more of a quandary with no clear-cut answers. "Are you going to help drive the cattle to the stockyards?"

"I'll take my mother back to town first before the road is a cloud of dust and mud. Then I'll circle back to help. The six of them can do it themselves, but another man will make it go smoother."

Cassandra stepped down one step and lowered her voice. "How long have you been doing these roundups?"

"Since I was fourteen. Mr. Stewart wanted Doug to know how tough the work was so that he'd respect the hands doing it. I skipped school and helped. I got paid after that first year."

Fourteen! "And you've been helping every year since?"

He nodded. "Though this will probably be my last here."

A lump formed in her throat. "Why didn't you become the foreman here? It's so obviously something you love."

"Doug and I… We talked about it. But when old Charlie left and the position opened up, my father came down with pneumonia. He needed me to run the store. Then Barker showed up."

"Family…"

Wolf nodded.

What was she to do? She had been so sure that selling the place was the best option. She simply had to make sure the new owners kept on the ranch hands. Trouble was, even if they did, that wouldn't include Wolf.

"That first day that you drove me here, you said that you'd stay until I settled in. I guess…all things considered, I've done that. Will you return tomorrow with the others?" She wanted him to come back. She wanted more time with him.

He blew out a breath. "Would it matter?"

Her world stilled at his question. It did matter to her… "I have come to depend on you here. I look forward to seeing you every day."

He snorted softly. "That's not what I mean."

She looked down, gathering her courage before meeting his steady gaze. "More than I can say."

He didn't respond immediately but seemed to weigh her words. "Yet you still won't consider staying on."

He was purposely pushing her into a corner. "I need time to think."

His mouth drew into a line. He took a deep breath. "I have some gun orders in town waiting to be filled. I've let them go so that I could help out with the roundup. It will take at least a week to catch up with them."

Her heart sank. He wasn't coming back. "And then?"

"I guess we'll see." No smile, no glance occurred as he climbed the steps and passed her. The sound of his boots was heavy against the wood planks of the porch as he headed into the house.

Wolf borrowed two horses from the ranch and took his mother back to town. When he returned, he changed out his mount for his own horse—a horse he could rely on if trouble happened on the trail. He spotted Cassandra watching from the porch while he switched saddles. He'd expected too much from her. And she'd put him in his place. Guess he'd learned his lesson.

The attraction between them must be more on his side than hers. He'd seen a lot of her over the past two weeks, and he'd let small touches and certain phrases mean more than they really did.

He'd always been good at closing off his heart and hiding his feelings. He'd had to among the whites— with the part of him that was Indian. And among the Indians—with the part of him that was white. He shouldn't have let down his guard with her. He'd been a fool to ask her that question. And a fool to let himself care too much. He had set himself up for a world of hurt.

He mounted and then reined his horse around toward the cattle pen where the other men had just opened the gate.

Chapter Eighteen

Otis remained at the ranch. Cassandra was glad for the company, even though he immediately started cleaning up and left her alone. With the others gone, the regular ranch chores needed doing—feeding and watering the horses, and mucking out the stables.

Cassandra wandered through the empty house in a state of disorientation. The last few days had been filled with so much work and excitement and men and noise, that to have everything suddenly quiet threw her. Although she was ready to have everything return to a more normal routine, she didn't quite know what to do with herself.

She drew a heart in the dust on the dining-room table. Dirt from the constant churning of the soil underfoot by the cattle had found its way into everything from the dishes in the cupboard to the pores in her skin. The house was in need of a good cleaning, and then afterward she would see about a bath for herself. Over the days of the roundup, she had used the wash-basin in her room. The men were working far too hard to be bothered with fetching and heating water for a full bath for her.

With that thought, she set to work dusting the house with a feather duster she'd found in a box by the kitchen door. By the time Otis called her for the noon meal, dust was flying everywhere and mostly landing right back on the flat surface that she had just finished dusting.

She sat down to a light meal of chicken soup, glad she'd had the foresight to stay out of the kitchen or dust would have been in the soup! "I may as well open all the doors and windows and let this constant Kansas wind blow the dust away. My attempt is not helping much at all," she complained.

"You ever done any housecleanin' before?" he asked with a doubtful expression.

"How difficult can it be?"

He still looked unsure whether to say anything.

"Who usually sees to the cleaning?" she asked, remembering that she'd wanted to thoroughly clean Douglas's old room.

"I do—when I get a stretch of time. Might not be up to your highfalutin standards from Virginy, but we get by."

"Oh, Otis," she hurried to say. "I meant no offense. Goodness, but you and everyone else have not had a minute to spare with all that's been going on this week. I only wondered because Mr. Barker's room has been a mess since he moved out."

"Well, just shut the door and don't look. I'll get to it when I get to it."

"I don't mind helping as long as I'm not making more work for you."

"Just don't use water on Mrs. Stewart's fine furniture. She used an oil she got from town." He got up from the table and produced a small bottle from the cupboard. "Not much. Just a dot on an old rag."

"I wish I'd known about this earlier," she said.

The rest of the dusting went much better, although she quickly saw that it would take more than a day to finish the thorough cleaning she had envisioned.

As she worked, she noticed places where a small improvement would be beneficial—a few more hooks at the back door for coats, a new mat at the back door for the hands to wipe their feet before entering the kitchen.

In the evening, Otis helped her pull in the tub from the back pantry and set it up in the kitchen. It took a long time to fill it with hot water from the stove. While they waited for the water to warm, Otis taught her a game of cards. Not poker. Poker was for the men, he said. But it was a simple, fun game. Once the tub was full enough—and a little extra—he excused himself to the bunkhouse so that she could have some privacy.

As she sank into the water, she considered it a fitting end to the day. Her thoughts drifted over all that had happened since she had arrived at the ranch—visiting Doug's grave, the roundup, the branding. Every thought, every image in her mind was intermixed with Wolf being near. She couldn't think of one without the other. How much lonelier would her time here have been if he had not made it a point to make sure she settled in. She couldn't have asked for more.

Even at the cattle sale in the morning, she was depending on him to be her eyes and ears. How would the sale of the cattle go? Were the men having a good time in town? Was Wolf? She knew that Roth and Barker wouldn't include him, but Jordan would. And

Fitch. They would all probably stop by the bathhouse on the main street to get cleaned up.

The image lingered in her mind of Wolf sitting in a bathtub, his skin wet and slippery. The thought was indecent…and she should feel guilty for even thinking it. But it warmed her all over. She shook her head and sat up in the tub, letting the cool evening air against her wet skin drive the thought from her mind.

She stepped from the tub and toweled off. Slipping on her wrap and slippers, she climbed the stairs to her room. It was a marvel to her, how comfortable she felt here in only a few short weeks. Before this journey, she had assumed that living on the prairie would be lonely and boring compared to the entertainment she found in Alexandria. Yet nothing was as she expected. The ranch was proving to be anything but boring. Every moment held a bit of adventure or something new to learn. Quiet though today had been, she was more content than she had been in a long time.

The only thing marring that contentment was the last words she'd had with Wolf. *Would it matter?* Of course it would! He mattered. He had mattered to Douglas, to this ranch, and he mattered to her. In the short time she had known him, he had come to matter so much more than anyone else in her life.

She had jumped so fast into marriage with Douglas, and the results had been disastrous. Now at the end of her mourning period, she wouldn't let herself do it again. She *had* learned her lesson. In ignoring the rules of her family and common propriety with her rapid engagement and marriage to Douglas, life had been swift to retaliate, slapping her down with Doug's death and the loss of his baby.

Even her friends had distanced themselves, thinking her tainted. She had scoffed at the idea when Chloe first mentioned it, but after all that had happened, maybe there was a tiny measure of truth to what she said. How could she ignore such harsh instruction? If she gave in to her growing feelings for Wolf, she had the horrible feeling that something bad would happen. And this time, it would happen to him. She couldn't let that happen. Not after all he'd done for her.

She had answered him with the only possible honest answer. She was confused. And likely would stay that way. She doubted that he would ever try to kiss her again after the words they'd just spoken. He was angry. But it was better to keep him at a distance. That way when she left, no one's heart would be aching but hers.

Chapter Nineteen

The next morning, Cassandra and Otis emptied the bathwater, pan by pan, onto the garden. While Otis stayed and harvested the last of his pumpkins and squash, Cassandra started back to the house.

A horse whinnied from inside the stable. Then it neighed again, this time sounding agitated. Board clattered against board. What was going on? She altered her course, crossed the drive and entered the stable.

Many of the horses were gone, used for the cattle drive to town. Patsy, her horse, remained and now pranced nervously about in her stall.

"There, there, girl," Cassandra murmured. "What has you in knots?"

She inched up to the stall, her heart pounding. A snake perhaps? She hoped not. She was afraid of the slithery things. With that thought, she looked about for a handy weapon. She found a pitchfork nearby in a mound of straw and grabbed it in front of her as she inched forward. Whatever had caused Patsy's agitation sounded like it was in the stall with her.

Suddenly an earsplitting cry screeched from the rafters above her, and a large bird swooped down. She screamed and ducked low, holding the pitchfork over her head for protection. The bird's talons scratched her fingers, drawing blood. The bird—an owl—soared back up to the rafters and sat near a nest where it screeched down at her, disturbed and angry.

More screeching occurred in Patsy's stall. Cassandra inched forward until she could see another owl, this one sporting fluff instead of feathers. It hobbled around, scrunching up its shoulders and puffing out its chest in an attempt to appear larger than it was and scare off Patsy. Apparently, it had fallen from its nest.

Cassandra relaxed slightly. At least it wasn't a snake. If she remembered correctly, owls ate snakes. She leaned the pitchfork against the stall. "Come on, girl. Let's get you outside and away from the fussing. No wonder you weren't happy."

Patsy turned slightly, and Cassandra slipped a halter over her head. She'd leave her in the corral for a few hours until she could figure out what to do with the baby owl. Maybe Otis would have an idea.

"Well, look who we've got here."

She looked up from Patsy. "Mr. Roth! Is everyone back?" She looked behind him to see if the others had accompanied him. No one had followed.

"Forgot something in the bunkhouse," he said, moving his gaze down her lazily. The stub of a rolled cigarette hung from his mouth. "What's got you all pink and out of breath?"

His tone, and the way he looked at her, made her grip the leather she held tighter, wishing she had held on to that pitchfork. She took a step back. "Move aside," she said, keeping her tone firm. "I need to put Patsy in the corral."

He jerked the lead line from her hands. "Ask me nice-like. Say please."

She tried to step farther away, but he grabbed her arm and held her in place. Her body tensed in fear.

"What do you think you are doing? Let go of me."

"Now, you don't need to be like that. You being a widow and all… I thought you might like a little attention. No one needs to know, not even Barker. It'll be our secret."

"Let go of me or I'll scream."

He snickered. "Aw. Come on now. I ain't going to hurt you." He pushed her farther into the stall.

She glanced at the pitchfork. She could almost reach it.

He noticed and chuckled cruelly. "You forget. I saw what happened at the branding the other day. You ain't got enough sass in you to use that on me. Besides, cross me and I might have to do a little branding of my own." Amused at his own idea, he laughed—a mean bark of a laugh—and strode into the stall.

At that, the owlet flapped frantically, stirring up the straw and dirt. It let out a piercing screech.

Cassandra screamed.

Roth looked to see what the commotion was in the straw, and the mother owl swooped down from the rafters, her talons extended, her shriek so loud and drawn out that Cassandra wanted to cringe and hold her ears.

Roth released her to defend himself against the large bird, and in that moment, Cassandra ducked low and ran from the stable. Behind her, the angry owl hissed and make a clicking sound, pummeling Roth with its talons and beak and large wings.

Cassandra raced across the drive and up to the house. She slammed the front door and turned the key in the lock, then ran to the kitchen door and locked it too. Her pulse pounded in her ears. If Roth was determined to get in, the locks would not hold, but at least they would make him think twice or at least slow him down.

She rummaged through the cupboard for the small derringer. Her hands shook as she loaded the bullets into the chambers, at the same time saying a prayer for help. Would she be able to use it if necessary? A snake was one thing. A human being entirely different.

She walked into the parlor and peered through the window. Roth stood in the stable doorway and looked around the yard. Two long red lines marked the left side of his face, adding to his brutal expression.

He focused on the house. She drew back into the shadows, her heart thumping wildly in her chest. Where was Otis? Hadn't he heard her scream?

Then Otis appeared at the cookhouse door. Leaning on his tall walking stick, he limped over to the stable. "What's all the commotion?"

Roth's reply was too low for her to hear, but while he spoke, he pulled out his pistol, flipped open the cartridge and examined the chambers. He wouldn't hurt Otis, would he? She couldn't let that happen.

Roth tilted his head toward the stable door while he spoke. A moment later, Otis ducked inside the building.

What was he up to? Cassandra noticed more blood on his hands.

Closing the cartridge, he slowly clicked it around

before holstering the gun. In that moment, she knew that he could have shot Otis at any time and thought nothing of it. He knew it, and he was letting her know it. He had the upper hand. He looked across to the house and tipped his hat, that horrible smirk present on his face again. Then he wiped his hands on his pants, untied his horse, mounted and rode down the lane.

Cassandra let out a shaky breath. Thank God he hadn't hurt Otis. Would he come back? Would he dare to return? He was a horrid beast of a man. Why had Cleve Barker hired him in the first place?

She walked back into the kitchen just as the door jiggled.

"Ma'am? Miss Cassandra?" Otis called out.

She rushed to the door and opened it for him.

"What's this doin' locked?" Otis said, a frown of consternation on his brow. "Is this because of all that commotion?"

It was a plausible explanation. "Yes. Do you know what it was?"

"Just an old barn owl. That Mr. Roth happened to come back and found it botherin' Patsy. He bare-handed broke the bird's neck. It's not a pretty sight. Don't go near there until I get it cleaned up." Otis peered at her closely. "You all right? You look a bit peaked."

"I am now," she said, relieved that along with Otis came a feeling of normalcy.

He straightened. "Guess all the commotion was a mite upsettin'."

"Did Mr. Roth say why he had returned to the ranch?"

"Somethin' about forgettin' his lucky cards." Otis looked over her shoulder. "What are you up to in my kitchen? I just put it all back together, and you got all the cupboard doors open."

Impulsively, she hugged him. He was so very down-to-earth that he helped to settle her jumpy nerves.

By the look on his face, it took him by surprise.

"I'm thankful no one was hurt." She glanced about the room. Things were a bit scattered. "I'll put it all back perfectly. I promise."

"Hurt? Why would either one of us be hurt?"

Should she say anything about Roth scaring her? If she did and Otis chose to go after him, Roth wouldn't hesitate to use that gun on him. She couldn't have Otis getting hurt on her conscience.

When she didn't answer, Otis scrutinized her closely. "Mind tellin' me what it was you were a-lookin' for?"

"Scissors," she answered quickly. "I've mislaid the ones in Mrs. Stewart's sewing basket and thought there might be some in here."

Otis yanked on the drawer in the hutch. Large scissors, in obvious view, sat on top of everything else in the drawer.

She plucked them up. "Thank you! These will do fine." She turned and headed up the stairs.

Chapter Twenty

Wolf removed his mustang's bridle and saddle, stowing them on the rack in the shed behind his parents' store. This was the first day he'd had a chance to exercise the gelding since returning to town. A few gun orders had piled up while he'd been helping at the Rocking S, and he'd been buried under them for the past four days.

He picked up a brush and began currying the mustang.

Of one thing he was certain after the time he'd spent on the ranch and with the roundup—Cleve Barker had no business being foreman. He might have done a fair job of negotiating the price of the cattle at the stockyards, but if Wolf hadn't stepped in at the last moment, the Rocking S wouldn't have gotten the full price that other cattlemen had received this season in Dodge City. Besides that, the man disappeared at key moments, leaving the decisions up to others. After seeing that, Wolf had stayed with the man until all the ranch hands were paid and the rest of the money was safely in the bank.

He'd have to let Cassandra know about his misgivings. Then it would be up to her to relay that to the new owners if she thought it necessary. They would be the ones to keep an eye on the sale next spring—whether Barker was involved or not.

He already missed the ranch. And he missed Cassandra. She'd been on his mind constantly since he returned to town. At any given moment, he wondered what she was doing. Was there any way that he could change her mind about staying and running the ranch?

Why had he put her on the spot the way he did? Guess he'd asked for the disappointment. Confused, she'd said. What the heck did that mean? He hadn't imagined her warm response in the kiss they'd shared. It was there. She had feelings for him. Going by the kiss, he'd say they were strong feelings too.

He'd thought they had drawn closer when she'd confessed about losing the baby. The way she had confided in him had stirred up his desire to protect her and then some.

When Doug had written and asked him to come out East for the wedding, he'd worried that Doug wasn't seeing clearly. His friend's letter had overflowed with excitement and the rush of his feelings. But Doug was one to jump headlong into things, and Wolf figured that this had been one more thing.

As he struggled to stifle the urges that kept rising in him each time he was near Cassandra—urges to touch her and to take her hand—he understood how Doug had fallen so hard and fast for her. She was smart and compassionate and had a gentle nature. That nature had been battered over the past year with all that had happened, but it still showed through. It showed in her strong reaction to the calf being hurt at the branding, and it showed in the way she had come to care for Otis and Jordan.

But he wasn't anything like his best friend. Of them both, he was the careful and methodical one. It wasn't like him to let a woman play havoc with his senses.

Yet it was becoming more and more difficult for him to keep his distance from Cassandra. Her questions revealed her intelligence, and her desire to understand and do the right thing about the ranch. Her wit, her caring for Otis and the others, and her determination to keep her promise to Doug—all told him what a special woman she was. She had integrity and she was loyal. Everything about her drew him closer.

He kept telling himself that she was only here because of her promise—not because the ranch meant anything to her and definitely not because he meant enough. Eight more days and her promise would be fulfilled. Then she would leave. Not nearly enough time to convince her of anything, let alone staying.

He should keep far, far away. Any more contact with her would only bring him a wagonload of hurt and frustration.

Footsteps sounded outside the doorway. Otis walked in, favoring his right leg more than usual. Wolf checked behind him for Cassandra.

"She ain't here so stop stretchin' your neck."

Guess more than Barker had noticed things between him and Cassandra. "What happened to you?" he asked, indicating the old man's leg.

"Weather's changed. Colder last night."

"Hmph." Wolf continued with his horse, moving from its withers to curry its flank.

Otis paced the length of the small shed. For a man bothered by rheumatism, he was moving slower than usual. "Miss Cassandra has a few stops to make. We came early to get things done 'cause she wants to go to the harvest shindig later on. She's wantin' to send a telegram and other things. I dropped her off at the sheriff's."

He paused, turning to Otis. "Something wrong?"

"We got to talk and I mean here in private. Somethin's happened. Been a few days back. Seein' as how you're Doug's friend and you take a particular interest in Miss Cassandra, it's somethin' you should know."

Wolf threw the currycomb into a nearby barrel filled with other tools. Whatever it was must be important. He'd never seen Otis so agitated. "Have a seat. I'm listening."

Otis sank down onto a three-legged stool in the corner. "After you and the others left for the stockyards, who should come a-callin' but that weasel Tom Roth? Sunday mornin' it was, bright and early—a time when the only men up and about are ones with a mind for religion. I was workin' in the garden when I heard a ruckus in the stable. Then I heard a scream—'least I thought that's what I heard. It could have been that old barn owl that's been roostin' in the rafters.

"I headed for the stable, when who should step through the door casually as you please but Tom Roth. I asked him why he was back so soon on his own without the others, and he said he'd forgotten a deck of lucky cards that he wanted to use on the other cowpokes. His gloves were all bloody, and he had scratches on his face. I feared for Miss Cassandra, but he said smooth as could be that a baby owl fell from its nest and when he went to put it back, the mother owl attacked him. He ended up wringin' the baby's neck. Said the thing wasn't going to survive anyway, so it was the compassionate thing to do."

"That's hard to believe," Wolf said with a grunt. "Roth doesn't have a compassionate bone in his body."

"I'm thinkin' along those lines too. More likely it was out of pure orneriness that he killed the thing. Well, I ducked inside to check about the bird, and sure enough there lay a dead baby owl on the straw with its neck broke."

"Where was Cassandra while all this was going on?"

"Well, that's the thing. When I came inside to check on her, both doors were locked, which you know ain't usual. She let me in. When I asked her about the doors being locked, she said she didn't realize that she'd done that and had been busy searchin' through drawers for scissors for her sewin'. Trouble is, later, I found a pair of small sewin' scissors in Mrs. Stewart's basket layin' right on top of the thread."

"Her story doesn't hold water."

Otis nodded. "That screech—it could have been her and not the owl. On top of that, she's been actin' different."

Wolf didn't like the sound of things. "What do you mean by different?"

"Like she got the wind knocked out of her. She won't go into the stable. She ain't ridin' Patsy, ain't hardly leavin' her room, and when she does leave the house, she makes sure that me or Jordan or Fitch is right beside her. I gotta say, the way she's been actin', that I'm surprised she'll walk to the mercantile here in town without me in tow."

A weight dropped in Wolf's gut. Something was definitely wrong. Cassandra loved riding that sweet little mare. If something more had happened… If Roth had harmed her…Wolf would never forgive himself for leaving her on her own. He'd known the man was a bad seed ever since that day he'd helped him get that steer out of the muck. Jarvis wasn't any better, but followed Roth around like a half-whipped pup most of the time. At least Jarvis didn't go out of his way looking for trouble. Roth did…with anything or anyone that crossed him.

"Have you seen Roth since then?"

Otis shook his head.

"Barker have anything to say about that?"

"Just that he'd sent Roth and Jarvis back out to fix some fencing he knew needed work."

Wolf debated telling Otis about his suspicions of Roth and Jarvis rustling cattle. Trouble was, he wasn't sure if Barker was involved. Still—it was better to be forewarned…

"Keep your wits about you around those two."

"You ain't tellin' me anythin' I don't already know."

"Good. I came across things that point to rustlers taking advantage of the ranch."

Otis frowned. "Guess with no real boss around the Rockin' S we made it easy. You think it's Roth and Jarvis?"

"I do, but I also need proof to pin it on them."

"Winston?"

Wolf shook his head.

"Barker?"

"I'm not sure about him. Cassandra knows."

"Cassandra is it now?"

Wolf grunted.

A twinkle returned to the old man's eyes. "All right. I'll keep an eye out. You'll see to the other?"

"I'll talk to her."

"Good. Now, don't let on that I said anythin'. She's a proud little thing and won't take it kindly that we was talkin' about her." Otis walked to the door. "She's wantin' to see the mayor while she is in town too. Do you know anything about that?"

"He's the only lawyer in town, so I figure she's talking to him about selling or staying."

"Can't see her stayin' now. Not the way she's acting lately," he muttered and then pinned Wolf with his gaze. "Ain't she said anythin' to you one way or the other? Which way is she leanin'?"

It was Cassandra's place to explain her plans for the ranch, not his. He hesitated a bit too long as he considered how to answer Otis.

"I see the answer right there on your face," Otis said, pointing at him with a gnarled index finger.

"It's not for me to say anything."

"Right," Otis said flatly. "We go way back, you whippersnapper. I'd say that makes it your place. Don't you try to fool me."

"She's the one dragging her heels. Now that the cattle have been sold and the money is in the bank, she is probably getting a new figure of her assets from Micah." He looked Otis square in the eyes. "Yeah… she's going to sell."

Otis's shoulders lowered in defeat as he backed up and sat down again on the stool. "I've been at that ranch since the beginnin'. This old leg took a bullet for Doug Senior durin' the war, and he said he'd never forget.

Thought I'd live the rest of my days there. Guess I better start ruminatin' on what I'll do."

At sixty-plus hard years, few options existed for the old man. "I keep hoping she'll change her mind and stay."

Otis eyed him closely. "I thought that might be the way of it."

More than you know, he wanted to say, but it wasn't something men said to each other. His expression must have communicated something of his thoughts by the way Otis continued.

"Now, hold on. Maybe she don't know what she wants. Maybe there's still time. She might be searchin' for a reason to stay. T'ain't nothin' for her back in Virginy but kowtowin' to her folks. Heck…everyone there thinks she won't have no choice but to go back with her tail between her legs."

"How'd you learn about that?"

Otis grinned. "She told me. Said when you drove her out to the ranch and she saw it for the first time, her jaw just about dropped to the ground."

The irony of his situation had caught up and tromped on him. He remembered that day and how he'd accused Cassandra of being a gold digger. He'd been so wrong about her! Nothing like chewing on a mouthful of shoe leather. His accusation taunted him now.

"So, you gotta talk to her," Otis said.

"What do you mean?" He had a feeling he knew.

"I've seen the way you look at her. And she ain't exactly blind to you. Get yourself all spiffed up and make your case at the party tonight. You got lots of time. She's stayin' at the hotel afterward and travelin' back in the mornin'."

He wasn't sure she'd appreciate any advances from him, and he wasn't sure this was the right time for them if Roth had done something to scare or harm her. And likely with her seeing Mayor Melbourne and Micah Swift about selling, she was no longer interested in picking things back up with him.

What did remain between them was their kiss. He couldn't forget it. And he wanted more. He wanted her.

After Otis left for the mercantile, Wolf entered his parents' store through the back door. He always thought better when he could work with his hands, and he had that gun to finish on his workbench. He had to think about what he'd say the next time he saw Cassandra. He had to find out what was going on and what Roth had to do with it. Talk like this required careful words.

He pushed open the curtain that separated the storage room and the front area of the store, and pulled up short. Cassandra was standing there at the front window, staring down at his worktable. In her hands, she held a Colt .45 that he'd been working on. So much for having time to think about his words.

"Hello, Cassandra."

She looked up as he strode toward her. "Oh, hello, Wolf. Is this yours?"

He'd forgotten how soft and sweet her voice was— like a clear bell on a quiet morning. Then he took in her appearance. Something about her seemed different. She was as delicate…as fine-boned and pretty as ever, but instead of the slight tan she had acquired the last time he'd seen her, now she looked pale again… and haunted. The shadows under her eyes were back.

"It's Sheriff Baniff's. He asked me to take a look at it. It's shooting to the left." She bounced it as if weighing it again in her hands. "It's quite heavy."

"Not for a man's hand."

He took the .45 from her and set it back on his workbench. "What's going on, Cassandra?"

Her gaze darted away, rather than meet his. "I...I'd like to buy more bullets."

"For the derringer?"

"Yes. I'll need more for practice. You said yourself...or perhaps it was Mr. Barker...that there are dangerous animals on the prairie."

He didn't think it was dangerous animals that had her acting so strange. "I can get more bullets for you, but putting a gun in your hand means dealing with the consequences. Are you prepared for that?"

"I hope so," she whispered.

He took her shoulders gently in his hands. "Look at me, Cassandra. Tell me what frightened you."

She swallowed. "It's nothing. Really. I can handle it. I just need to learn to shoot. You'll teach me, won't you?" she said the last, her large blue eyes full of hope as she looked up at him. There was no way he would deny her request.

"I think it's a good thing for a woman to know how to protect herself."

"Did the first Mrs. Stewart know how to use one?"

"Yes. And I remember her using it once on a rabid coyote."

She shivered. "I could do that. If I had to. What about your mother? I imagine she knows how also."

"She carries a knife." He rummaged in his drawer and withdrew a box, handing it to her.

She loosened the drawstring on her purse.

He closed his hand over hers. "I don't want your money. Tell me what is going on, and you can have this."

Her lids shuttered down.

She walked to the door and looked out on the main street of town. He had the feeling she wasn't seeing the buildings or the train depot, but looking beyond them, inside to her thoughts. Then she glanced around the store, her gaze roaming the bins full of wheat flour and cornmeal, taking in his cluttered workbench and chair last.

"You have your own work to tend to here, and I know you can't always be at the ranch. But…you were there, and now you are gone." She swallowed. "I don't feel safe…without you at the ranch."

Her admission sent a jolt through him. The urge to protect her rose inside and with it the tentative hope that he could be more than a protector in her eyes. Perhaps…more than a friend. Hope filled him. Maybe he did matter…and she'd been afraid to admit it. At least now he knew that she needed him. That was enough… for now.

He took a step toward her. He wanted to hold her. Tell her that she was safe. She stood only six feet from him, but in that distance, there was a chasm that separated them that was more than physical. Her husband had been his closest friend. How could either one of them get beyond that?

Something had happened after he left the ranch and before the rest of the ranch hands had returned from Oak Grove late last Sunday afternoon. Something that had frightened her. And he couldn't let that happen again. Not because of some duty to her late husband, but because *he* couldn't stand by and see her worried or frightened.

"Otis says that you are staying for the harvest dance."

She nodded.

"When you head back to the ranch tomorrow, I'll go with you. We'll get in some practice shooting over the next couple days."

The hope that sprang up in her blue eyes quickened his heartbeat. "You will? Are you sure?"

"I'm sure."

She visibly relaxed and grasped the back of his chair to steady herself.

He wasn't going to let her off that easy. She still owed him the truth. "I need to know what happened."

"Of course." Voices coming from the back room had her adding quickly, "As soon as we get back."

His father entered the room carrying a large sack of oats over his shoulder. He nodded to Cassandra but then continued out the door to the waiting flatbed wagon. His mother and Otis followed, each carrying a box of supplies.

"I'm coming with you tomorrow," Wolf said.

Otis grumbled good-naturedly. "Good thing I figured on it with these supplies. But I can always use another turkey."

The quip was an old one. "You mean that you want me to hunt up a turkey."

Otis grinned. "Caught that, did you? How long are you fixin' to stay?"

He met her gaze. He had a few conditions of his own

if he was going out to the Rocking S. "I'll be staying until Mrs. Stewart asks me to leave."

If he thought his answer would surprise her, he was wrong. The soft, trusting smile she bestowed on him caught again at the edges of his hope. Maybe, just maybe, he could convince her to stay.

Chapter Twenty-One

After storing the flatbed wagon safely in the livery for the night, Otis walked Cassandra to the hotel. He promised to come back at the time of the party to escort her to the dance and introduce her to some of the townsfolk.

In her room, she removed her Stetson and tossed it to the foot of the bed. After speaking with the banker and then the mayor, she had a good idea of the ranch's finances. They'd done well this year. The profit from the cattle, along with the money she would make with the sale of the property, would be enough to see her comfortable for many years to come, and also leave enough to care for Otis for the rest of his days. The others would get a severance amount that would see to them until they found new positions.

As she spoke with the two men, her resolve to follow Barker's advice had weakened. It didn't seem right to keep her intentions of selling from the men who worked for her. She would call a meeting with them when she returned to the ranch tomorrow and let them know. It was time. They should know her thoughts. Even finding out that she was undecided about what to do with every detail would let them know that she was trying to make wise decisions for everyone.

She laid her black skirt and a white blouse for the dance over the bed. If only it could have been her autumn silk dress, but that was back in Alexandria. Oh, how she missed colors, but the black skirt, once more, would have to do. It was nearly worn-out with all the use it had had. When her year was complete, she would burn it—happily. Doug had loved her in bright colors. He'd bought her red and yellow and vibrant blue material, and soon she would wear them again and never, never don another black dress.

A knock sounded.

When Cassandra opened the door, Sadie Austin, the hotel owner's wife, stepped into her room. She was a pert, freckled woman with thick auburn hair pulled into a knot at her nape. "Is everything satisfactory?" she asked.

"It is fine, Mrs. Austin."

"Sadie. Please. I'm so glad you came early today. The rooms are filling up fast with people from afar that have come for the dance." Her gaze flitted over the room with a practiced eye. She walked over and picked up a piece of thread from the floor. "My son, Wylie, swept up in here. He doesn't have quite the eye for detail," she said with a smile.

She indicated the clothes on the bed. "For the party?"

Cassandra sighed. "I'm officially in mourning until the end of this month. I probably shouldn't even go to the dance, but I wanted to meet some of the people who knew my husband. I think he would want that. And to tell the truth. I could use some conversation other than cattle prices and the cost of feed and grain."

Sadie's smile grew. "I haven't lived here all that long, so I didn't know your late husband, but I know everyone will be happy to meet you. Most people here don't stand on ceremony. We've all had our trials, and because of them we tend to judge each other a bit more gently."

Cassandra remembered some of the attitudes she'd observed of people around Wolf. She didn't think that he would completely agree with Sadie about the generous spirit of the town. "I'm afraid that sounds too good to be true."

"Perhaps," Sadie said, amending her words, "but we do try."

Cassandra studied her black skirt, but she wasn't really seeing it, she was imagining another. "I have a lovely silk, the color of pumpkin, with a deep green sash, hanging in my closet back in Alexandria. It's so perfect for this time of year." If only Wolf could see her in something other than black.

"Well, no matter what you choose to wear, you are welcome to come to the dance. I hope everyone will make you feel that way." She glanced about the room one last time. "Is there anything else you need?"

"I'd like to post a letter and I also need to see someone about a headstone for my late husband's grave."

"Mr. Gallagher is the postmaster for Oak Grove. That would be across the street at the mercantile. If you draw up what you want for a headstone, he'll get it to Mr. Moyer, who does the carving."

"Thank you."

"There won't be much of a supper here at the hotel

restaurant since we've been preparing all day for the festival, but if you want a cup of tea, please feel free to come down." Sadie walked out of the room, closing the door behind her.

From her carpetbag, Cassandra withdrew paper and a pen that she'd brought from the ranch's study. She sat down at the table in her room and wrote a letter to her parents, letting them know how she was doing.

Wolf followed his parents out of the store. "I'll catch up with you," he told them. As they locked arms and started down the boardwalk, he turned to lock the door.

He had cleaned up and put on his only suit—a black one—along with boots and a black Stetson. That was about as fancy as he got. He had come to this annual dance that marked the end of the harvest ever since it started when he was seventeen, but he'd never been so nervous as tonight. He meant to dance with Cassandra.

The last rays of the sun lit the horizon a pale lavender, and overhead the stars twinkled—more appearing every minute. The storefronts along the boardwalk on either side of Main Street were dark and quiet. Everyone was at the party. At the end of the street near the schoolhouse, the light streamed from the tall windows of the town hall out onto the road. The new building served as a community center for meetings and whatever was needed—dances included.

As he drew near, three young boys—Kade, Wyatt and Tommy, Doc Graham's new son by marriage—ran out the front door and across the street. They crouched behind a water barrel in front of the *Oak Grove Ga-*

zette, their loud whispers and laughing leaving no doubt as to their hiding place. Suddenly the sound of firecrackers popping in uncoordinated sequence filled the town hall. Ladies shrieked, and men laughed. "Yes!" Wyatt yelled, holding up his fist. Then the boys danced a bit and laughed before sneaking back around to the side door of the busy building.

A moment later, Sylvia Graham stepped from the town hall, her hands on her hips. "Tommy!"

"He got away, ma'am," Wolf said, climbing the steps to the half-curved platform at the entry.

"Well, I guess no harm's been done. And I'm glad he's having a good time." She looked him over with a pert smile on her face. "How are you, Mr. Wolf? You've been making yourself scarce around here of late."

He removed his hat. "Been busy with the roundup out at the Rocking S."

"That's right. Nelson was called out of church to take care of Jordan on Sunday. That boy did a little too much celebrating Saturday night."

"He'll learn. It was his first roundup."

"I suppose he will. At that age it always takes a bit of experience to figure out up and down, don't it?"

He couldn't help grinning at her way of speech. It reminded him of Otis.

"Oh—speaking of the roundup," she continued. "Steve Putnam is looking for you inside."

He held the door as she walked past him and into the large entryway. "Thanks. I'll find him."

On one side of the room, women from town and the neighboring farms and ranches bustled about, setting food and drinks and plates and cups on tables. On the other side, the new schoolteacher attempted to keep the children entertained with a game of musical chairs to the tune of her own singing and clapping. Toward the back of the room on the small stage, four men gathered with their instruments—a banjo, fiddle and a bass guitar. Men lined the perimeter of the room as they watched the hubbub.

He looked about for Cassandra but didn't see her. She had to be there, seeing as how Otis had already claimed a chair by the punch bowl and was talking recipes with Maggie Miller. Maggie looked ready to pop with that baby she was carrying. Wolf was glad to see her husband, Jackson, carry a chair over to her so that she could sit down.

He spotted Steve Putnam with Doc Graham and headed over to see what it was the rancher had wanted to see him about.

He was halfway there when he saw Cassandra. She stood with Fiona Blackwell and Sadie Austin, looking prettier than any woman in the room. She wore a white blouse and her black skirt, but somewhere, she'd latched onto a wide pumpkin-colored sash that banded her torso, the ends tied in a big bow in back and hanging decoratively to the floor. Her blond hair was piled high on the top of her head with black glass beads sprinkled here and there that caught the lamplight and sparkled. High color stained her cheeks, and her eyes twinkled when she suddenly caught sight of him.

He walked toward her, and it was as if the entire room melted away. She turned from the other women and waited for him.

"You came!" she said softly. "I was worried you'd change your mind."

"Why did you think that?"

"Well...you are a man who is more at home on a horse than in town."

He smiled. She was getting to know him. "Are you having a good time?"

"I am. And I'm a bit surprised. I don't know that many people, but the ones I've met are friendly." She glanced over his shoulder. "Oh, look! There's Mr. Putnam. He's coming this way."

"Gotta proposition for you," Putnam said to Wolf as soon as he'd greeted them both. "You know Mary is about to have our first at any moment now."

Wolf wondered what all this had to do with him, but he nodded.

"Well, she wants me home more so that she can get used to being a mother. The boys and I have been talking about the next year of roundups. We took a poll to pick a boss for the next spring and fall roundups. Your name came up. More than once."

Wolf swallowed. "But I don't even own a ranch."

"We all know that. But you are a natural leader, and you know ranching as well—or better—as any of us. Plus, the boys think the fact that you don't own a ranch will keep things fair. You won't play favorites. They even said something about paying you enough to make it worth your while. What do you say? Are you willing?"

A few other men had gathered around, listening. He felt their interest in what he would answer. Cassandra waited too. Among ranchers, this was an honor. He felt the weight of it.

"Yes," he said simply.

Putnam stuck out his hand.

When Wolf shook on the deal, several men moved

in and congratulated him. A few slapped him on the back. It was then he noticed Cleve Barker standing back against the wall with three other men, watching. By the look on their faces, they weren't happy with the decision. Seems the votes hadn't been unanimous. He wondered how things would shake out at the next roundup with them.

"Mrs. Stewart, you missed quite a show last Saturday at the stockyards between your foreman, the cattle buyers and Wolf here. Since your cattle were the first to the yards, that set the price for the rest of us."

"They did a good job?" she asked.

"Barker did a fair job, but once Wolf arrived negotiations definitely improved. Because of his skill, we all got a bigger slice of the pie."

The smile Cassandra gave Wolf made him feel ten feet tall.

Steve Putnam's wife sidled up to her husband. "I'm glad you accepted, Wolf. With our baby coming, it will be nice to have my husband home more."

"But…" Cassandra brows drew together as she looked from Mary to Steve and back to Mary again. "I saw you…"

Steve grinned. "I've seen the look that's on your face before—on others. Mrs. Stewart…this is my wife, Mary. She has a twin sister, Maggie, who is also expecting her first."

Cassandra breathed out in relief. "I'm glad you made that clear. Very nice to meet you, Mrs. Putnam."

"Call me Mary, please. And welcome."

"You're not from around here." Cassandra tilted her head. "Your accent…"

"I'm from the East, although I would wager not as far east as you."

"And you've adjusted? With no trees, no green…"

"Ah… I felt that way at first. You'll find weather in this part of Kansas a bit harsher, but I wouldn't trade places with my old life. I'm much happier here."

Keep talking like that, Mary. Maybe Mary's attitude would rub off on Cassandra. Wolf wasn't about to stop her.

Suddenly, Mary gripped her middle and her eyes widened. "I do believe I'd better sit down. Steve—a hand, please. Very nice to have met you, Mrs. Stewart, and to see you, Wolf."

With that Steve walked with his wife over to the chair vacated by Otis. She sat down with a relieved sigh beside her sister.

When Wolf turned back to Cassandra, she was still watching Mary. The expression on her face was a valiant effort to cover up that she was hurting. It had to be Mary's condition. He didn't know how to ease that particular ache in Cassandra.

She glanced up at him. When her gaze connected with his, he knew he was right. A tremulous smile tilted one side of her mouth. "Some punch?"

"This way." He put his hand to the small of her back, steering her toward the refreshments.

She slowed as they neared the table, her focus on Mary and Maggie sitting just to the side of the table.

He leaned down to her ear and lowered his voice. "How about I get the punch and we step outside for some fresh air."

"I'd like that." She smiled gratefully.

A moment later, he walked with her outside into the cool night air.

"Thank you. I… It's hard to be around…"

"You don't have to explain."

She visibly relaxed, her shoulders lowering. "Talking with you…being here with you… It helps." She looked up at him. "I'm glad you will be coming back to the ranch tomorrow."

The light from the lanterns on each side of the town hall door sparkled in her eyes and sent shadows playing across her face. Inside, the party continued, the music growing louder, but all he saw was her. She was the most beautiful thing he'd ever seen.

"Cassandra…you look at me like that, and I forget my promise to keep my distance."

"The minute you rode away I started missing you. I meant it when I said that I needed time, that I was confused." She drew in a breath. "All I know is that I like when you are there at the ranch with me. You make me feel safe. I looked forward to seeing you, talking to you every day. Wolf… You *do* matter so much to me."

He swallowed. "Why are you doing this? It makes no sense to talk like that. You are leaving in a week."

"I'm not sure what I am doing at this point. But staying or going, it doesn't change how I feel about you."

Common sense told him that she was still in a vulnerable state. Certain men would take advantage of that and use it to get what they wanted—namely the ranch. He wouldn't do that. He didn't want her to stay because of coercion or manipulation. He wanted her to stay for the right reasons—because she loved the ranch and maybe, because she loved him. He wanted to be a part of her life—a part of her future. But first she had to make the decision to stay on her own accord.

"Well, well, well. Look who's out here getting some night air," Cleve Barker said as he stepped from the town hall.

"Hello, Mr. Barker," Cassandra said, her voice cool. "I see you made it into town with the others. Were things taken care of before you left the ranch?"

"If you mean did I get a chance to talk to Roth and Jarvis... No. The men didn't come in, and I didn't ride out to find them. Seemed like a waste of my time to go hunting them down." Cleve pulled a cigarette paper from his pocket, filled it with tobacco and rolled it up, wetting the edge with his tongue. "I can't say if they'll show up here. If they do, I'll take care of it."

"Take care of what?" Wolf asked. He still had to find out what had happened to her.

Barker sneered. "Ranch business. Nothing to do with you."

Wolf squared off to him. "You say that often, Barker. And we both know why you are wrong."

"I think the new owner's wishes pull a sight more weight than what a dead man asked you to do. Cassandra is the one calling the shots now. You were a big help at the roundup and the sale, but now that's over. You are back in town and don't know what's going on out at the ranch, so keep your nose out it."

"Cleve Barker!" Cassandra said sharply. "How can you say that? Wolf knows the ranch better than any of the rest of us. He was a trusted friend of my late husband."

"Sure. That might have been at one time. But now

his whole purpose for hanging around the place is to lay claim to it. He can't get a loan, so now he is trying to romance his way to it." Cleve stared at Wolf. "Why don't you tell my cousin about your meeting with Micah Swift?"

Wolf's jaw tensed.

"Let me help you," Cleve said, continuing. "He asked for a loan this past week. It's the second time the bank has turned him down."

"And you? What were you doing at the bank?" Wolf accused.

"I happen to keep my money there and the ranch's payroll," Cleve said smoothly.

Cassandra glared at Barker. "You are not yourself, Mr. Barker. Have you been imbibing?"

Wolf touched her arm. "I'll handle this. Go back inside."

The look she gave him—one full of irritation—made him pull back his hand.

"You are smart not to trust him," Cleve said. "It's no secret he wants that ranch for his own. He's already been to the bank about it. And if he gets you along with it… Well, wouldn't that just be dandy? Simpler even—to get what he wants by marrying into it. That's something you know about, ain't it? You married my cousin to get your hands on the ranch in the first place, and now you are all set to turn a profit with it."

Cassandra's eyes widened in shock.

"Keep your mouth shut, Barker," Wolf said, his gaze on Cassandra.

"Is what he says true?" she asked him. "Not about me…but about you?"

He hesitated, his thoughts jumbled. Part was true—

the part about wanting the ranch. But to go so far as marrying? He knew he didn't stand a chance with someone like her. Whether he loved her or not, it didn't matter.

Barker chuckled. "Can't even answer it, can you? You know it's true. Ha!"

The smug look on Barker's face did it. He hauled back his fist and popped Cleve in the mouth.

Barker stumbled backward and then wiped the blood from his split lip with the back of his hand. He spit into the dirt. "Didn't know you had it in you." He shuffled sideways, his fists in front of him, ready to retaliate.

"No! Stop this!" Cassandra cried out.

He heard Cassandra, her voice filled with distress. He wasn't about to stop. Once and for all, he would square things with Barker. He'd had enough of his insinuations and snide remarks ever since Doug had hired him on.

Barker rammed his fist into Wolf's gut. For a shorter man, he packed a powerful punch. Wolf doubled over, the air rushing out of him.

Barker followed up with a fist to his chin. Pain exploded through Wolf's jaw and neck as his head flew backward. When his vision cleared, he realized men from inside the town hall had stepped outside to watch the fight.

"Somebody stop them! Please!" Cassandra wailed, drawing too close.

Wolf glanced meaningfully at Putnam. In answer, Steve pulled her back and stepped slightly in front of her, protecting her from the fray. Seeing that she was safe, Wolf turned and pummeled Barker, one, two, three times. Each time the man backed up two steps, and each time his eyes went a bit more out of focus. With the third jab, he fell to the dirt—dazed.

"Stay down if you know what's good for you," Wolf said, standing over him.

"Not till you're down here instead of me!"

"They're here!" Cassandra suddenly cried out, her tone insistent as she pointed down the street. "Mr. Jarvis and Mr. Roth. Down at the saloon."

Wolf looked down the street where two men dismounted from their horses. Cleve got to his feet. He worked his jaw, checking that it wasn't broken.

"Mr. Barker. Make sure Roth never returns to the ranch. Not ever." Her voice shook with emotion.

Barker picked up his hat from the dirt and batted it against his thigh. "What about Jarvis?"

Cassandra hesitated, then said, "He can stay or go. Whatever he chooses."

Barker narrowed his gaze at Wolf. "We'll finish this another time."

"Fine by me," Wolf said.

Cleve strode down the street toward the saloon.

The men who had piled out onto the street to watch started back inside the dance until he was left standing there, alone with Cassandra.

"Was that necessary?" she asked in an exasperated tone.

He touched his cut lip gingerly. "Yes."

"I'll never understand men. Never."

He didn't need her censure. "You fired Roth?"

She looked away rather than meet his gaze. "Mr. Barker will take care of it."

He grabbed her arm, making her look up at him. "Why?"

She wrenched from his grasp. "Do you really care about me? Or is it like Barker said? Is it all about the land?"

Her words stung. Barker had opened up a trainload of doubt inside her with his insinuations about the bank and speculating on Wolf's intentions. Heck, even he didn't know his intentions past getting her to stay and run the ranch herself. He cared about her—yes. In all truth, he loved her. But that didn't amount to being able to marry her! He couldn't ask her. He had nothing to offer someone born to money like her.

"Cassandra…" He didn't know what to say. Again. Seemed whatever he said, she wasn't ready to hear it or believe him. He shook his head. How had things gotten to this point? He retrieved his hat from the ground.

"I'll admit I'd like to own that property. I've always felt that way. It's a beautiful piece of land. But when you showed up, all I ever wanted was to do right by Doug. At least, that's how I felt at the start. Now—" He blew out a breath. "Now all I can think about is you. But to marry you, just to get the land… I wouldn't go that far. And I know you wouldn't have me. So that doesn't figure into any of this at all. I don't expect you to believe me. Not after what Barker said. But I don't lie."

He nodded to her, settled his Stetson on his head and strode down the street.

Chapter Twenty-Two

After a restless night, Cassandra was sure she would be returning to the ranch alone. Wolf was a man of his word. She knew that. But she had questioned him where it mattered most—his pride. After all that had been said last evening, how could she hope that he would accompany them back to the ranch? She might have garnered his promise yesterday afternoon, but their words last evening hung between them like a dark curtain and changed everything.

The restaurant was filled with people she had seen at the dance. Many would be heading home today, just like her.

Sadie brought a cup of tea to her table. "Are you sure you wouldn't like more than toast? It won't take me a minute to dish you out some porridge or sausage."

"No. This is enough." She reached out, stopping Sadie from leaving. "By the way, you were right yesterday. Everyone was very welcoming. I heard not one disparaging remark about me attending the party."

"It wasn't anyone's business but your own. Oak Grove does have its charm. Despite the brawl in the street last night, it is a good place to settle down." Her green eyes sparkled with excitement. "Especially now!"

"What do you mean? Why now?" Cassandra asked, drawn in by her air of mystery.

Sadie slid into the chair across from her. "Our little town is growing! Mary and Maggie... You met them at the dance last night, didn't you?"

"Yes."

"They had to leave early. Both of them started having birthing pains."

Cassandra braced herself, but instead of the familiar envy she usually felt at the mention of babies, she realized she was more curious than ever to know the outcome.

"Twins having babies," Sadie mused in a whisper. "Those two have done everything together their entire lives. What happens if one has a boy and the other a girl?"

Cassandra felt the tug of a smile. "That might really throw them."

"It just might. The entire town is eager to find out." She leaned forward. "I think some of the men have even placed bets."

"And what about the women?"

Sadie grinned. "Well, now. I did hear that something was said at the quilting bee last Tuesday night, but that's all I have a right to share. Now that you are a part of Oak Grove, perhaps you would like to join our quilting group?"

"Oh... I don't know." The invitation to stay and be a part of this community wrapped around her. It sounded wonderful.

She realized that Sadie was waiting for her answer. As friendly and open as the woman was, Cassandra didn't want to say anything to her of her plans—especially since she wasn't sure of them herself. It wouldn't be right. Her first words should be to her ranch hands. She smiled at Sadie. "Thank you for inviting me."

"More coffee!" A man raised his mug at a neighboring table.

Sadie stood. "Well, back to work. I hope I will see you the next time you are in town, Mrs. Stewart."

"I'll be sure to stop in. You've made me curious. I'd like to know the outcome of the twins—whether they have boys or girls or one of each."

After Sadie left, Cassandra finished her tea and then stepped outside on the boardwalk. Otis had moved the flatbed wagon from the livery to in front of the hotel. She glanced down the street, wondering if Wolf was up. There was no sign of him.

She picked up her carpetbag from the hotel lobby where she had left it and swung it into the back of the wagon.

"Mrs. Stewart!" Cleve Barker strode toward her.

"Good morning, Mr. Barker." She squared her shoulders, facing him. A heavy day's growth of beard stubbled his jaw, and his upper lip was swollen and scabbed over where Wolf had punched him.

"I talked to Roth. He lit out early this morning. You won't see him again."

"Did he leave anything in the bunkhouse?" She had to make sure there wasn't even a remote chance of running into him.

"He keeps all he owns in his saddlebags." His bushy

brows drew together. "Guess it's no loss—especially since you're selling the place. It's one less worry."

"About that. When we get back to the ranch today, I want to talk to all the hands."

A shimmery flash of red from down the street pulled her gaze. Gertie leaned out a second-story window of the saloon and waved a sparkly cloth. "Yoo-hoo! Forgot your hat, Cleve."

Cleve waved a hand in acknowledgment, then turned back to Cassandra. "I was hoping I could work something out with you before you say something to the rest of the men. I can't buy the place outright, but maybe you'd be willing to go in with me on time. Why don't we go talk to Micah at the bank? Maybe he's got a way this could work out for the both of us."

She'd been honest with him the entire time, ever since she'd written her first letter to the ranch. And for that, he'd been secretive and often gone when she needed him. Then to hear last night from Mr. Putnam that he hadn't been the best negotiator at the stockyards, she was certain now that it would not do to sell the ranch to him. He wasn't the right person. Blood relative or not, she couldn't have Doug's heritage, and all the family had worked for, ruined. She would let the new owners know of her qualms so that they could either keep him on with guidance, or hire their own choice of ranch foreman.

"I already have a buyer waiting for word in Denver. I'm sorry, Cleve, but if I sell, I want a clean break. I want the money up front…not pieced out a little at a time." Her talk yesterday afternoon with Mayor Melbourne had convinced her that she needed it that way to see to herself and Otis and the rest of the hands properly.

"You gotta give me a chance!" Frustration filled his strong voice. Several passersby glanced at them.

"Please, Cleve, lower your voice. You've already had three weeks since we first talked of this. Today, I just want to get back to the ranch."

He scowled. "Well then... Can't have you upset now, can we?"

It was a churlish thing to say. "What do you mean by that?"

"Just what I said."

At his moody look, she stepped back.

"Everything all right?" Wolf said, striding toward them from the street, his horse in tow.

"What are you doing here?" Cleve asked.

"Mrs. Stewart asked me back out to her ranch." He tied his horse to the back of the wagon.

She couldn't have been more relieved! "I thought..."

"Like you, ma'am, I keep my word." He gave an extra tug on the tether line, then grabbed the burlap sack from his horse's saddle and settled it into the back of the wagon with her carpetbag and the supplies.

Cleve glared at the both of them, a suspicious expression on his face. "Looks like you are planning to stay awhile." He spun on his heel and stormed off in the direction of the saloon.

They watched him go. Wolf turned to her. "My being out at the ranch might cause more problems than it helps."

"Perhaps. But I'm glad you will be there anyway."

She let him help her into the wagon.

Then he climbed up beside her. "I expect some answers about Roth and Jarvis. You worried Otis too. He deserves to hear your explanation, as well."

"All right. We'll talk on the ride home."

He smiled and raised his dark brows.

She realized suddenly what she'd said. "I mean ranch. I'll tell you both on the ride to the ranch."

"I liked how you said it the first time." He snapped the reins lightly and drove the horse and wagon in a big half circle, stopping before the mercantile's front doors. "Otis thought of two more things he wanted before leaving town."

They sat there for a moment, waiting.

"About last night," Wolf said. "You looked nice. Just thought you should know."

A small glow flickered inside and held. In his quiet, understated way, he'd made her feel feminine and pretty. She wanted to believe him, but Cleve's comments still lingered, creating a cloud of suspicion about his motives. Since hearing them, she'd questioned all the things that had happened and everything Wolf had told her. Still, the part inside her that was all woman was glad Wolf liked the way she looked at the dance.

When Otis stepped from the mercantile, she could tell he had mischief up his sleeve. He carried a bundle of fluff that wiggled and squirmed and yipped under one arm and a thin rope and collar in the other.

"A puppy?" Cassandra said. "Are you serious?"

"She's to even out things at the ranch," Otis said. "Figured you could use some female company. And she'll grow up to be a right fine guard dog for the place."

"A girl? Here...give her to me so you can get in the wagon."

When Otis handed the puppy off, it almost jumped

out of her arms. Wolf helped subdue the wiggling mass of fur. A giggle bubbled up, surprising her, as the pup on her lap stood on its hind legs and tried to lick her chin.

Wolf smiled. "She's taking to you right off."

"I know very little about dogs, but I believe it will be some time before I can count on this one for protection."

"She'll grow." Wolf snapped the reins, and they headed out of town.

"Where did you find her, Otis?" she asked.

"Wally Brown at the livery had her. 'Bout eight weeks ago, a mother dog came in and promptly dropped six babies. Wally's been lookin' for homes for them." He slipped the leather collar around the pup's neck and attached the rope. "Mother was a shepherd. Don't know about the sire."

"You'll have to come up with a name," Wolf said.

Otis looked at her expectantly.

"Not me. She belongs to you and the ranch. Otis, you name her." She didn't want to name a dog and then leave it behind.

"I ain't no good at names. If you ask me, I'd call her Sissy, and that ain't no name for a pup who will grow up to be a guard dog."

"Well, we'll have to put our heads together and think of something."

The puppy jumped between her lap and Otis's lap, and finally settled down to take a nap. The rocking of the wagon might have had something to do with it. Wolf, she noticed, became quieter the farther they got from town. He became silently alert to every noise around them. Had she missed that the first time he'd taken her to the ranch? Had she misinterpreted his watchfulness as uninterest? If so, what else was she mistaken about?

They were nearly to the edge of the ranch property when she caught a look from Wolf. He was waiting for her to explain about what had happened with Tom Roth. She told him and Otis of the baby owl and Roth's sudden appearance while everyone was in town on Sunday morning, as well as her concern for Otis's safety. As she talked, it was as if a weight lifted from her shoulders.

"Why didn't you say somethin' sooner, Miss Cassandra?" Otis said. "I would have been on the lookout for you, 'case he showed up."

"I…I guess I didn't want to appear weak."

"No one thinks of you that way," Otis said.

She caught the look that passed between him and Wolf. Both set their jaws. "Mr. Barker has fired him. He won't be back."

"Never should have been hired in the first place, if you ask me," Otis grumbled. "What about Jarvis? He came right along with Roth."

"I don't know. He hasn't disobeyed any of Barker's orders or my requests…although he is very disagreeable to be around."

"We'll keep an eye on him," Wolf said.

"Right!" Otis seconded. "The moment he crosses a line, he's gone."

"And you'll have that shooting lesson today," Wolf said darkly.

Chapter Twenty-Three

After hearing of Cassandra's narrow escape with Roth, it was all Wolf could do not to hand the reins to Otis, jump on his horse and chase after the scoundrel. He was frustrated with her too—that she hadn't said something sooner, that she'd suffered in silence, frightened and unsure if Roth was going to appear around a corner and threaten her again.

And he was angry with himself too. It was his job to keep an eye on her while she was here. He figured once she left that would put an end to anything he could do for her. But here at the ranch, he'd made the commitment to be here for her, and he'd left right after the roundup, letting his pride get in the way of his duty.

The pressure built up inside him so much that the moment he pulled the wagon up to the front of the ranch house and stopped, he set the brake lever, swung down and began unhitching the wagon without a word, leaving Otis to help Cassandra down with the puppy.

"What's wrong, Wolf?" Cassandra asked from the wagon seat.

He didn't answer, afraid he'd probably rail at her

when it was himself he was angry with. He'd learned long ago it was better to keep silent. He unbuckled and then flipped the traces from each horse, feeling Cassandra watching him. His thoughts were dark—of himself and of Roth.

With a confused look on her face, she handed the puppy to Otis and then climbed down by herself. She watched him a moment longer. "Once Mr. Barker returns, I'd like everyone to gather in the study. You too, Wolf. I have a few things to say." She turned and carried the puppy into the house.

Two hours later, Wolf finished repairing several broken slats on a crate he'd fixed up for the pup. He carried the crate to the porch, where Cassandra sat in the swing. "Thought you could use this for the pup. Maybe find an old blanket in the house, or Otis could make a small pillow with those feathers he is always collecting."

The sound of hooves on dirt had them both glancing toward the lane.

Barker rode into the yard. He tied his horse to the corral fencing and strode up to the house.

"I'm glad you are back," Cassandra said. "We need to have that meeting."

"If this is about last night…" Barker said.

"It isn't."

They assembled in the study. Wolf folded his arms over his chest and stood at the back.

Cassandra stood beside the desk and surveyed the men. "First off, I'd like to say thank you for how welcome you have all made me feel. You have been gracious in sharing your expertise about this ranch business that I know nothing of. I can see why my late husband felt so strongly about this place and all of you.

"When I first arrived, Otis asked if I was going to sell the ranch, and my answer was evasive. I was cautioned against saying anything at first by my lawyer. Wolf has challenged that from the start." She stopped for a breath and glanced at him. "He has never known for sure if I was going to sell, but in his quiet way, every day he has championed your cause.

"You all know that I spoke to my lawyer while in town yesterday—Mayor Melbourne. Although I have not yet signed any sale papers, that will be done in town on the day I leave, which is one week from today. There is a man from Denver who is interested in the land, however, I don't know any details about whether he already has a crew to work the land, or whether he will absorb you into the mix."

She stopped for another deep breath. "Because of your loyalty to my husband and to this ranch, I've worked out a few things legally. I hope for the better for all of you. Hopefully, you will be able to continue working here if that is what you want. Either way, whether you stay or whether you leave for a different place, you will each get severance pay to see you through until spring."

Disappointment filled their faces. Jarvis looked angry. It was obvious they didn't want things to change. All except Otis. He looked heartbroken.

"Otis?" she continued. "You have been loyal to the Stewarts since you rode with Douglas's father in the war. You took that bullet for him. I have worked out a monthly stipend for you. It's yours whether you chose to stay on here or not. The new owners would be fools not to hire you back—" she looked over everyone "—not to hire any of you back." She struggled to keep control of her emotions. "That's all I really have to say. If you think of something I've forgotten, please let me know. I want this transition to be as easy as possible for all of you."

"Well, since you asked, I got a thing or two to say, and then I'll keep quiet," Otis said. "I appreciate your seeing to all those things, particularly me, but it ain't right. What are you goin' back to Virginy for? You got people here that care about you and that'll help you. Don't leave. Don't sell out. Doug had a reason for wantin' you to come and stay here for a spell. Keep this place like Doug would have wanted."

"Yeah," Jordan said.

"That goes for my thoughts too," Fitch said. "Seems like you're giving up too quick. Give it another month… Give it a year…"

Jarvis didn't say a word.

She glanced his way. "I…" Her voice trembled. Then, composing herself, she tried again. "Thank you… I just can't."

Wolf was proud of the way she'd handled the meeting. He could tell it wasn't easy for her. Her voice shook a time or two as she spoke. He was glad that Otis had spoken up, giving voice to what the rest of the men were thinking.

The men filed out. Otis shook his head as he left. It would probably take a while for all she'd said to sink in. He turned to go.

"Wolf? Do you have time this afternoon to teach me to shoot?"

He nodded.

"Do you think the men will be all right?"

The worry in her eyes stopped him. "You did a good thing here today. You were honest with them—and that means something. They have a short amount of time now to work through what you said. And they'll likely stay to see what happens with the sale."

She breathed a sigh of relief. "Good. I...don't want them to hate me."

He nearly smiled at that. "Hate you? You included them—which made them feel a part of your decision. You did the unexpected. It is more than most bosses would do."

She turned away, but not before he saw her relieved expression.

Did his approval mean that much to her? It was hard to believe. Barker's words from last night must still be ringing in her ears. He hadn't imagined the suspicion that leaped into her eyes then—or the rush of anger that overwhelmed him.

"Cassandra... About what Barker said last night..."

"You don't need to explain again."

"I think I do. I do want to buy the land, and I did go to the bank to take out a loan for it. So that much of what Barker said is true."

"Then buy me out, Wolf. All you had to do was tell me."

She still didn't understand. "I didn't get the loan. Micah Swift has strong thoughts on loaning money to someone like me."

"Oh. I see. Then I guess that would make marrying me an opportune way to get hold of the land."

"It would."

She stepped back from him. "Then do you admit that you've been helping me as a ruse to get hold of the ranch? That...that kiss meant nothing?"

"You know me better than that," he said, his frustration growing. "You are a beautiful, strong woman, Cassandra. Any man would be a fool not to want you for his own." *Not to love you.* "We both feel something for each other. There's no lie in that. But marriage to me wouldn't be easy. I've seen it with my own parents. I wouldn't wish that for you. Not after all you have been through."

"So, you aren't giving me a choice. How noble of you."

She didn't, or wasn't trying to, understand. He'd put his feelings, all of himself into that kiss, fearing it would be all he'd ever have of her. "I asked you to stay," he reminded her.

"You did. To run the ranch."

He scowled, then stuffed his hat on his head. "I'll meet you on the porch after dinner for that shooting lesson. If you don't show up, I'll assume you've changed your mind about it." He spun on his heel and headed outside.

Waiting for Otis to call her for dinner, Cassandra stayed in her room and thought over the conversation she'd had with the men. They were unhappy with all that she'd said, but she hadn't expected them to come right out and ask her to stay. It was so heartfelt. Her eyes burned with unshed tears, thinking of it. She was torn between a wild desire to stay and give ranching her best effort or to listen to the sensible voice inside that told her she had to return to her home in Alexandria.

If she stayed, would it be one more example of her selfishness? Her choices had once brought disaster on Douglas and the baby. Would choosing to stay in some way bring disaster on the men here in the same way? She couldn't live with that. She had no business running a ranch. Yet a small voice inside told her that she was smart, that she was capable. As long as Otis and Jordan and Fitch helped her, maybe she could do it. And most important, as long as Wolf stayed and helped.

Was she tempting fate?

With her thoughts so muddled, it was a good thing she had a few hours to calm down before heading out to the west field with a gun for shooting practice. Wolf chose an area free of cattle.

They were careful to keep their comments to the lesson at hand. A good thing, because in trying to decide what was the best course for everyone else at the ranch, it was really her own heart she needed to figure out.

The day she would be leaving the ranch was barreling down on her. And after all that they had shared, she found herself more and more reluctant to go. It was crazy and ridiculous, and she could think of many reasons why she must keep to her original plans. She was all bound up in a jumble of feelings and thoughts and couldn't trust herself to speak of it.

Patiently, he adjusted her grip on the derringer. "Hold it up so that you can look right down the barrel and use the sight. With a short barrel like this, it is easy to shoot wide of your target, so you want to move slow and steady. You've only got two shots."

At her side, Wolf touched her elbow, raising her arm. His calloused fingers were rough on her skin, and his warm breath on her cheek sent shivers down her spine. The urge to turn to him came over her. She wanted his kiss. Knowing that he had set his feelings for her aside, that he would not pursue her because he thought she would be leaving, made the shooting lesson nearly unbearable.

Looking up into his warm brown eyes, she finally admitted to herself the feelings that she'd held at bay— what she really wanted. She loved him. She truly loved him. He thought marriage to him would be too hard on her. But staying here in Kansas, near enough to see him often and yet not be a part of his life, would be so much worse. If only he would ask her to stay—not as the owner of the Rocking S, but as his wife.

The next morning, she awoke to someone pounding on the downstairs door. She rose quickly and donned her clothes. Downstairs, a man spoke with Otis on the porch. She knotted her hair quickly and joined them.

"Mrs. Stewart," Sheriff Baniff said. "Sorry to disturb you so early, but I received that telegram you were waiting on."

"Come in. Please. Otis? Please put on some coffee for the sheriff."

As Otis left to do her bidding, she ushered the sheriff into the study.

Chapter Twenty-Four

"Wolf? Would you mind staying for a moment? You too, Mr. Barker."

Dinner was finished and the rest of the hands were heading back to their chores. Wolf glanced at Otis. Did he know what was going on? He received a small shrug before Otis began clearing the dishes.

"We can talk in the parlor," Cassandra said.

They followed her into the front room.

Now what? What more was there to say between him and Barker? They'd hashed out everything the night at the dance and hadn't spoken sense. As it stood, he'd rather not be in the same room with the man.

"What's this all about?" Barker asked.

Wolf was glad to see that the man was as much in the dark about it as he was. Cassandra didn't sit down, so he took it this wasn't a social call. He remained on his feet, as did Barker.

Behind her, light from outside streamed in through the window. "I want to hear where you first ran into Roth and Jarvis."

"I already told you. At a job just outside of Dodge City."

"And how did they know that you came this way?"

He shrugged. "I must have mentioned that I was headed here."

"Do you know the reason they left their last employer?"

"Something about not getting paid after they'd done good work." Barker frowned and rubbed his chin. "Look. If there's been a problem, I'll take care of it. I took care of Roth for you, didn't I?"

"Yes. And I appreciate that. But if you had been careful about hiring him in the first place, it would have been better for the ranch. You see, I sent a telegram a while back—to Mr. Turnage—and received an answer this morning."

The sudden tension in the small room put Wolf on alert.

"Truly, Cleve, I like to think that family looks out for family. But you haven't, have you? You've done my late husband a disservice and only looked out for yourself. Very well, as a matter of fact. The three of you rustled cattle from Mr. Turnage's ranch until he became suspicious. And now, under the name of being family, you have quietly taken cattle from my husband's ranch."

"You can't prove anything," Barker said.

"Cassandra," Wolf warned, moving his hand to his holstered gun. "You should have the sheriff here."

"But I'm not going to press charges. He is family after all." Her eyes narrowed. "But you are not going to continue working here, Cleve. You must leave. I think that is more than what my late husband would have done. You and Jarvis are to get your things immediately and get off my land."

Barker's chin raised defiantly, his eyes cold. "Wolf put you up to this."

"All he did was come across a calf tied out and explained the implications to me. I'm the one who talked to the sheriff and Steve Putnam. They suggested I send a telegram to Mr. Turnage. Then Winston found two more calves tied out.

"You are right," she continued. "I cannot prove that you were involved with stealing my cattle, but too many other things have happened that make it clear to me you should not be the foreman here or anywhere near the Rocking S. You lied about the reason Jarvis and Roth left Mr. Turnage. You shouldn't have hired them in the first place. Plus, you are often gone when decisions are needed. You may be my cousin by marriage, but I can no longer have you on this place. You may as well know that I intend to alert my neighbors, so do not expect to work at any ranches around Oak Grove. You won't be welcome."

"You're making a mistake," Barker said.

"Don't you dare threaten me. Yours is a much better outcome than other cattle thieves'. I've been told they are most often hanged. Now, please, go."

She stood proud and in control, but Wolf had a bad feeling about this. Barker wasn't the type to let a woman get the better of him.

The man slapped on his hat and stormed from the house.

Wolf removed his hand from his gun and followed.

He'd keep an eye on Barker and Jarvis until they were both off the ranch. It looked like he had three men to watch out for now.

The next three days brought a quiet to the ranch that Cassandra had not experienced before. She let the others know about Roth, Jarvis and Mr. Barker in case any of them happened back to the ranch. She practiced shooting with Wolf in the morning and then went riding with him in the afternoon. After chores in the evening, Otis placed supper in the dining room and Otis, Jordan, Fitch and Wolf sat down with her. They'd linger for one game of chess or checkers, but then they returned to the bunkhouse where they could smoke and play poker and would not have to watch their manners so closely.

All with the exception of Wolf. Each night, despite the progressing chill in the air, he sat on the porch steps while she rocked in the swing with the puppy in her lap, and they talked.

Tonight, she studied his strong profile as he rubbed oil over the handle of his rifle, working it into the wood until a sheen appeared. His face was mostly in shadows, but she knew it as well as she knew her own. Her thoughts, this evening as always of late, centered on him and on how very special he had become to her. Leaving the ranch would be difficult, but leaving him? The more she thought of stepping on the train, the more something inside her rebelled.

"You figured out a name for that pup yet?" Wolf asked.

"Sheba. I've named her Sheba. It means *queenly*."

"Sounds like a good strong name for a guard dog. She'll grow into it."

"I thought so. I'm tempted to take her with me when I leave," she said.

He shrugged. "Suit yourself."

"I suppose you will be happy to get back to your regular routine. I've pulled you away from your business in town and your friends there."

He stopped polishing and looked over at her. "I have friends here. And I wouldn't have stayed if I didn't want to."

"I don't suppose you do anything you don't want to."

A spare smile was her reply.

"Where is the line, Wolf?"

"What line?"

"The line that separates what we are doing for Doug from what we want for ourselves?"

He was quiet for a moment. "Oh. That line."

"Really. I want to know. I need to know. Because it has become very blurry to me. And lately, it's not Doug that I'm thinking about at all."

He didn't answer her. Not for a long time. "You said it yourself. You'll be leaving soon. Let's not do anything that we will regret."

It wasn't what she wanted to hear. She wanted him to hold her again, to kiss her again. But she knew he spoke the truth. Taking the puppy in her arms, she rose from the swing. "Good night. I'll see you in the morning."

"Make sure the windows are all closed. A storm is coming."

"How can you tell?"

When he stood, the look he gave her left no doubt in her mind that he wanted her. She nearly stopped breathing. Hunger and desire swirled in his dark gaze.

"The air is damp, warmer than usual. And I'm restless."

Chapter Twenty-Five

He'd spoken the truth. Sleep didn't come to him for a long time, and when it did, he tossed and turned in a fitful rest. Cassandra consumed his thoughts. Memories of their short time together hounded him. He loved her. He wanted her for his own. And he couldn't bear to let her leave. But he had no right at all to ask her to stay for him.

It was in the early hours of the morning, before sunrise, that the wind came up and the rain started. Lightning cracked across the sky, lighting up the inside of the bunkhouse with an eerie blue flash. He wouldn't have thought anything of it, except that in between the wind and the rain, he thought he heard Sheba yipping and whining. It was probably the thunder that frightened the pup—that and the need for attention in a strange place. He would have ignored it, except something told him to check it out.

He opened the bunkhouse door and a sheet of rain whipped against him. The ranch house was dark. He was halfway across the yard when the odor of burning wood came to him. A light flickered from within the stable. He changed his course and threw open the stable doors. Heat billowed out from inside. Flames burned high in a pile of straw by the wall of tack. The horses whinnied and stomped in their stalls.

He grabbed an armful of horse blankets and doused them in the watering trough, then raced back into the stable and threw them over the worst of the flames. He couldn't do much alone. He needed more help.

He ran back to the bunkhouse and yelled at Jordan and Fitch to get a move on and help. Then he returned to the stable, grabbed two buckets and went for more water. He handed the buckets to the other men, who had appeared by then, and headed back into the stable. Opening each stall, he and Fitch shooed the horses out, forcing them past the flames that drew perilously close to the doorway.

As he batted the fire with more wet blankets, he zeroed in on the thought that this fire hadn't been started by lightning. It was too neatly set inside the stable with no evidence of destruction of the stable's roof.

"Take care of the fire," Wolf instructed the two men. "I'm going to check on Mrs. Stewart."

He left them and headed out through the rain toward the kitchen door. Lightning split the sky again, and in the bright flash of light, he saw that footprints in the mud led up to the house. He sneaked into the kitchen. The sound of voices came from the dining room.

"You think you can just sashay right in and take what should go to Barker? He's the rightful owner of this here ranch. And he owes me big-time."

Roth!

"Get out this instant!" Cassandra said. There was an edge of steel in her tone.

"Not until I've taken what I want."

"I said to get out!"

"Ha! You ain't going to use that on me," Roth said. "Besides, mine's bigger." An evil chuckle slipped out.

So Cassandra had her gun pointed at Roth. But Roth had one too. Wolf cracked open the door. Cassandra stood halfway up the stairs in her nightgown, her derringer in front of her and pointed at Roth.

In the next instant, the door creaked, alerting both Cassandra and Roth to his presence. He thrust it open completely, knocking Roth off balance. It was only for a second, but it was enough that Wolf could grab his arm and wrench it up, aiming the gun he held away from Cassandra. The sudden explosion of Roth's fist into his stomach had him doubling over, yet he still held on to the gun.

They both wrestled for the firearm. Roth, being larger, had the advantage. As he pushed Wolf down and forced the gun at his adversary's head, Wolf ripped his knife from its sheath.

A shot rang out. Suddenly Roth froze and then crumpled on top of him.

Wolf pushed the man off him. He looked at Cassandra, surprised that she'd had the nerve to fire her gun. He rose to his feet and then rushed to her, grabbing her shoulders and looking her over. "Are you all right? He didn't hurt you?"

She shook her head. "I'm fine."

He let out a relieved breath and hugged her to him. Her arms slipped around his waist, and she laid her head against his shoulder. She was shaking.

"What about you?" she asked, the words muffled against his shirt.

He was all right, but looking down, he saw blood on his shirt. Roth's blood.

The man stirred.

"Grab some rope," Wolf said, releasing her. "I'll tie him up and then send Jordan for the sheriff. By the way, Roth—or someone else—set the stable on fire. Otis, Jordan and Fitch are putting it out. I was suspicious that the fire might be a diversion, so I came to check on you."

She brought some twine from the kitchen. "Will this do?"

He took it and tied up Roth's hands behind his back. Then, for good measure, he tied his ankles together too.

"I should go see if I can help," Cassandra said as she grabbed her shawl from the back of a nearby chair.

"Too dangerous," he said, standing. "I don't know if Jarvis or Barker are around. Besides, that shawl won't keep you dry in the rain."

He walked to the kitchen and pulled the oilcloth from a shelf. Throwing it over her head, he hugged her to his side and together, they strode out to the stable to see about the fire.

Once inside, she stayed near his side. The fire was nearly out, the entire dirt floor of the stable muddy and wet.

"Good thing it was raining so hard," Jordan said. "We opened the door and the rain blew right in and doused the fire."

"And the horses?" Cassandra asked.

"We'll round them up soon as it's light, ma'am," Fitch said.

Wolf told them who he'd caught in the house.

Otis grumbled. "Varmints one and all. Don't deserve the sheriff. In my day we would have strung them up for thievin' cattle and botherin' women."

"I'm going to keep an eye on Roth until the sheriff arrives," Wolf said. "But we all need to watch out for the other two in case they are around. Jordan, head into town and get the sheriff. Take my horse. He's still in the corral."

"Yes, sir," Jordan said, and left immediately.

"Fitch? Keep an eye on the fire. Make sure it doesn't start back up."

"Yes, sir."

"Otis? How about some coffee for all of us? I don't think we will get any more sleep tonight."

Otis grinned. "Sounds good. I'll bring you out a cup soon as it's ready, Fitch."

Otis walked with Cassandra and Wolf back to the ranch house.

After Sheriff Baniff had obtained statements from each of them and hauled Roth away to jail, exhaustion and fatigue finally claimed both Wolf and Cassandra.

Wolf fell asleep on the settee in the parlor, still determined to keep an eye on her. She pulled off his boots and swung his legs up on the leather ottoman. As she stuffed a pillow behind his head, she paused and raked the hair on his head back with her fingers. He'd become so dear to her. Didn't he know that she loved him?

He'd saved her life. She would never have had the nerve to shoot a man before the lessons he'd given her. She still didn't know for sure if she would have gone through with it. It was only when Roth threatened Wolf that she found the courage to pull the trigger.

He'd saved her life and she'd saved his, but that still didn't make things even between them. He'd given her more than his protection over the past four weeks. Doug had given her life a purpose by asking her to stay on the ranch for a month, but Wolf... He'd given her time to heal.

She leaned over him, brushed his black hair out of the way once more and kissed him lightly on the forehead. "I love you, Wolf."

With her murmur, he stirred but didn't awaken.

She climbed the stairs to her bedroom and fell into bed, fully clothed.

When she woke up, the sun was going down. She straightened her dress and combed her hair as best she could. It saddened her to realize that she'd slept away the entire day. Tomorrow...tomorrow was her last full day at the ranch.

The table was set, and Otis rang the triangle bell to call Fitch and Jordan and Wolf to the table. From the very unlively conversation that ensued, apparently everyone had slogged through the day, half-awake.

"One thing I haven't heard yet, and you promised to tell me," she said to Wolf at the table, "is the way you and Doug became blood brothers."

Jordan put his fork down. "I ain't heard it either."

Wolf shook his head. "It's between Doug and me."

"Go on," Otis urged. "It's a good story."

"Yes. Please," Cassandra said. "If anyone should know, it is me, don't you think?"

A furrow deepened between his eyes. "Yes," he said reluctantly.

She smiled. And waited.

"It was two years after we met. Doug and I went

hunting. I always used a bow. I liked the quiet, the stealth of an arrow cutting through the wind over the loud crack of a rifle shot. That day though, it would have been smarter to take my father's rifle.

"We hunted for deer. No small birds or rabbits. It had to be big game, Doug said. We didn't see anything the first half of the day even though we'd risen early, hoping to find a deer when they went down to the creek to drink. A little after noon we saw the fresh tracks of a large deer and followed them. The tracks disappeared on a patch of hard-packed dirt, and we saw the flash of tan hide through the tall prairie grass. It wasn't a deer. It was a longhorn that had strayed far from the herd.

"'Let's rope him,' Doug said. He had just been talking about the next roundup. He wanted to prove to his father that he was old enough to help out on it. It was a foolish idea. We had a rope, but we were on foot. We'd left our horses tied up half a mile away. And the bull—a maverick—had other ideas for his day than being caught.

"Before I could tell Doug my doubts about his plan, he whirled that rope over his head and set it neatly over the bull's head. And the bull went wild. It jerked on the rope, and Doug flew through the air and landed facedown on the ground. Then the bull charged him. I shot an arrow—and another. I'd never seen such a large animal cover a distance so fast. I shouted and waved my arms, running at it, trying to get its attention. Anything to make it turn toward me or veer away. At the last second, it turned—toward me. It hooked me with its horn—" he pointed to his left side "—and tossed me in the air. While it was busy with me, Doug grabbed his rifle and shot it twice. It finally went down.

"I was angry. It was a fool thing to do. I'd been hurt, and the ranch had lost valuable beef that could have gone to market. Doug didn't want to hear any of it. He ran back to get the horses and helped me back to the ranch where his mother stitched me up. I had a broken rib and had to stay a few days while it mended enough to go home."

"You still haven't explained about…" Jordan said.

"I'm getting to it." Wolf glanced at Cassandra. "While I was here at the house, Doug's father told us about fighting for the Union and how Otis took a bullet for him. He pledged from that time on, to look out for Otis no matter what. Doug heard that and said that what happened to us was even bigger. We had both saved each other's life. So we made a pledge to each other, and we sealed it with our blood.

"After that, I started saving up for a rifle of my own. I wasn't ever going to let myself be in that position again with only a bow. I ended up buying an old revolver—one that needed fixing."

"And I imagine that that is how you came into your livelihood," Cassandra said. "I'm glad you told me."

"Wow," Jordan said. "I wanna know about how you did the oath."

Wolf touched the piece of turquoise at his throat. "We both had these stones—presents from my mother on each of our birthdays. We exchanged them in a ceremony." He showed the long thin white scar that bisected his palm. "I cut my hand here. Doug too. Then we shook, mixing the blood, and gave each other our Wichita names."

"New names? Are you permitted to tell us?" Cassandra asked. "Or are they a secret?"

"No real secret. Doug was *wira'a*. It means *bear*."

"And yours?"

"Wáse'ekhaar'a."

"Wolf?" Jordan guessed.

"Yes."

A strange feeling came over her. "I've heard that word before."

"Maybe Doug told you," Wolf said.

"I'm not sure…" Where had she come across those names before? They tugged at the corner of her memory.

The men finished their supper, and Jordan and Fitch headed to the bunkhouse. Cassandra helped Otis clear the used dishes.

"Now, don't be doin' that," Otis said, taking the dishes from her hands. "You go on into the parlor and I'll bring coffee."

"No coffee, Otis, unless you would like some. Just come and sit with us for a bit, if you'd like."

He looked from her to Wolf and gave a lopsided smile. "Beggin' your pardon, ma'am, but I'd like to get in a game of poker with the boys before shut-eye."

Was he purposely trying to leave her alone with Wolf? What was going on? "All right. Then I'll see you in the morning."

She walked into the parlor and found Wolf reading the thick book on animal husbandry again. "I imagine someday you will have your own ranch. You may as well have that book."

He put the book aside.

"I've even thought to give you the ranch as a gift, Wolf, but I know your pride won't let you accept it."

"You're right. I wouldn't let you do that. You shouldn't give up what is rightfully yours."

She heard the unspoken underlying message…he meant by leaving the ranch or by selling it. He was relentless in that. "Tomorrow is my last day here, and I have one more request. Go with me to the Stewarts' grave sites? I wish to say goodbye to Doug."

"I'll go with you. But I still wish you would stay. Live here. Run the ranch. Otis could help. Fitch too."

"After yesterday and the incident with Roth, I do feel stronger. He didn't cow me the way he did in the stable."

"You are a warrior," he said quietly. "Stronger than when you first arrived."

"Only because you taught me how to protect myself."

"You would have learned it on your own."

His confidence in her had always encouraged her. "If I changed my mind… If I stayed and ran the ranch… would you help?"

He let out a sigh. "It is one thing for me to help you for a few weeks because you are Doug's widow. If you stayed…it would be different."

"Why? It doesn't have to be."

"Says the woman who still wears black."

"What do you mean by that?"

"You care deeply what others think."

"That's not a bad thing."

"No. But when you base your decisions on what others expect, you become their prisoner."

She didn't care for him analyzing her. He hadn't held Doug as he died. He hadn't lost a baby. "You wouldn't understand!"

"What wouldn't I understand? You are ready to move on. Your clothes, the Stetson you wear, even attending the dance… All are signs that you are ready."

She sat down in the chair across from him, thinking over his words. What he said was true. "Ever since you held me while I cried buckets of tears there has been change…"

"You are healing. You only need to see it for yourself."

Perhaps he was right. She had thought following the rules would be a way to atone for her waywardness. That it would make things "right." But in the end, she hadn't followed the rules. At least not as strictly as she should. Nothing bad had happened. Maybe it was all right to listen to her heart instead of what others dictated. She was a grown woman now. Maybe she was healing and finding bits of herself that she had once lost. She could make her own decisions and handle the consequences. She was strong enough…

Did she dare ask him to stay? Regret would hound her if she left without trying. But she couldn't live with a halfway arrangement, not with how much she loved him. Sharing him with his life in town wouldn't work. She wanted him here—with her.

She met his gaze. "If I stayed here at the ranch, would you stay?"

By his expression, she had surprised him.

He shook his head. "As a ranch hand? No."

"I don't mean as a ranch hand."

"Then what?"

As my husband, she wanted to say, but she couldn't very well ask him to marry her. It wasn't proper. A woman simply did not do the asking. "I don't know. As a partner?" She watched him, waiting…hopeful…

He raked his hair back with his fingers. "The truth,

Cassandra? I wouldn't be able to keep my hands off you."

Her breath caught. "You wouldn't?" Her heart skipped a beat as she imagined him holding her, loving her. She stood, willing him silently to agree before she'd even uttered the words. "Then marry me."

His gaze pinned her—deep, quiet, moody. His expression was so still that she had no idea what was going through his thoughts.

Nervous now, that he'd refuse, the words tumbled out. "I love you, Wolf. It doesn't seem to matter anymore whether it is appropriate or not. It just is. Will you... Would you consider staying and marrying me?"

The weight of her request hovered suspended between them. The parlor...the entire house was awkwardly still as she waited for his answer. The only sound came from the ticktock of the clock on the mantel.

A furrow formed between his dark brows. Slowly, he stood. "You don't really mean it. You are frightened of what the future holds for you back in Virginia."

"That's not true."

He studied her silently and then picked up his Stetson.

"You're leaving?" A lead weight dropped in her stomach.

"Your offer is very tempting. *You*...are very tempting. But you know if I agree, you'd always wonder what it was I wanted most. You? Or the ranch. Eventually that distrust would ruin any true feelings between us." He plopped his hat on his head. "I do care for you, Cassandra. But I don't have anything to offer you."

The room, the house, was utterly silent as he walked

to the front door. He stopped before opening it, turning to her once more. "When I decide to marry, I'll do my own asking."

She stared at the door as it closed behind him. Heat flamed her cheeks. What had she done? She'd been an impulsive fool! A lovesick, ridiculous fool!

Chapter Twenty-Six

Wolf stormed across the yard. He was itching to take a ride. A long hard ride. His hands clenched into fists at his side and then unclenched, over and over. He could have had the ranch. All it would take was for him to say yes to her wild proposal.

To ride hard at this hour on horseback would only put his horse at risk, so he strode past the bunkhouse and kept walking. The screech of an owl overhead sounded as he followed a narrow deer trail away from the house.

He came to the creek and realized that he'd walked two miles. His thoughts were calming down. They were almost coherent. He sat down on the sandy bank.

All his life he had done the sensible thing. When Doug would pull one of his harebrained ideas, Wolf would stop him by speaking truth or if that didn't work, he'd get him out of the trouble that would ensue—or face it with him.

Now he had the chance to own the land. The one thing he'd always wanted was within reach.

And yet he hesitated—practical once more.

He wanted to spit the word out… *Practical!* It had never brought him what he wanted, and what he wanted even more than the land was Cassandra.

Yet he knew what would happen if he forgot caution and did the very thing he ached to do—to be Cassandra's husband in every way. To marry her in this way would scar her reputation and Doug's memory. She would come to hate him. Maybe not right away, but eventually. He would not be able to live with himself. He had nothing of true value to offer her—no money, no land of his own, no cattle, no horses. He would be less of a man if he selfishly gave in to his desires.

It could not happen.

So…on Saturday, he would stand by silently and watch the woman he loved sign over the ranch and board the train to leave Kansas for good.

And he would do nothing to stop her.

Chapter Twenty-Seven

The next morning, Cassandra avoided breakfast in the kitchen with the men. She couldn't bear to see Wolf after the words they'd last spoken. She was too embarrassed.

Instead of going downstairs, she gathered her things to pack, putting the clothing she would wear that day in a small pile on the bed. She opened her trunk and stared down at her corset. That was one item she'd stopped wearing, finding it snug as she'd put on a few pounds with Otis's meals and the fresh air. Riding astride was much more comfortable without the confines of the corset, which tended to dig into her thighs while she was astride.

She closed her eyes and remembered the feel of Wolf's strong hands on her waist and then splayed on her back the night of the dance. She hadn't even had a chance to dance with him that night!

She picked up the undergarment, analyzing it critically. Corsets were as much a prison as some rules of etiquette. Yet, no doubt tomorrow she would once again don it for the trip to town and the train ride to Virginia. Irritated at the thought, she tossed the corset aside on the bed.

Last night, Wolf had mentioned something about the things she wore—the white blouse instead of the black one and the colorful sash. Even the hat he'd given her was a deep tan rather than black, yet she'd worn it to ward off the sun. Maybe he needed to see that things like a black wardrobe didn't matter as much to her as they once had, that she could still respect Doug's passing in other ways.

She searched the very bottom of the trunk and pulled out her favorite blue skirt. It had been Doug's favorite color on her. He'd said it brought out the blue in her eyes. What better day to wear it than the day she would say goodbye to him?

She dressed quickly—the blue skirt, her white blouse. Last, she laced up her high-top shoes. Then she rummaged through her trunk once more and withdrew a lace handkerchief that held the large blue brooch Doug had given her. She would wear that too. As she pulled the handkerchief from its place at the bottom of the trunk, her gaze fell upon a small box.

Oh, my word! The box Mr. Edelman had given her! She'd completely forgotten it!

She withdrew the box. Opening the lid, she once again saw the bullet, the lock of red hair, the feather and the turquoise stone. Her breath caught, remembering the ceremony Wolf had spoken of between him and Douglas. The stone was similar to the one Wolf wore at his neck. She unfolded the note.

Wáse'ekhaar'a—
You will know what to do.
Wira'a

Of course! The story Wolf had told her of becoming blood brothers flooded back to her. The wolf. The bear. It made sense now. This was for Wolf. A memento perhaps of their days together as boys.

She would have to give it to him. She slipped it into her satchel.

Wolf watched for signs of Cassandra stirring. She hadn't been at breakfast, and it was halfway to noon now. After the way things had ended last night, he didn't know what to expect. Would she still want his company on the ride out to the grave site today? Would she want anything to do with him?

He saddled Patsy and got his own horse ready, then led both horses out to the corral. At the least, that would signal to her that he was ready to accompany her.

Finally, he headed up to the porch and knocked on the door. A moment later, she stepped outside.

He wasn't sure what to make of her. She wore her golden blond hair pulled back at the nape, loosely braided a few times and tied with a blue ribbon. The long strands hung down her back to her waist. She'd chosen a white blouse to wear and a darker blue skirt he'd never seen before. The Stetson he'd given her dangled from her hand. She looked fresh and sun kissed and sweet.

Taking a deep breath, she met his gaze. "What do you think?"

He grinned. "Doug would be proud."

Her lashes fluttered down, and she fingered a brooch at her throat. "Thank you. I'm glad you remembered about today. Are you ready?"

He nodded.

They descended the steps and crossed the yard to the horses. He helped her to mount. "Cassandra…about last night."

"It's all right. You don't need to say anything," she said quickly. "I was wrong. That's all. Absolutely wrong to push you. It was me, being…me. I tend to be impulsive. I guess I have always been a bit like Douglas in that."

"You must have been unstoppable when you both wanted the same thing."

"Oh, we were!" She smiled softly. "It's been tempered somewhat with all that has happened this year, but once in a while, I can't contain it. I guess it's just me. Consider yourself lucky. You only got a small dose of it."

She was enchanting him all over again. Here he'd thought the ride would be silent and stilted and uncomfortable, and in only a few sentences she'd changed it—made him feel comfortable with her openness. He reined his horse around and together they rode out to the grave site.

"I wish I had flowers," she said, dismounting on her own. "But this late in autumn, they've withered and died."

"Another year and the prairie grass and wildflowers will cover the grave. Doug will be happy with them."

"I suppose you are right. He didn't care for hothouse flowers anyway."

That's why he picked you, he thought. To make it out here on the prairie, a woman had to be smart and resourceful and tough. Cassandra was all those things and more. He held the gate to the picket fence open for her. "I'll give you a moment," he said as she stepped through.

"Thank you."

He walked back to the horses, turning his back to her to give her privacy.

In every fiber of his being, he wanted her to stay. He thought back to all that had happened during her time on the ranch. Was there something more he could have done? Was there any other way that he could buy the ranch from her? A way that didn't go through the bank? Then he would have the right to ask her to stay. Then he would ask for her hand.

"Wolf? Come here," she said quietly.

He joined her at the grave, relieved to find her composed. Her cheek, however, showed the silvery trace of a tear. He reached out to wipe it away, his hand trembling as he touched her soft skin.

"I'm all right." She took a deep breath. "I'm fine."

He nodded, waiting.

"I ordered a headstone in town the day of the dance. You'll make sure to place it when Mr. Moyer finishes with it? And you'll watch over things here when I'm gone?"

He nodded again.

"Thank you. Knowing that will make it easier when I am back in Virginia."

She squared her shoulders and met his gaze. "Wait here. I have something for you. I think here is the proper place for me to give it to you."

He waited while she walked back to her horse and withdrew a package wrapped in a dark cloth and tied with twine. Returning to him, she held it out with both hands. "This was found with Douglas's important papers. I had forgotten it was in my things and didn't realize it until this morning when I looked for this skirt. I believe he meant it for you."

He removed the wrapping and twine, hesitating when he recognized the box. "He kept this? All these years?"

"Then you recognize it?"

"I made it. My first attempt at a box. I was probably fourteen." He opened the lid. "I can't believe this. He kept these? I knew he was a sap, sentimental and all, but this still surprises me." His eyes prickled with emotion.

"What do all of these things mean? The bullet, the hair and all. Do you know?"

"The bullet? Well, that is the one that crippled Otis when he dashed in front of Douglas's father. Otis wanted to throw it out, but Doug said it should be a badge of honor because if Otis hadn't done that, his father would have been killed and Doug wouldn't have been born."

"And the lock of hair?"

"That's a lock of his mother's hair." He picked up the turquoise stone. "You know about this."

"And the feather?"

"That's a quail feather. It's from the first bird he ever shot with a bow and arrow. He taught me to shoot a gun. I taught him to hunt with a bow and arrow."

He opened the note.

You will know what to do.

"What does it mean?" Cassandra asked.

"I'm not sure," he said, reading the cryptic note

again. "It is like him though, to stay one step ahead
of me. He always liked a good puzzle." He turned the
box over, noting Doug's initials on the bottom and remembering the day he'd burned them into the wood.
The answer was close. If only he could feel it.

Wait!

"Hold out your hands," he said.

He opened the lid again and dumped the few con-
tents into her cupped hands. "I remember this box
now." He jiggled each plane of the box, searching for
the loose one. Finally, the back slid up slightly and the
bottom slid out.

"You made a secret compartment?"

He handed the bottom to her. "There's a paper here."
He took it out and unfolded the paper. And swallowed.
Hard. "It's a will." he said, his heart beating hard.

Cassandra stepped closer, her head near his shoulder. "And the date?"

He showed her, watching her face for a sign of what
she must be feeling. If this was legal, it could change
a lot of things.

"It's 1875. Four years ago," she said and then pulled
back from him. "Long before he met me."

"Right after his mother died. Guess you should read
this." He held out the paper for her.

She pushed it back toward him, her light touch tickling his hand. "I don't think so. I wouldn't have had
a clue about the hidden compartment. It is for you."

Wolf raked his hand through his hair. Unbeliev-
able. "All right. Let's sit down. We'll read it together."

He found an area of thick grass, and they both sat
down with their backs against the fence. Then he read

the will out loud for them both. He spoke slowly, so that he could absorb each word that was written in Doug's own hand, but stopped when he came to the part about the ranch. In the end, Doug had bequeathed the ranch property and cattle to Wolf.

He was dumbfounded. What did this mean for Cassandra?

"Doug wrote this way before he met you," he said, unable to look directly into her troubled blue gaze. "If he'd had the chance, he would have changed it. I'm sure he would have crossed out my name and written in yours instead."

"I'm not so sure," she said slowly. "Not after the four weeks that I've spent here. Not after knowing you as I do now."

He dropped his shoulders. "Cassandra… He would have made sure to take care of you. Doug might have taken risks in all other areas of his life, but he wouldn't take a risk with this ranch. I'm sure of it."

"But he did take a risk!" she said, her brows knitting. "Don't you see? It would have been so easy for me to forget about the box, and then where would your inheritance be? Sold out from under you!" She blew out a breath, her face hardening with irritation. "He was brash and larger-than-life…and…and I loved him. But in this, he took an unnecessary risk."

"He thought he'd bring you back here. I'm sure he would have updated the will once he got back to Oak Grove. This is all a mess because of his accident."

She turned her face away. "He wanted you to have this land. He had time to tell me of the will. It will always be a mystery whether he simply didn't think of it at the last or whether he purposely left its finding to chance."

She had never said a disparaging word about Doug other than to be angry he'd left her to go boating the day of the storm. Up to that moment, she seemed to think everything about him was perfect.

"He had time enough to extract my promise to come here and stay for a month! He knew exactly what he was doing."

Wolf jumped to his feet and walked to Doug's grave. He had always been the one to clean up Doug's messes. What the heck was he supposed to do with this one? Cassandra deserved something left to her for being the man's wife, for going through all she had with his baby.

Cassandra rose slowly to her feet and brushed the dried grasses off her skirt. "This is a bit of an adjustment for me. I had just started to think of the ranch as mine."

Her voice was controlled—too controlled. And her smile didn't quite reach her eyes.

"But this is as it should be. You'll do a great job with the property, and you'll do right by Doug. He knew you would care for it. After all, you are his brother. He made a good choice in you."

This didn't feel right. "Cassandra…"

She glanced at him. "It's all right, Wolf. It will work out well. I've kept my promise to Doug, and now it is time for me to return home."

"But you are not yourself."

"I'm just emotional, is all. Doug barreled into my life and five weeks later we married. Everything changed with that. And now it's as if he has reached back from the grave and changed the direction of my life again. He was like that during our marriage too. I never knew what to expect from him. In a way it was exhilarating. In a way it was exhausting. But it was always an adventure. Believe me, part of me is relieved to have this settled. What if I'd forgotten about the box completely and traveled all the way back to Alexandria, finding it only after the ranch had been sold? What a mess that would have created!"

"He took risks. For him, they usually turned out well, although not always for the people around him," Wolf said.

"And the few times they didn't turn out well, he trusted you to step in and fix things."

He nodded, wondering if she was including herself in that thought.

Suddenly, her eyes lit up. "Oh, my goodness, Wolf. This just changes everything! We have to get back to the ranch! We have to tell Otis and everyone!"

She ran toward the gate.

"Now, hold on," he said, catching her arm and spinning her around to face him. "I need more time to think about all this."

Her lips trembled, and she looked dangerously close to crying. Something more was going on inside her. "You stay, then," she said. "Take your time here. But I need to go back and pack. I'll…I'll see you at the house."

"Not a word to anybody," he cautioned. He was still unsure whether he should let her leave in the state that she was in, but he needed to think through this sudden change.

"No. Of course not." She wrenched her arm from his grip and hurried to her horse, mounted and galloped down the hillside.

Chapter Twenty-Eight

Cassandra rode like the very devil chased her. Her hair came loose from the ribbon, and as the wind caught her hat, it fell off and bounced between her shoulders, held there by the chin ties. She had made a fool of herself in believing that Doug would actually leave the ranch to her. Wolf's diatribe on her first day as he brought her to the ranch came back to torment her.

You are from the East. You are from the city. And you are a woman. You know nothing about ranching.

Doug had never meant for her to have the land! Never meant for her to have anything. It hurt her to the quick. She had impulsively assumed—and been wrong.

Well, she had kept her promise. A month had passed. It was time to go home. Wolf didn't need her to take the will to the land office and switch the title of the land into his name. She wasn't needed for anything. She would gather her things quickly, say a hasty goodbye to Jordan, Otis and Fitch, and then have Otis take her to town. She could spend one last night in Oak Grove at the hotel and get on the train first thing in the morning.

The decision was made in her mind, but as she drew close to the ranch and heard the chickens clucking in the henhouse and Sheba yipping happily at her return, her heart splintered into a million pieces. She passed the soddie, and suddenly Sheba veered around the side of the earth house and raced toward her. She stopped Patsy and dismounted. Cassandra didn't want Patsy rearing or stumbling because of the overanxious pup, and she didn't want Sheba getting stepped on.

She scooped up Sheba in one arm, burrowing her nose into the soft fluffy puppy.

"Oh, Sheba... I don't want to go, and yet I feel that I must." Her breast ached with the admission. Leaving had been her plan all along, yet now that it was time, now that she should, she didn't want to go.

But what other choice did she have?

This was not her home. This was not her land. And Wolf didn't want to marry—at least not her.

At the stable, she handed Patsy's reins to Jordan and then took Sheba to the porch and tied her so that she couldn't run farther than the steps. Then she went inside to find Otis.

He was in the kitchen.

"Otis? I will need you to drive me into town as soon as I am finished packing my trunk. It won't take me long."

He looked up from the squash he was cutting into small chunks. "You mean it? You're really headin' back to Virginy?" He wiped his hands on his apron. "Guess I always hoped you'd change your mind and stay. You could have done it, you know."

She shook her head. "It would take me years and years to learn all that you know about ranching. Besides, I need to get to my parents' home before the weather turns colder. It won't be long and snow will be falling." She couldn't very well tell him that the ranch was no longer hers to call home.

"Well, Miss Cassandra, you just give a holler when you got everythin' ready. I'll get one of the boys to hitch up the wagon and help me tote that trunk down the stairs."

"Thank you." She turned away.

She finished packing and was closing the lid to her trunk when she heard the pounding of horse hooves outside. She looked out the window and saw Wolf's horse in the yard surrounded by a cloud of dust. The sound of boots on the stairs made her step to the hall-way.

"Cassandra!" Wolf stopped short when he saw her. Then he looked behind her at the open trunk. "You're going now?"

"I have to. This isn't my home anymore…if it ever really was."

"You are leaving without even saying goodbye?" He whipped his Stetson off and hooked it over the banister post. "But you said you loved me."

"I do. I do love you…completely."

He strode toward her. "Leaving isn't the way to show it."

"Please, Wolf. Don't make this any harder than it already is for me. You said you wouldn't marry me, and I cannot stay with less than that."

"I wouldn't marry you because I had nothing to bring to the marriage."

"Oh, Wolf," she cried. Tears blurred his face. "I didn't want anything. I only wanted you."

"And I feel the same way about you." He swallowed, taking her hands in his. "It looks like I do have something to offer now…"

She went still, focused acutely on him.

"Marry me. Stay here and make this our home."

Her heart pounded against her rib cage. Was this really happening?

He cupped her chin with his warm palm, holding her gaze. In his dark eyes she saw uncertainty and desire all rolled into one big ball of hope. Her own face probably mirrored those feelings right back.

"It won't be easy."

"Oh, Wolf!" she murmured. "I don't need easy. I just need you."

He lowered his chin, holding her captive with his gaze. "Then kiss me and tell me you'll be my wife."

Her heart, so very shattered only minutes before, now beat steadily, the cracks filling up and spilling over with love. She stood on tiptoe, leaning toward him, and brushed her lips lightly over his. A shiver coursed through her. "Yes. I love you so very much. I'll happily stay here with you forever."

He pressed his mouth against hers and kissed her hard, drawing her tight against him.

And, oh, my, she kissed him right back with the same fervor. Her heart thudded in her chest. She was home.

He drew back then, holding her hands against his chest. "When?"

She swallowed. "Next month?"

"That's too long to wait."

"Now who is impulsive?" she teased.

He grinned. "Now that you've said yes, I don't want you to have the chance to change your mind."

"Believe me. I won't change my mind. I have a feeling that life with you is going to be a wonderful adventure. One I want to share. One I don't want to miss."

"Miss Cassandra?" Otis called up the stairwell. "Wagon is all hitched up and ready."

Wolf smiled down at her. "Are you ready to tell everyone?"

She nodded.

He smiled then and kissed her once more. And she knew, as his lips touched hers, that without a doubt, the love they shared would be more than enough to see them through a lifetime.

Chapter Twenty-Nine

*O*ak Grove *Gazette*
Article by Abigail White

The wedding of Mr. Raymond Wolf, Rocking S Ranch, Oak Grove, Kansas, and Cassandra Stewart, Alexandria, Virginia, took place in a quiet ceremony at the Oak Grove Community Church on November 26, 1879. Officiating was Parson Conner Flaherty. Attending the bride was Sadie Austin. Standing with the groom was Otis Klap. All from Oak Grove, Kansas.

The groom's parents, Lily and Homer Wolf, along with ranch hands Jordan Hughes, "Fitch" and Royce Winston were present to witness the vows.

The entire town of Oak Grove was invited to the reception that followed at the new town hall, and many showed up to offer the newlyweds congratulations.

Mary Putnam and Maggie Miller led the music with several Irish ballads, punctuated by the happy gurgles of the newest additions to our community, Brent Putnam, age six weeks, and Charlotte Miller, also age six weeks.

Shortly after Cassandra Wolf threw the bouquet—caught by Abigail White—the two newlyweds slipped away from the celebration and back to the Rocking S Ranch to start their married life together.

* * * * *

If you enjoyed this story,
try these other great Western reads
by Kathryn Albright

The Prairie Doctor's Bride
Christmas Kiss from the Sheriff
Familiar Stranger in Clear Springs
The Gunslinger and the Heiress